SMALL CHANGE

Keddie Hughes

KEDDIE HUGHES

And though I'm poisoned
choking on the small change

of human hope,
daily beaten into me

look: I am still alive
in fact, in bud.

Kathleen Jamie

For Bob. Always for you.

CHAPTER 1

4:40 p.m. His file was marked "Urgent". Izzy took a deep breath and prepared herself for bad news. Redundancy from a plumbing agency, job allowance stopped following missed appointments and housing benefit about to be cut. The welfare system was like a set of dominoes, when one fell, the others soon came clattering down. She sighed and reminded herself that giving up was not an option; whatever help she could offer her clients, whatever small change they could make to improve their circumstances, was cause for hope.

Connor Docherty was forty-two years old, lived in the East End of Glasgow and was married, with one son, deceased, aged seventeen. Izzy had been trained not to make assumptions about people, but she couldn't help thinking that this terrible event had probably triggered his decline. His son had been the same age as Davy. She gazed into space. Davy was now six feet tall with a tousle of blue-black hair. Pride bloomed in her chest, followed by a dull ache. He was hoping to go to university next year and the time was fast approaching for her to admit defeat in the unwinnable war of keeping him young.

She stood and stretched, easing the stiffness in her back from sitting all day. The office was spartan, just big enough for a desk with a computer on it, a filing cabinet, three chairs and a box of tissues. A client had once told her that the cells in Barlinnie looked more inviting, but she liked to think that people soon came to know the Bureau as a place of refuge, a place of comfort.

4:55 p.m. Mr Docherty was late. A small window high up in the wall let in a shaft of bright light. The sun was still high and pale; it wouldn't get dark until after 10 p.m. She thought about leaving and walking home, enjoying the balmy, summer evening – a minor miracle for the west of Scotland. She could take the long way round, through Glasgow Green, buy a ninety-nine from the Mr Whippy van, then sit for a while by the playground, watching the children swinging on swings while trying to eat their ice creams at the same time. But no, tonight, she was going to the company party at the Caledonian Hotel with Jim. Her mind emptied at the prospect of it. Over breakfast that morning, he had told her he was going to make a big announcement about the business. An announcement so significant, it would make Verisafe the biggest installer of domestic and commercial alarms in Glasgow. She hadn't pressed him for details and he'd left the table, leaving his cornflakes half-eaten, telling her not to be late. She felt a stab of guilt at how easy it had been to needle him.

5:00 p.m. The book from college was lying on her desk, next to Mr Docherty's file. She picked it up and examined the cover: a painting of trees, tall and willowy, as if flowing in a light breeze. It was a gentle picture, although no one would describe the contents as friendly. *Steps to an Ecology of Mind* by Gregory Bateson, '*a synthesis of philosophical and scientific imagination that is tantalising and cryptically suggestive.*' She had told her tutor that she was looking forward to reading it, though she felt the exact opposite. When he had suggested she write her term essay on it, she hadn't hesitated in saying she'd give it a go. Pleasing authority had been a lifelong habit. Sometimes she despaired about herself.

5:10 p.m. Mr Docherty looked like a no-show and she felt a pinch of sadness. When people faced reality and admitted they had a problem with debt, it was what Shona called a "breakthrough moment." Izzy hadn't contradicted her. Shona was her boss, one of the few full-time employees at The Citizen's Advice Bureau, with over twenty years' service. However, in Izzy's experience, it wasn't unusual for there to be quite a few "breakthrough moments", with false starts and ups and downs. It was more a case of walking alongside people and doing your best to pull them back onto the path whenever they wandered off. But, maybe when you've lost a child, you lose interest in getting back on the path. Perhaps even the idea of there being a path no longer made sense to him.

Either way, it was time to go home. She picked up Mr Docherty's file and turned to put it back in the cabinet. Her eyes met those of a man standing in the doorway. He was tall, slim and looked lost, as if he'd been travelling through space and found himself in the wrong universe. She frowned, puzzled that she hadn't heard the click of the buzzer, or a call from Alan, the receptionist, to let her know that her client was on his way.

'Mr Docherty?' she asked.

He nodded but didn't move. She thought she could smell alcohol, but she could have been mistaken. He was wearing a Celtic football strip. It was immaculately clean, the green and white hoops looking jolly against his thin face.

'I was expecting you. Well, thirty minutes ago,' she said. Mr Docherty ignored her mild rebuke and sat down in the chair at right angles to hers, his bony knees jutting through his faded jeans.

He had fine, brown hair, the sort that often thins with age, so it was unusual to see a man in his forties with a full head of it. It was a little on the long side and curled at the edge of his collar, the first dustings of grey at the temples. Stubble covered his chin, softening his chiselled features, and his eyes were a mix of yellow and green, the colours swirling together like the glass marbles she'd had as a child. She felt her face prickle with heat and looked away, concentrating on his Celtic shirt instead. The green and white was dazzling.

'I'm Izzy,' she said, pulling at her wild hair, 'Frizzy Izzy.' She wondered why she'd said that. She must sound like a numpty. She tucked a stray lock behind her ear and gave him a professional smile.

'Sorry I'm late,' he began. 'I was in the pub. Celebrating. Lost track of time.'

His English accent was as modulated as a London BBC presenter. It was so unexpected that she had to look down and pretend to read his file, silently chastising herself for allowing herself to slip into stereotypes.

'That's nice. What were you celebrating?' she asked.

His eyes widened. She felt pleased to have surprised him. He was probably expecting disapproval for drinking in the pub when he was up to his armpits in debt.

'The Huns are finished,' he said, smiling. His teeth were white and well cared for, and his smile transformed him into an attractive man, a person capable of coping with life.

'Huns?' she asked, feigning ignorance. She knew full well it was an insulting term for Rangers football supporters.

'The Sheriff paid a visit to Ibrox today. Rangers are going bust and the pubs around here are full of Celtic fans celebrating.'

Her mind tumbled. Jim and Davy were both fanatical Rangers fans – she could barely imagine their grief if this was true. She sat back in her chair, suspecting her jaw had dropped. Mr Docherty leaned towards her, rubbing his hands together.

'They owe the taxman millions. But they're in denial. Massive denial,' he added. His eyes glittered.

'Denial is a common reaction to debt. In fact, facing up to the reality of your situation is what we call a "breakthrough moment," she said, relieved to be back on familiar ground.

Mr Docherty leaned closer towards her, like a spring about to be released. Izzy felt a frisson of alarm and her fingers moved under the desk to feel for the panic button. He began to speak slowly, as if the words were being pulled out of his mouth, one by one. 'Rangers might not be willing to face the facts about their debts, but I'm not going to make the same mistake.'

Alan would be round any minute to lock up. She felt a nudge of regret, this was a man with energy and focus. 'I'm glad you came, Mr Docherty, I really am, but unfortunately, the office is about to close.' She said this as gently as she could, but he still looked dismayed.

'Please, Izzy,' he said.

He remembered her name and she felt herself soften. 'Let me ask Alan if we can stay a bit longer.'

Alan sat in a small cubicle in the reception area. She tapped on his hatch door. It took a moment to open. He was sitting on a chair that was too small for him and his flesh spilled over the sides.

'Alan, my client turned up late. Do you mind ...'

Alan was bent over his phone and didn't look up. 'The office shuts at five-thirty.'

'Please. It's important.'

He sighed. 'Lucky for you, I'm only at level three. You're fine until six.'

She walked back to her office, buoyed with a sense of achievement. Alan was a long-term volunteer at the Bureau and had a reputation for sticking to the rules. Mr Docherty was sitting where she had left him, his arms and legs crossed, his foot tapping on the floor as if anxious to get on with things. She felt her mood brighten, reassured in her judgement to give him extra time.

The Verisafe Summer Party! She checked her watch. 5:35 p.m. If they finished at 6:00 p.m. and she got a taxi home, she would have enough time to get ready. Just.

'Right, Mr Docherty. We've got a little more time,' she said. 'Is it OK if I call you Connor?'

'I'm not Connor,' he said.

'You're not Connor Docherty, living at 82 Muirfield Drive?' asked Izzy, feeling the first stirrings of confusion.

'He's still in the pub. Celebrating.'

'I don't understand …' she said. She re-read the details in his file to check if she had missed something. She looked up, frowning.

'I'm Sean, Connor's brother. Unfortunately, Connor's not in a fit state to attend. I told him I would come in his place. I knew there would be a long waiting list for another appointment if he didn't show up.'

He was smiling broadly and she felt torn between wanting to continue the meeting and the rules of client confidentiality. 'I'm sorry, Sean, but I can't discuss your brother's case with anyone but him,' she said, slowly closing the folder. A silence opened up between them, full of disappointment.

'The last few months have been very difficult for my brother. For all the family,' he said quietly, raking his fingers through his hair.

She felt a rush of remorse remembering that Connor's son had died. 'I've a seventeen-year-old son myself. I don't know how you can survive such a loss.' She saw him flinch, two small spots of colour forming in his pale face.

'Connor was asked to fill out some forms,' he said, suddenly business-like, 'and bring as much paperwork as he could find.' He held up a plastic carrier bag. She was surprised she hadn't noticed it before. He emptied the contents of it onto the table, facing her squarely in the eye. A scatter of letters and unopened envelopes lay on her desk.

'OK. Let's take a look,' she said, matching his efficient tone. She began opening envelopes and sorting the letters into various piles. There were several from the council demanding rent, electricity final demands, hire purchase agreements in arrears and bank statements showing an escalating overdraft. The Income and Creditors form that itemised all outgoings and income had been sparsely completed in small, spidery handwriting.

Sean put on his glasses and picked up one of the letters. He had long, elegant fingers; the sort that would be good for guitar playing. There was an imperceptible shake of his head. 'I knew Connor had money problems, but I had no idea he was in this much trouble,' he said, putting the letter back and picking up another.

'He's lucky to have a brother like you to help because there's a lot of information that's missing. It's important to work out how much he owes and how much money comes in, plus all the supporting documentation: court orders, unpaid invoices, statements, final demands, that sort of thing,' she said.

Sean continued to read and she wondered if he had heard her. His nose was straight and he needed to keep pushing his glasses up. It gave him an educated look, like a teacher, or maybe a lawyer.

'And then what happens?' he asked, looking up at her.

She stared back at him blankly, blinking foolishly.

'What happens after the forms have been completed and we've got all the documentation?' he repeated.

Her attention snapped back to the Income and Creditors form. 'Then we look at his options. The important thing to remember is that there are always options.'

'Finding all that paperwork's going to be a challenge. You haven't seen the state of his flat,' he said.

'Look in drawers, dig out any unopened envelopes – you'd be surprised at how much you find. Meanwhile, I'll make another appointment for Connor.' She clicked on the office calendar on her computer. 'Great. Shona has a cancellation at 11 a.m. on Monday.' She felt pleased with herself, as if she had solved a difficult crossword clue.

'The appointment won't be with you?' he asked.

She heard an edge of disappointment in his voice and felt her face warming. 'Shona's the Senior Advisor here at the Gallowgate Office. He'll be in good hands. I go to Glasgow Tech on Mondays,' she said, keeping her eyes on the screen.

'Is that why you're reading Gregory Bateson?' he asked.

She turned to face him. 'You've read *Steps to an Ecology of Mind*?' Her tone was incredulous. Unforgivable, she knew, but it was out of her mouth before she could stop it.

'A long time ago,' he replied, smiling. The laughter lines at the side of his eyes were like tiny tributaries of a river.

'I'm studying for a degree in Social Science. I have to write an essay on the book, but I don't know where to start.' She knew she was veering off script but there was something about his interest that was difficult to resist. He was leafing through the book, a small murmur of recognition escaping from him, as if he were meeting a friend he hadn't seen for a while.

'The problem is, I don't think I'm clever enough for it,' she added, rubbing the back of her neck, inwardly wincing. Another numpty remark.

'Cleverness is overrated. In my experience, curiosity is a more useful quality,' he said, placing the book back on the desk. 'Pick a chapter that catches your attention. Any chapter. Then just start writing about why it interests you, or why it confuses you.'

Despite herself, she felt startled. It was a good idea. Who was he? Where did he live? Where did that English accent come from? She wished they had more time.

'I'll give that a go, thanks. I'm so sorry, Sean, but we have to finish now. Is it clear what Connor has to do for Monday?'

'To be honest, I don't think he's up to it,' he admitted quietly. His shoulders had slumped.

Instinctively, she reached over and touched his hand. She felt a small charge pass between them. 'Once he gets started, he'll see it's not as bad as he thinks. We can write to creditors and request copies of any necessary documentation. We'll help him as much as we can.'

She heard the buzzer and the click of the door. Alan stood in the doorway, his arms folded, his legs akimbo.

'Everything all right, Izzy?' he said, looking at Sean through narrowed eyes.

'Fine thanks, Alan. We're just finishing,' she said, quietly withdrawing her hand.

Alan gave Sean another hostile look and mumbled, 'It's already past six.'

Sean stood up. 'Thanks, Izzy. You've been very kind.' He held out his hand and she shook it. It was warm and dry and she felt the same charge pass between them, only this time, it was a little stronger.

Alan moved sideways to let him pass. 'I'll see Mr Docherty out.'

She heard Alan lumber down the corridor and then the click of the security door. She filed Connor's folder, locked the cabinet and began typing.

Saw Mr Docherty on Friday. Encouraged him to complete Income and Creditor form as fully as possible, including as much supporting documentation as possible. Booked in to see Shona on Monday at 11 a.m.

She sat back in her seat and re-read her notes. Best not to mention which Mr Docherty had shown up as it would only complicate matters. Absentmindedly, she threaded her arms through the sleeves of her jacket. She predicted that the chances of Connor turning up on Monday were slim, but maybe Sean had some money to help his brother. She stood for a moment, allowing her mind to drift. Sean was different to most of the men she met at the Bureau. He was cultured, intelligent and sensitive. He was different to most men she knew, full stop. She picked up the Bateson book, looking again at the pretty cover. Sean had said curiosity was a useful quality, but she wondered if it could be a dangerous one, too.

***

Therapist:	Hello, Jim. Welcome. It's good to meet you.
Jim:	Aye. Me too. I can't stay long though. I've got a big company party tonight.
Therapist:	So, what brings you here?
Jim:	My mum was worried about my drinking. She made me promise to speak to someone about it.
Therapist:	She'll be pleased you're here then.
Jim:	She died three months ago.
Therapist:	(Silence)

Jim:	I can't take it in. She was such a strong woman. I never thought she'd go. (Begins to cough)
Therapist:	It's OK. Take your time.
Jim:	I'm fine. I'm fine.
Therapist:	Why d'you think your mum was worried about your drinking?
Jim:	God knows. Her brother, my Uncle Andy, was an alcoholic. Died from drink. I suppose she didn't want me heading the same way.
Therapist:	And are you? I mean, do you think you're heading the same way?
Jim:	Nae chance. I like a drink, who doesn't? This is Glasgow, after all. But normal drinking, social drinking. Sorry, I don't know why I'm here. I'm wasting your time.
Therapist:	You mentioned a party tonight?
Jim:	It's our annual summer party. My first since becoming Managing Director. I'm feeling as nervous as a kitten. How daft is that?
Therapist:	Parties can be very stressful. Have you had a drink already today?

Jim: I'm not going to lie to you.

Therapist: Is that a worry for you?

Jim: Drinking gives me confidence. Makes me feel good about myself. I can always rely on it. I suppose you think that's a problem right there?

Therapist: Why don't you come and see me again? We can chat more about it then.

CHAPTER 2

Jim's face was florid and Izzy could feel the heat radiating from him. 'Was it too much to expect?' he hissed. They were sitting in the car outside the Caledonian Hotel, the atmosphere between them was tense and unyielding. Izzy flattened her cloud of hair and pinched her cheeks. 'ready,' she said. Even to her ears, her upbeat voice sounded forced.

Jim was biting his nails. He favoured the outside edge of his pinkie finger. It was an oddly dainty, feminine gesture. 'I wanted to be early so I could greet everyone. Now, thanks to you, we're going to be the last ones to arrive.'

She reached into the back seat for her shawl and opened her door. It was still bright, but the air had lost its earlier warmth; it felt as cool as water. Jim remained seated in the driver's seat like a stubborn toddler. 'C'mon then, let's not keep them waiting any longer,' she soothed. It was a familiar dance, to smooth things over, to cajole him back into a good mood.

'I'm telling you, Izzy, you're overdoing things. Volunteering. College. You're wearing yourself out,' he grumbled as he got out the car. 'Look at the hours you do at the Bureau. All the training you've done and you're still just a volunteer. It's exploitation, pure and simple.'

She smiled thinly. It was an old conversation: Jim pretending to be worried about her, when they both knew the real reason for his disapproval was that he thought a captain of industry deserved the attention of a full-time wife. He shook his head and gave her one of his "I-don't–know-why-you-put-yourself through-it" looks. She linked her arm through his and an uneasy truce settled between them.

The Caledonian Hotel was a handsome Georgian townhouse. Chandeliers shone from its curtain-less windows and two pillars flanked a sweep of stairs leading up to the entrance. The lobby was deserted, but the muffled sounds of the party floated through from the lounge.

'Let me have a look at you,' she said, brushing down the sleeves of his sports jacket. He was wearing his new blue shirt; it looked a little on the tight side. 'Everything's going to be fine,' she said, pulling down his sleeves and straightening his cufflinks. The Rangers logo gleamed blue, red and white. She frowned, remembering what Sean had said about the club going bust, but dismissed the thought. Jim would have mentioned something by now if there was any truth to it.

Jim turned and examined himself in the hall mirror. He had become prosperous-looking in recent years, a padding of flesh settling around his cheeks and jowls, his eyes sparkling and beady. His nose, red and mottled with tiny pin pricks, reminded her of a strawberry. He was smoothing down his short hair. The black and grey bristles were gleaming with gel and there were patches of pink scalp on top where it was thinning. Only his moustache, black and luxurious, was unchanged from the young man she had married twenty years ago. She stared at their reflection as they stood side by side. They were both forty-one. Their marriage could last for another thirty years or more. She looked away, her heart fluttering in dismay.

'I know what you're thinking,' he said.

She felt herself blushing. 'You do?'

'What a hunk of a man you're married to.'

He was grinning like a schoolboy. 'You could earn a fortune as a mind reader, Jim Campbell,' she replied, laughing.

He pulled himself up to his full stocky height, as if reminding himself of the importance of good posture. He cocked his head and beamed, his moustache moving with his face. 'Will I do?' he asked.

'You look grand,' she replied.

He opened the door to the lounge and strode in. 'Call this a party?' he shouted. She heard cries of approval at his entrance before he was swallowed up by the crowd without a backward glance.

An hour later, and Izzy was alone in the corner. Jim was in the thick of it, loosened by alcohol and relief that the party was a success. He was dancing with his arms in the air. She imagined dark patches of sweat were forming under his armpits. The table in front of her was crammed with glasses and plates loaded with half-eaten hamburgers and chips. The ketchup made the food look like the carnage of roadkill. She had a powerful urge to scrape the plates clean and take them through to the kitchen, just to be useful.

'So, this is where you're hiding.' Moira from Finance landed heavily beside her. She was squeezed into a tight dress, her creamy breasts on full display. 'Jim's done awfy well for himself, hasn't he? He's got massive plans for the business. But why am I telling you this? You must know all about them.' She took a gulp of wine, but her timing was off and some of it spilt down her low-cut dress, running like bloody rivulets between her cleavage. She laughed loudly, as if she had done something clever. Izzy felt a mild weariness descend and had to remind herself that she was the odd one out: one of the few people in Glasgow who didn't drink and wasn't a recovering alcoholic.

She offered Moira a tissue and watched as she pawed herself dry. 'Yes. Jim's loving the job,' she said, biting her lip. Most nights, he came to bed late, smelling of whisky and toothpaste, his sleep restless and troubled. She gave him quite a few "why-are-you-putting-yourself through-this" looks herself these days.

'I expect things will change for you,' said Moira.

'Change? In what way?'

'For starters, if I was tall and slim like you, and had a husband with plenty of cash, I would buy a new wardrobe for myself.'

Izzy looked down at her dress. It was a simple cotton frock with a floral pattern of green and blue. It was so comfortable, it was easy to forget she was wearing it. 'What's wrong with my dress? I bought this at *Vanessa's Once Loved* in Byres Road last year. She sells some lovely vintage things.'

'I don't think Jim will want his wife buying second-hand clothes from now on,' said Moira, pursing her lips and handing back the tissue. It was scrunched up into a gory ball. Izzy flushed, her pale skin betraying her inner irritation.

'Look over there,' said Moira, lowering her voice.

Izzy followed her gaze to a group of young girls standing by the bar. They were like a flock of pretty birds in brightly-coloured mini dresses that were nipped in at the waist, their dimpled thighs tottering on killer heels. Their faces were painted; their smiles fixed like a clown's.

'They're temps. Jim's hired them to cope with the new orders. They're all in love with him, you know.'

Izzy wanted to laugh. They weren't much older than Davy.

'They love his banter and jokes. Plus, he's very generous.

Always gets a round in at lunchtime.'

Izzy nodded, as if agreeing that would explain his popularity with young girls. She had a sudden fear he might be making a fool of himself, or worse, opening himself up to harassment claims. 'Yes, Jim's quite a character,' she said, resolving to have a quiet word with him later.

Moira shrugged. 'I'm just saying you could do more with yourself, Izzy. A lot more.' She heaved herself up and swayed gently back to the bar.

The heat in the room was making Izzy feel clammy. One of the temps was staring at her, pity and boldness shining from her kohl-lined eyes. Izzy looked away. She fingered the row of pearl buttons below the V-neck of her dress and had a fleeting impulse to undo one or two of them, before dismissing the idea as ridiculous.

She looked at the clock and yawned. Time seemed to be going backwards. A rogue thought entered her mind: men like Sean Docherty probably preferred natural-looking women. She wondered what he was doing at that moment. In a bar with his brother, maybe? It would be easy enough to find out. The east end of Glasgow was like a village. She would only have to ask in one or two of the pubs if anyone had seen them. She could buy them a drink or two – pick Sean's brains about Gregory Bateson for her essay and encourage Connor not to lose hope. The Gallowgate was a ten-minute taxi ride from the hotel. The thought made the hairs on her arms stand up.

She moved like a ghost, unseen, as she made her way out of the lounge. The hotel lobby was empty; no one came or went. She opened the front door and stood on the top step. Her heart was racing and she took a deep breath to calm herself, pulling her shawl across her shoulders. The light still lingered but the sky was clouding over; she could smell the rain in the air.

'Izzy? Is that you?' Bill was walking towards her, his gait a mixture of arthritis and too many whiskies. Her disobedient heart sank and her limbs deadened.

'Just needed some fresh air,' she explained.

He stubbed out his cigar and stumbled up the steps, pausing for a moment at the top to catch his breath. 'How's my lovely girl?' he mumbled, leaning over and kissing her on the cheek. She could identify the individual elements of his bad breath: whisky, hamburger and the rich loamy smell of nicotine.

'I'm fine, Bill. How are you? Enjoying life as the Chairman?' she asked. He had taken her arm and was guiding her back into the hotel lobby, as if he had decided that she'd had enough fresh air for the evening. It was pointless to resist.

'I suppose Jim told you that being the Chairman is the same as retiring? That all I do is play golf? Don't believe a word of it. I let him have his head, but I watch his every move. I don't miss a thing.'

She allowed him to take her shawl from her shoulders. The *thud thud* of bass notes rumbled in the air and one or two stray shouts escaped from the lounge. Bill took her hand as if she was a child who needed help crossing the road.

'So many people I don't know. I feel like a stranger,' she said, dropping his hand. Her fingers felt moist and clammy. She wanted to wipe them dry.

'It was Jim's idea to invite the sub-contractors and their partners. Since we expanded into industrial alarms, we've got an army of them working for us.'

'That's a good thing, I suppose. That the business is expanding.'

'Of course it is,' but he looked more worried than pleased. 'Best get back in there. We don't want to set tongues wagging,' he said, winking at her. Disgust rose briefly in the back of her throat. The door opened and a blast of hot air, flashing lights and music assaulted her senses. It took a moment to orientate herself. Jim was standing on the stage, coughing into a microphone.

'Your attention, please,' he shouted. She could hear a slight slurring in his voice. People stopped dancing and the place stilled. 'Izzy? Where are you?' He was shielding his eyes and looking out beyond the dance floor. Bill nudged her gently. Slowly, she made her way towards the stage. Jim helped her up some stairs at the side and then pressed her into his side. A smile stuck to her face and her skin burned with embarrassment.

'Sales are up. Customer satisfaction is up. Profits are up.'

Someone from the back of the crowd shouted: 'Go on yersel', son.' Jim paused, waiting for the cheers and clapping to subside. 'Today, I'm also proud to announce that Verisafe is on the shortlist to update the alarm system of none other than the most famous football club in the world ... Glasgow Rangers.'

More whoops and yells rose from the crowd. Izzy felt the blood drain from her face. She wanted to shout, 'Wait a minute, I'm not sure this is a good idea.' Instead, she stood as silent as a mannequin. The DJ started playing 'Here come the billy boys' at top volume. People were jumping like pogo sticks to the music. Strobe lights in the Rangers' colours of red, white and blue danced over their heads. She suddenly felt disconnected, as if she was leaving this world for another.

The music ended and the jumping subsided. People stood, looking towards the platform, staring at Jim and Izzy. Seconds passed; her flesh crawled under their scrutiny. Jim moved the microphone closer to his mouth and whispered huskily, 'And none of this would be possible if it weren't for all of you.'

There was a spontaneous round of applause. Someone from the back shouted, 'Gie us a pay rise,' followed by an even louder round of applause. Jim held up his hand to silence them. 'There's one person I'd like to single out for a special mention: my wonderful, beautiful wife, Izzy.'

He kissed her. There were more shouts and whistles. She tried to soften the tension in her face, but when he released her, her cheeks felt rigid.

'Now, let's have you all on the dance floor,' cried Jim.

She slipped her arm from his. 'You go. I'll keep Bill company.'

The music had shifted to a slow smooch. The dance floor lights dimmed and the knot of people tightened in on themselves. Bill was observing her carefully. 'The deal's worth hundreds of thousands if he pulls it off.'

'I heard at the Bureau today that Rangers are in financial trouble,' she said, keeping her voice low.

'There's always talk about football clubs having money troubles. A new management team bought the club in the summer. They've got deep pockets, so there's no need to worry.'

'But, Bill, this was more than talk. The sheriff visited Ibrox today.' A small ball of dread was forming, pressing like a weight against her chest.

'Just a wee show of strength from the powers-that-be, to make it look like they're doing something. It means nothing.' He patted her hand, his eyes rheumy with desire.

Suddenly, a burst of shouting erupted from the back of the dance floor. The crowd had parted and she could see Jim grappling with a young man. One of the temps was standing to the side. Izzy thought she might be crying. Moira from Finance bustled over and separated the two men, before turning to Jim to straighten the lapels of his shirt, laughing that loud laugh of hers. Jim brushed his shirt sleeves vigorously, as if trying to rid himself of dog hair.

'Just a bit of pushing and shoving by the looks of it,' said Bill.

Her face was on fire. She knew Bill was trying to reassure her, but she felt overwhelmed by embarrassment. The upset girl and boy walked off together and the space closed over. Jim was breathing heavily as he approached their table, wiping spittle from his mouth with his handkerchief. Sweat stood out on his moustache.

'Did you see that, Bill? I was assaulted by that wee bastard,' said Jim. He was part angry, part ashamed, but mostly drunk. He avoided Izzy's eye.

'Best to walk away,' said Bill.

He hadn't made room for Jim to sit down and Izzy took that as her cue and got to her feet.

'Time to go home, Jim,' she said.

'I'll go home when I'm fucking ready to go home.' Jim's face was red and raw-looking, his eyes glassy and unfocused. Turning, he bumped into the back of a chair, kicking it out of his way as he walked back to the bar. A few people were looking in their direction. Bill caught her eye and passed her Jim's jacket. She moved instinctively, picked up her bag and walked to the bar. She linked her arm through Jim's and tried to pull him away. 'Time to go,' she insisted.

'What can I get anyone?' Jim shouted, shrugging her off. No one replied or took him up on his offer. Izzy smiled, grateful, and firmly pulled him away.

She sat quietly in the driver's seat as Jim fell in beside her. Night had fallen and with it had come the rain. It was pelting down, pounding on the bonnet. 'I bet that wee bugger of a boyfriend was high on drugs. I'll make sure he never works for us again,' he said. She didn't reply. Instead, she started the car. The windscreen wipers came to life, pushing aside a curtain of rain.

'Apart from that wee strammy, the night went well, don't you think?' he asked.

'Very well,' she said, pulling out onto the road and slowing as she approached some traffic lights, the red stop light blazing in the wet darkness.

'You're not saying much, Izzy.'

'I hope Rangers' new management have as much money as they say they have,' she said. Her tone was mild but she knew her words would anger him.

'All this talk about the club going bust is pish. Bloody pish. We're talking about the oldest football club in the world. We're talking about the most successful football club … in … the … world.'

She moved away from the light, stepping on the accelerator, and indicated to overtake the car in front. Her heart was quickening as she switched the wipers to double speed. 'The club owes the taxman millions, Jim. They're going bust.' She paused. 'It's common knowledge to everyone except Ranger supporters. And their suppliers.' She felt a small thrill of rebellion before pulling the car back into the slow lane, the wipers resuming their normal rhythm. She kept her eyes on the road but could feel Jim's stare drill into her.

'You know what your trouble is, missus? You're spending too much time with Rangers haters. All those sad, wee feniens in the Gallowgate. It's jealousy, pure and simple. League champions for the past two years? It must make every Celtic supporter feel like shite.'

She gripped the steering wheel tightly. 'Let's hope you're right and I'm wrong,' she said, slowing the car to a stop at the next set of lights.

He lurched over to her side. 'Let's not argue, Izzy love. D'you know how beautiful you are?' He slipped his hand into her dress and squeezed her breast.

'Jim, I'm driving,' she said, removing his hand. The light changed to green and she put the car in gear. Jim slumped back in his seat. Wine fumes seeped from his flesh, mingling with the warm fug of the car. A moment later, his snores filled the silence. She had a wild thought. She could park in a side road, slip his seat belt off and take his door off the latch. Then drive back to the expressway and, when she reached a decent speed, she could reach over and push him out. His body would roly poly across the carriageway, his head bouncing like a burst turnip. It would be obvious to everyone that he was drunk: disorientated and not wearing his seatbelt, who opened his door by mistake. No one would suspect her. Her heart began to pound.

She took a sharp intake of breath. The vividness of the image frightened her. The thrill of it frightened her even more. A pulse beat in her ear as she drew up outside the house and turned off the engine. Jim was still slumped in the passenger seat, snoring softly, his face guileless and trusting. His mouth was gaping; the saliva dribbling from his lips, leaving a silvery trail. She gently prodded him. He stirred and his eyes opened, suddenly focused.

'We're home, Jim. Safe and sound.'

***

Therapist:	Jim? I'm glad you called. How did the party go?
Jim:	It was magic. A triumph, even though I say so myself.
Therapist:	Good to hear. How about your drinking?
Jim:	Oh, you know. Work in progress.
Therapist:	Are you planning to come and see me this week? I hope so.

Jim: I don't think Izzy loves me anymore.

Therapist: (Silence)

Jim: I think she's having an affair.

Therapist: I've got time to see you this afternoon.

CHAPTER 3

The three tower blocks of Glasgow Technical College stood at the top end of the High Street. Build in the 1960s, the concrete facings were streaked with damp, the window frames chipped and some of the upper floors looked like they'd already been condemned as unfit for habitation. Izzy gazed up at the buildings and felt her heart swell with gratitude.

Students were milling around the cafeteria. A TV monitor in the corner was advertising how to apply for hardship funds, but no one was paying any attention to it. Most of the students were wearing expensive, branded sportswear with their ubiquitous stripes and ticks. Izzy glanced at her jeans, cotton blouse and denim jacket. She'd tried her best to fit in, to look understated and casual, but somehow, she had only succeeded in looking like one of their teachers.

From a distance, the lady at the coffee counter could have been mistaken for a student. When she turned to serve her, Izzy was shocked by her lined, leathery face and felt a pinch of shame at feeling pleased she wasn't the oldest-looking person in the place.

She took a seat by the window and waited for Bridget. A cluster of girls sat nearby, discussing their hairdressing class. Their hair, nails, make-up and clothes were immaculate. She wondered what had happened to the days of student rebellion, of protest, of grunge and squalor. Perhaps that was a luxury young people couldn't afford in 2011 …

Bridget floated in wearing a cheesecloth blouse, stretched tight over her bosom, and loose, denim dungarees with a dropped waist; clothes better suited to a teenager than a forty-year-old woman. Izzy felt disloyal thinking like that. Bridget wore her outfits with such joy. Her hair was cut close to her head, like a coating of thick, dark fur and her over-sized, black-rimmed glasses gave her an owl-like look. The overall effect might have been masculine, but her mouth was generous and her full lips were painted a bright slut red.

Bridget looked across at the hairdressing girls. 'Jesus, I can't believe those bimbos attend a seat of learning,' she said, loud enough for them to hear her. 'Their obsession with looking like Barbie dolls is driving back the cause of feminism faster than it takes for their mascara to dry.'

'Now, Bridget,' Izzy chastened softly.

'You're right, Izzy. Appearances can be deceptive. For all we know, they could be the Tech's first Nobel prize winners – for discovering the cure for split ends.'

'I suppose they're refining their skills on themselves. There'll be a lot of competition for jobs in the beauty industry after they leave here.'

'What self-respecting person would want to be part of an industry whose sole aim is to make women feel inadequate and ugly?'

'Oh, come on. We were the same at their age, more interested in fashion than studying.'

'We weren't interested in studying because we were indoctrinated into thinking that the only career we were fit for was marriage and children.'

'I left school at sixteen. No one mentioned going to college. It was normal back then,' said Izzy.

'Well, it's 2011. Forgive me if I get cross when I see young girls, who are capable of so much more, dedicating their lives to looking like a bunch of living corpses.'

Bridget had a point, the girl at the centre of the group looked like she was wearing a death mask. Her perfect, heart-shaped face was thickly coated in a dun-coloured foundation. Only her candyfloss lips moved, mobile with indignation about the college lacking the latest technology in laser hair removal treatments.

'How was your weekend?' asked Izzy.

'I went on that *Plenty of Fish* date with Bruno,' said Bridget.

'The one who works out in the gym and plays the cornet?'

'Well, the last time he saw the inside of a gym was when I went to confession and, believe me, Izzy, that was a very long time ago. His arms shoogled like bags of blubber every time he lifted his pint. Mind you, I couldn't take my eyes off his face …'

'He was good-looking then?'

'… His face was covered in these wee warts and skin tags. I wanted to snip them off with my nail scissors. D'you think they would have bled?'

'Probably best not to have risked it,' said Izzy.

'Anyhow, he was nice enough. Works at Morrisons. Plays in a brass band. Offered to pay for the drinks. But no, I didn't fancy him.'

'So the date ended at the pub?'

'I went back to his flat. He was gagging for it and so was I. You know, just a fuck buddy thing,' she said, shrugging her fleshy shoulders. 'It wasn't that brilliant, sad to say. For such a big lad, he was a tad disappointing in the downstairs department. I didn't even feel it going into me. We didn't have a condom and his jism landed on my new black skirt. It's left a white mark that I can't sponge off. It's dry-clean only, too.'

Izzy was half horrified, half captivated. Bridget burst out laughing. 'Your face is priceless. Of course the date ended after the pub. Went straight home. Tended to myself.'

Izzy didn't know whether to laugh or show sympathy, so she settled on an encouraging smile.

'And how was your weekend? Mrs-Happily-Married-Ever-After?' asked Bridget.

'I met an interesting man at the Bureau. Tall, slim and good-looking in an intense kind of way. He had read Bateson. I wanted to go to the pub with him to discuss my essay, but didn't manage to escape from the Verisafe Summer Party. Jim got drunk and was beaten up by the jealous boyfriend of a girl half his age. On the way home, I came up with a plan to push him out of the car when driving at speed. He wouldn't have felt a thing.'

Bridget was looking at her curiously. Waiting. Izzy realised she hadn't spoken out loud.

'Rangers won on Saturday, so Jim was happy. Davy spent all weekend practicing with his new band so he was happy, too. Though, God knows how he'll pass his exams at this rate. I wrote my Bateson essay, so yes, a happy family all round.'

'You wee girlie swot. I can't make head nor tail of Gregory Bateson,' said Bridget.

'In my essay, I wrote that curiosity, not cleverness, was a better starting point.' As the words left her mouth, she could hear Sean's English accent in her head.

'Jesus, Izzy. You're even beginning to sound like Bateson. So, tell me, where did your curiosity take you?'

'There's a chapter called *Why Do Things Get in a Muddle?* I thought that was a good place to start since my work at the Bureau is all about helping people tidy up their financial muddles. In my essay, I questioned whether my clients' muddles were a consequence of people making bad choices, or whether they weren't in a muddle at all; just facing the logical outcome of a society designed to encourage debt by making it ridiculously easy for people to borrow more than they can afford.'

'And what was your conclusion?'

'I'm not sure I came to one, except to say that the world still seems to be in a muddle and I keep trying to tidy it as best I can,' admitted Izzy.

'Brilliant. Academics love it when you admire a problem. I mean, God forbid that anyone actually comes up with solutions.'

'Perhaps there aren't any solutions? Perhaps Bateson's right in saying the world is destined to remain in a constant state of muddle.'

'Crap. Of course there are solutions, if there's the political will to implement them. There are massive changes afoot in this country, and I'm going to be part of it.'

'What massive changes?'

Bridget hunkered down and lowered her voice. 'There's going to be a referendum on Scottish Independence. No date has been confirmed, but the Scottish National Party gains at the last election make it inevitable.'

The hairdressing girls erupted in laughter. Izzy looked over, wondering if they had overheard them and were laughing at the idea of Scottish Independence, but they were clustered around a phone. 'Look at the size of that one,' one of them shouted, pointing at the screen. The others screamed in response.

Bridget's eyes were dancing. 'I've joined the Scottish National Party.'

'I thought you were a lifelong Labour supporter?' asked Izzy.

'I was. As was my dad before me, and his dad before him. But this country needs to take charge of its own destiny and only the SNP seem to understand that.'

Izzy wanted to confess she had never voted at any general election, but thought it best not to admit the true extent of her apathy.

'I've not just joined them, Izzy, I've applied to be a candidate at the next general election,' added Bridget, her shoulders back, her head held high.

'A Member of Parliament? But what about your studies?' asked Izzy.

'It'll be four years before the next general election. Anyhow, there's no guarantee I'll be selected. The competition will be incredible.'

'You'll be brilliant,' breathed Izzy, giving her a hug.

Izzy's phone pinged with a text from Shona: *Call me. It's about Mr Docherty.* She felt a small start of pleasure at seeing the name. 'I have to call the Bureau. You go on ahead. Save me a seat.'

'No problem, it's the first lecture on a Monday morning. Only the sad old gits like us and the weirdos who didn't get their leg over at the weekend will be there. Sometimes that can be the same person,' she said, as she slouched off.

Shona picked up straight away. 'Izzy, do you remember Connor Docherty? Last appointment on Friday? His wife's just been on the phone. He's not coming in for his appointment at eleven.'

Izzy felt her shoulders slump. No surprise, but still a shame.

'She said he tried to commit suicide over the weekend.'

***

Therapist:	Did something happen at the party to make you think Izzy's having an affair?
Jim:	I announced we're on the shortlist for a deal with Rangers, worth hundreds of thousands. Everyone was ecstatic, but she didn't even smile. Her face was the length of Sauchiehall Street. She couldn't wait to get away and cosy up to Bill, the Chairman.
Therapist:	You think Izzy's having an affair with him?
Jim:	(Holds his head in his hands) I don't know what to think. Bill's over seventy. I doubt he can even get it up these days. I'm probably just being paranoid. Sometimes, I feel like my head's going to burst.
Therapist:	Your mum's death, the stress of your new job and drinking more than usual – it's not surprising you feel anxious.
Jim:	There's something else I haven't told you.
Therapist:	(Silence)
Jim:	Is everything I say completely confidential?

Therapist: Absolutely.

Jim: You promise you won't tell anyone?

Therapist: I promise.

Jim: I witnessed a fight. A young lad was hurt. He died ... and it's my fault.

CHAPTER 4

'I didn't mean for you to drop everything and come over. It could have waited until tomorrow,' said Shona. Her office was slightly larger than Izzy's but with the same bare look of institutional underfunding. Her long service certificate hung on the wall behind her desk. Its gold frame shone like a prize.

Izzy took off her denim jacket and draped it across the back of her chair. Shona, she noticed, still had her jacket on. It was black and a little tight across her chest. A thread was unravelling from one of the buttons. She would need to be careful or she'd lose it. Shona was appraising her carefully whilst warming her hands on an outsized mug of tea.

'I had to come and find out if Mr Docherty is OK,' said Izzy. She could feel her chest tightening.

'He's alive. That's about all we know,' replied Shona.

'Is he in hospital?' asked Izzy.

'Izzy,' Shona started, then paused. She put down her cup, got up and closed the door. Izzy prepared herself for bad news.

'Izzy, I've been speaking to Alan.'

'Alan? Alan, the receptionist?'

'He told me that you saw Mr Docherty out of hours. That he had to break up the meeting because it was already after six, and that he found you in, well, a slightly *compromising* position.'

'A what?'

'He said you were holding hands.'

'I was reassuring him as he was worried about filling in the Income and Creditors form,' explained Izzy, feeling a sense of injustice building.

'I've spoken to you before about the importance of keeping an emotional distance. Of course, we must apply empathy, but we mustn't over relate with our clients.'

'Apply empathy? What? Like a coat of paint? Empathy is about putting yourself in someone else's shoes. Seeing the world from their perspective. It's something you feel,' said Izzy, struggling to control her rising voice.

Shona's expression was blank, her face closed off. So, this was what you looked like when practising emotional distance.

'I've read his file, Izzy. I see his son died. He was the same age as Davy, wasn't he? That must have been hard for you.'

Izzy felt her face stiffening in disbelief. Shona was applying empathy; applying it thickly with a trowel. 'I was totally professional in all my dealings with Mr Docherty. I conducted myself in a friendly, calm and reassuring manner.' Izzy saw a flicker of recognition in Shona's eyes on hearing one of her favourite mantras.

'The note you left on the system wasn't as detailed, or complete, as it should be,' said Shona. Her voice was gentle, but insistent. 'You know you must cross-reference all advice with the relative rule number in the database.' Izzy felt her sense of unfairness deepening. Shona might be the most senior person in the office, but she hadn't mastered the latest system and depended on either Izzy or Alan to input data for her.

'It was late. Alan wanted to get away,' she said, sounding like Davy when giving excuses for not doing his homework.

'The office shuts at five-thirty. Only in emergencies, and with my approval, should it stay open longer. You knew I was at a meeting at the Council Chambers. I don't understand why you didn't call me.'

Izzy slumped back in her seat. Defeat settled on her like a chill. She could hear Shona's voice in the background, talking about how rules were there to protect both herself and the client, but her mind was in a swirl. What a terrible thing to have happened to Connor. She wondered where

Sean was. Perhaps he was at his bedside in the hospital, keeping vigil.

'Izzy.' The mention of her name brought her attention back to Shona. 'You've been with us for over three years. You're one of our most valued volunteers. We've all over-empathised at some point – it shows you care – but we must maintain boundaries, OK?'

A petty thought had wormed its way into her head: to resign. That would leave them in a right mess. Show them how much their bloody boundaries mattered. 'OK,' she mumbled.

'Good. Now go back to college and put this behind you,' Shona said, giving her a kindly smile. Izzy returned it with one of her own, but it was low wattage, like one of those Eco bulbs that do the job with the least amount of energy.

Shona was right. She must learn to keep a professional distance with clients, but a small knot of stubbornness was refusing to budge. Abandoning Connor felt wrong. His debts weren't going to go away. His creditors would be relentless in chasing him and his wife. His wife. Shona said she had been the one who had called in. Perhaps Izzy could speak to her? Offer her help? There was an outreach team who did home visits, but it would take weeks to organise. She slipped into her office next door. The cabinet wasn't locked and she found Connor's file right away. He lived around the corner; she didn't have to write down his address to remember it.

The Gallowgate was infamous for crime but there was no hint of its reputation that quiet Monday morning. A warm drizzle was falling, releasing the perfume of stale, fried food. Connor's flat was in a block of tenements, just beyond a run of tatty-looking shops. She stared at the building, feeling a sense of deep sorrow. The paintwork around the windows was peeling, exposing rotten woodwork, and some had sheets rigged up for curtains. The council had earmarked swathes of the area for redevelopment but, until then, the buildings had no choice but to wait, until decay, and then the bulldozers, claimed them.

A security system with a bank of buttons had been fitted by the building's entrance. Docherty was on the second floor. She pressed the buzzer and waited, feeling her pulse quicken. No reply. She pressed it again. If no one answered, she would take that as a sign that she was overstepping her remit and leave. She waited. No reply. She walked up to the main door and gave it a push; the lock was broken and it opened effortlessly. Inside, the hallway smelt of disinfectant and curry powder. She walked up the stairs and knocked on the Dochertys' door, the sound echoing along the stairwell. Silence. The loudest noise was her heart knocking against her ribs. She knocked again, more gently this time. She didn't want to sound like a bailiff battering their door down.

The door on the opposite side of the landing creaked. Izzy turned slowly and sensed, rather than saw, that someone was behind it.

'What do you want?' It was a woman's voice, croaky from smoking, crying or shouting, or perhaps all three.

'I'm here to see Mrs Docherty,' said Izzy, her middle-class accent amplified in the boom of the acoustic.

'Are you from the charity?' the voice asked. The door opened a fraction more.

Izzy replied without thinking, 'Yes.' It was a small lie as, technically, the Citizens Advice Bureau was a charity.

'Hold on. I've got something for you,' the voice said before closing the door. The dankness of the hallway felt ominous; she could feel a sense of threat closing in on her like a deepening twilight. The door opened again, this time wide enough to allow an arm to slip through and pass Izzy an envelope.

'Carol's been at the hospital since Friday night so I haven't been able to give her this. Andrew did well in his sponsored swim. Thirty lengths.'

Izzy took the envelope but the woman had closed her door before she could thank her.

Carol must be Connor's wife. So, given that she had been at the hospital since Friday night, Connor must have attempted suicide after Izzy's meeting with Sean. She looked at the envelope and felt the weight of the coins inside it. On the front was printed "SOS". Beneath it, in smaller letters: *Sense Over Sectarianism*. There was an address. It was close to Glasgow Tech – she could walk there in less than half an hour.

She must have passed the doorway a hundred times on her way to college, but never paid attention to it. It was set between a nightclub and a Korean restaurant. It looked like the offices of lawyers or surveyors, but, on closer inspection, she could see paint was peeling on the walls and the list of companies on the metal plate was a strange mix: *The Exchange, Dynamic Motion, The Snicket.* SOS was on the fifth floor. *Carol Docherty, Founder,* was printed under the company name.

The broad flight of stairs narrowed as she climbed up them. On the top floor, a door leading to a small reception area was wedged open. Izzy walked in. A poster had been stuck on the wall: *Boot out Bigotry!* Underneath was a picture of young people in Rangers and Celtic football strips with their arms round each other. It was a lovely picture, but she knew it must have been staged as no self-respecting football fan would want to be seen hugging the enemy. A girl in her early twenties was struggling to lift a large box onto the reception counter.

'Let me help you with that,' said Izzy.

'Thanks,' the girl said pleasantly. She had olive skin, black eyes and beautiful hair that fell like a bright, shiny curtain across her face. She pushed it aside as if it was alive, pestering her for attention.

'Posters for *The Shindig*,' said the girl, opening the box and handing Izzy a leaflet from the top of the pile. There was a photograph of Glasgow Green, packed with festivalgoers and a stage decked out in peace symbols. The banner across the front read: *Sense Over Sectarianism.*

'Looks like it'll be a great party,' said Izzy, handing it back.

'Keep it. Spread the word. *The Shindig* is our first big fundraising event. *Django, Django* are headlining. The lead singer is Will's older brother. Will was Mark's best friend, you know.'

Izzy didn't know who any of these people were, but she recognised a chatterbox. If she listened attentively and made encouraging gestures, the girl would talk all day. 'But *The Shindig* isn't just for famous bands, you know. There's a competition for new bands, too,' the girl went on.

'Brilliant,' said Izzy and then feeling guilty for pretending to know what the girl was talking about, added, 'My son, Davy, is in a band.'

'We've still got a place left if he wants to audition.'

'I'll tell him, he might well be interested,' said Izzy.

'Well, we've only got one place left so if he wants it, I need to know now.'

Izzy's mind raced. Davy had spent all weekend rehearsing with his new band and Jim had given him one of his father-son lectures about getting his priorities right. Davy had smiled politely and gone to his room, where he turned the music up extra loud.

'Oh, in that case, thanks. He'll take it,' she said.

The girl pulled out a large diary. 'Name of the band?' she asked.

Izzy's mind went blank. She didn't even know if the band had a name. 'No idea,' she said apologetically.

'Brilliant,' said the girl, 'how do you spell it?'

It took a moment for Izzy to register that the girl thought "no idea" to be the band's name. 'Lower case, all one word,' she said, and then, a flash of inspiration, 'the "i" is written as the number one.' The girl's tongue protruded from her lips in concentration, a small pink tip.

'Right. Tell *no1dea* to be at St Stephen's church hall at three this Saturday afternoon, with two numbers prepared and no longer than eight minutes. Got that? Here's their booking slip.' Her smile was luminous. Izzy stared at the piece of paper. She felt excited, as if she had bought Davy a surprise present.

'Tell your son to ask for Carol when he arrives.'

Carol. The name brought her back to the reason she was here in the first place.

'Oh, sorry. I actually came here to give you this,' she said, handing over the donation envelope.

'Magic. It's always a hassle to chase people for their sponsorship money,' she said.

'So, what's the charity all about?' asked Izzy.

'Our goal is to eradicate religious bigotry from Scottish culture. We run workshops in schools and youth clubs, promoting religious tolerance and respect,' she explained. 'Here's a brochure we did for Lothian Education Council.'

Izzy glanced at the leaflet. Her attention was caught by a photograph of a dark, slight woman. Even in the grainy picture, Izzy could tell that her deep-set eyes were tinged with sadness.

'Is this Carol?'

The girl nodded.

'I heard what happened to Connor over the weekend,' said Izzy.

The girl bit her lip, her brown eyes filling with tears. 'After all they've been through, it's just not fair,' she said.

'Do you know how Connor's doing?' asked Izzy.

'No. But here's someone who might know more.'

Izzy turned. He was wearing the same faded jeans and, although he was now clean shaven and the Celtic strip was gone, she recognised him immediately.

***

Therapist:	You saw a fight where a boy died?
Jim:	Four months ago. We won 4-2 against Celtic. I was on top of the fucking world.
Therapist:	So, this fight happened at a football match?
Jim:	No. After the match. If only I had gone straight home …
Therapist:	What happened?
Jim:	Some of the lads persuaded me to have a couple of swift ones after the match. I told Davy to go on home without me. I wouldn't be long. Izzy was cooking my favourite dinner. Lasagne and apple pie.
Therapist:	Go on.
Jim:	Well, after a couple of pints … or maybe three, I can't remember – but I wasn't pissed, OK?
Therapist:	OK.
Jim:	Well, I was walking down the alleyway between Duke Street and Tollcross and a lad was coming towards me. He was wearing a Celtic strip. I called out to him, to carry on past me. Instead, he turned and

ran in the other direction, smack into a gang of Rangers supporters.

Therapist: Oh no …

Jim: By the time I got to him, the Rangers supporters had run off, and he was sitting against the wall. I asked him if he was OK. He said he was fine but his face was so white, it scared me. I picked up a broken bottle that was lying beside him. That's when I saw the blood on his thigh.

Therapist: What did you do then?

Jim: I don't take my mobile to matches, so I ran out onto Duke Street and grabbed the first person I saw, a lassie coming back from the shops. I asked her to call an ambulance. She wasn't keen at first. She thought I was part of the trouble.

Therapist: What happened then?

Jim: I ran. I ran as fast as my legs would carry me. I could hear sirens, so I knew help was on the way. When I was a decent distance away, I went into a bar. I only meant to have one or two but … well … you know, I'd had a helluva shock.

Therapist: So, what makes you think the boy's death
                 was your fault?

CHAPTER 5

The day had transformed from a drizzly morning to a sunny afternoon in a way only a northern town could do. Heat was rising from the pavement and the sky was blue with fluffy clouds, like a child's drawing of a summer day. Izzy and Sean walked down Cathedral Street in silence. His expression was inscrutable; she couldn't work out if he was pleased or irritated to see her.

He opened the door of The Hungry Tum and motioned for her to enter first. The smell of fried food made her stomach rumble, though there was nothing appetising to eat. The photographs advertising the café's specialities – burgers, pizzas and all day breakfasts – were curled at the edges with grease. The café was empty but for an assortment of odd tables and chairs that looked like they had been picked up at various jumble sales. The floor tiles were chipped, revealing the black linoleum surface underneath. She dismissed a vivid image of insects crawling over every surface.

'Coffee?' he asked. She nodded and threaded her way through the jungle of tables and chairs, eventually deciding on a window seat at the back where she could watch him as he stood at the counter ordering their drinks. He was wearing a slim-fitting T-shirt and looked as fit as a marathon runner. His hair was slightly damp, as if he had just stepped out of the shower, and he was jingling loose change in his pocket whilst shifting his weight from foot to foot. She took off her jacket and fluffed her hair. Every nerve in her body was jangling.

'What were you doing at SOS?' he asked, putting two mugs on the table. His tone of voice was mild, as if asking a friend what brought them to town.

'I went to Connor's house. To ask Carol – Mrs Docherty – if there was anything I could do to help. She wasn't there, but a neighbour asked me to deliver some sponsorship money.'

He opened two sachets of sugar and poured them into his mug. 'Carol told me she had spoken to your boss, Sheila.'

'Shona.'

'Yes. She spoke to Shona and told her about Connor,' he said, raking his fingers through his hair. There was a blue vein lightly sketched on his temple. He was wearing a watch, which had a rose gold strap. Izzy was sure he hadn't been wearing that on Friday.

'How is he?' she asked.

'Not so good,' he said looking out of the window. The sun poured through the glass, highlighting its dirty streaks. The bus shelter across the road had a poster with the caption: *Calm your cravings and quit for good.*

There were posters like that plastered all over in Glasgow. What a waste of money. Their motivational slogans didn't change anything. Their bright, shiny promises so far out of reach, it was enough to drive folks to despair.

'Anyway, how are you?' he asked, changing the subject. His charming smile was back, but it hadn't reached his eyes.

'Me? Fine. Good. I got my Bateson essay written, thanks to you,' she said.

'I didn't do much, except encourage you not to feel intimidated, to trust your curiosity,' he said.

She felt a sudden boldness. 'I'm curious about you. Are you a teacher?'

'I suppose I asked for that. No, I'm not a teacher. I'm a journalist. Freelance. I live in London,' he said.

'You don't sound like you're from here,' Izzy stated, feeling an unexpected punch of disappointment that he didn't live closer.

'I was born in Glasgow but my parents split up when I was three. Mum and I went to live in Brighton. Dad re-married and Connor was born shortly afterwards.'

Sean had a far-away look in his eye, as if he was remembering a happier past.

'How did Connor's son die?' Izzy asked gently.

'Mark was murdered walking home from a football match. Just for wearing the wrong strip. He was attacked by a gang of Rangers supporters. Connor wasn't with him that day, something he can't forgive himself for. He believes that if he'd been there, he would've been able to protect him. But it's not just Connor who feels guilty, we all do.' There was a slight break in his voice and he looked down, stirring the sugar in his coffee.

Words dried up in her throat. 'I'm so sorry,' she said eventually. It was inadequate, but he nodded in acknowledgement.

'So, Carol founded SOS because of what happened to Mark?'

He drained his cup, sat back in his seat and looked at her, now fully composed. 'That's how she's dealt with her grief. She calls sectarianism "Scotland's secret shame."'

'I hate football,' Izzy admitted. 'It's hard to understand why football supporters fight each other because of religious differences when so few of them care about religion or even go to church,' she added.

Sean shifted in his seat and leaned forward, animated. 'Celtic and Rangers fans have a complicated hatred for each other. The only thing they seem to agree on is that they should be allowed to hate each other.'

'You must hate Rangers, too? Especially after what happened to your nephew,' she said.

Sean raised his eyebrows. 'No, I don't hate Rangers, but I hate what's happening to the club. The new management are incompetent clowns. The fans deserve better. It's bad for Celtic supporters, too, though they might not agree with me. Scottish football relies on the rivalry between the two clubs.'

'So, is it just a matter of time before Rangers goes bankrupt?' asked Izzy, bracing herself for his answer.

'The club owes the taxman millions. That's a fact everyone agrees on. But Rangers isn't just a football club, it's a Scottish institution with friends in high places. They think they're untouchable, that they'll find a way to avoid paying what they owe.'

'That can't be right, surely?' said Izzy.

'It's not,' he said, his hazel eyes alive with intensity. 'I've persuaded Matt, my editor in London, to give me three months to expose their corruption before it's too late and the club disappears forever.'

She felt a frisson of fear, the same fear she'd felt when they first met at the Bureau. His passion and desire scared her. Yet, at the same time, it felt as if she was being lit from the inside out. Her hands had begun to tremble, but when she looked at them, they were lying in her lap, still and composed.

'It's not going to be easy. I was told by a well-known newspaper editor that my interest in the club was "unhealthy". I've been refused a press pass for Ibrox.'

'So, how will you find out anything if no one will speak to you?' she asked, leaning forward.

'Good question,' he said.

'My husband's a fan. A big fan,' she blurted out.

'And, let me guess, he's not worried about the club's finances.'

'No, he's not,' she agreed. She wanted to add that Jim wasn't an ordinary fan, either, and that he was bidding for a huge alarm contract with them. He was friendly with all the senior managers. She wondered if she should tell him this. The minutes ticked by but she said nothing.

'Well, if he's interested in talking to a catholic journalist intent on exposing the corruption in the management of his beloved club, here's my card.'

They both laughed at the absurdity of such a thing.

'Go on. Take it.' He pushed his card across the table. It had his name and mobile number in a simple font. She put it her pocket, resolving to transfer it to her wallet later, for safekeeping. He looked around. He was getting ready to leave. Her mind was buzzing, trying to think of a way to delay him.

'I hope Connor will be OK. Carol must be beside herself with worry.'

'She is, but it's complicated. They're separated, on and off for the past two years,' he said, gathering up their mugs and taking them to the counter. He was moving quickly, in a way that discouraged any further conversation.

They stood side by side in the doorway of the café. Dust and diesel fumes from Buchanan Bus Station blew in the soft wind. She could see her reflection in the café window: she was flushed and smiling a little too brightly.

'Thanks for listening to my ranting about football corruption,' he said, 'and thanks for caring about Connor.' His eyes flickered over her, taking care not to linger on any feature too long, as if he was committing her face to memory.

She fingered the card in her pocket; she couldn't bear the thought of not seeing him again. 'I'll give you a call if I think of anything that may help with the Rangers story. You never know,' she said.

'You're right. You never know,' he replied, leaning towards her and brushing her cheek with his lips. It was a London kiss, meaningless. Yet, when she touched her cheek a moment later, she felt a wonderful heat.

**

Jim:	The boy bled to death in that alleyway. It was in the papers the next day. (Shakes his head) He was a just a kid. The same age as Davy.
Therapist:	Sectarian violence. It's a blight on our society.
Jim:	Aye, but it's the ways things are. It'll never change.
Therapist:	I still don't understand why you think you were responsible for the boy's death?
Jim	I keep thinking that, if I had stayed with him, did some first aid on him, things might have turned out different. But what could I have done? I'm no good with blood. I usually faint at the sight of it. I had to run away. There were bloodstains on my jacket and my prints were on the bottle. The lass that called the ambulance wanted to take a photo of me on her phone. If the police had caught me, I would've been in big trouble. Even if they believed I wasn't involved, the Celtic fans wouldn't. I'd be a wanted man.
Therapist:	Have you been involved in sectarian violence before?

Jim: No. And I wasn't involved this time, either. I had nothing to do with the fight. I was just in the wrong place at the wrong time.

Therapist: And have you told anyone about this? I mean, apart from me?

Jim: No. And that's how it's going to stay. OK? I only told you because I think it made me drink more. I keep seeing that boy's face. That fucking pale face.

Therapist: Alcohol helps you forget the horror of what you witnessed?

Jim: I wish it did. The boy's mother has set up an anti-sectarian charity. It's do-gooder nonsense, of course. There's no chance the football culture in Glasgow will change, but it's just another fucking thing I could do without.

CHAPTER 6

The curved roof of Queen Street Station arched over the platforms, light flooded down, bouncing off the tiled floor, and the temperature was soaring. Bridget had taken off her jacket and rolled her sleeves up beyond her elbows, but her makeup was melting and her skin looked like softened wax.

'You'll miss your train,' warned Izzy, as she watched Bridget's fingers dance across her computer keyboard.

'No bother. I'll get the next one.' She had a look of intense concentration, like a lioness circling her prey. 'Sean Docherty's LinkedIn page confirms what he told you. He's a freelance journalist with an occasional column in *The Independent*. Lives in London and is single.' She looked up to see if Izzy had registered an interest in the last point. Izzy gave her an exasperated look in return.

'Not much more on his Facebook page,' sighed Bridget. 'Let me have a look at his Twitter account.'

'I wish I hadn't mentioned him,' Izzy murmured as she glanced at Bridget's notes on the lecture she had missed that morning. Although, in the heat, she was finding it difficult to focus.

'Wait a minute, here's something interesting. He wrote an article about single parents, which JK Rowling endorsed,' said Bridget.

Izzy continued reading the lecture notes. 'Go on then,' she said finally, 'what did he say about single parents?'

'That we criticise them too much. His mum had two jobs as a cleaner, and encouraged him to be ambitious. He was the only member of his family to go to university. Cambridge, no less. On the day he left home, she gave him £1,600, the money she had scrimped and saved for over fifteen years because she wanted him to buy books, and not just borrow them from the library. Wow,' breathed Bridget. 'What a wonderful story. I'm not sure my lad would ever write about me like that.'

Izzy squeezed her arm. 'Of course he would. You've brought him up, single-handed, to believe in himself. He's travelling in Australia because you've been a brilliant mum and role model to him.'

'Maybe. Maybe he's just found a way to escape from me. But I do know Davy would write something like this about you. He loves you to bits,' said Bridget.

Izzy looked down at her lap with a rush of regret. 'I always thought I'd have a houseful of children but when nothing happened after

Davy was born, Jim and I just accepted it wasn't to be. We talked a bit about adoption but there were so few babies being put up for adoption in those days. Now, people have more options like surrogacy, IVF, going abroad for babies …'

Bridget looked worried. 'Jesus, Izzy, I didn't know you were feeling broody.'

Izzy laughed lightly. 'I'm not. I'm very happy with my family. I'm just glad that attitudes are changing; that it's OK to be proactive and not just accept what nature throws at you.'

Bridget was scrolling through online images of Sean. There was a photograph of him wearing a dinner jacket. It had been taken at night and the flash lit up his face, exaggerating its gauntness. His collar looked too big for his neck and he had day-old stubble. Izzy couldn't decide if it looked artful or unkempt. He was smiling but his eyes were guarded, as if he distrusted the person taking his photograph. His expression was a mixture of fierceness and vulnerability. She couldn't take her eyes off it.

'He's not bad looking. I quite like the skinny, creative type,' commented Bridget.

'For goodness sake,' sighed Izzy. 'He's probably got some gorgeous girlfriend who goes with him to dinner parties at JK Rowling's house.'

'OK. OK. I get the message. Out of my league,' said Bridget.

'I didn't mean that. Sorry. This heat's making me crabby,' said Izzy, flapping the course notes in front of her face.

'So, he's investigating potential corruption at Rangers?' asked Bridget.

'No one wants to speak to him but he's determined to find out the truth.'

'A man with principles and a Rangers hater, too? I'm liking him more and more.'

'He doesn't hate Rangers, he just feels for the fans who are being misled. He wants to expose the incompetent management before the club collapses for good.'

'What's Jim's theory about the truth?' asked Bridget.

'That this new management has plenty of cash but doesn't want to give it to the taxman. Who knows what to believe? I'd like to help Sean but Jim would never want anything to do with a catholic journalist, I'm ashamed to say.'

'Don't be ashamed, Izzy. We're all part of the same history. My dad would have skinned me alive if I had brought home a "Proddy" boyfriend. Even though he's in his eighties and desperate to see me hitched, he'd feel the same today.' Bridget's eyes seemed enormous behind her black-rimmed glasses. 'You say you want to help Sean, so, other than Jim, what's stopping you?' The vibrancy of her red lipstick was almost accusatory. 'Jim doesn't need to know. You could go undercover.'

'Go undercover?' Izzy laughed. 'That sounds like a film, not real-life. Not my life, anyhow.'

Bridget waved her hand. 'I don't know what it means, either, but Jim must know plenty of people at the club. You must know a few of them yourself. Investigative journalists rely on sources and whistle-blowers.'

The tannoy crackled into life. 'The train now leaving platform seven is the 16:57 to Coatbridge.'

Bridget shut her laptop and turned to Izzy. 'The question to ask yourself is, do you want to make a difference in this world? You say it's a good thing to be proactive. Well … now's your chance. Are you content with playing small, or do you want to play big?'

'You're as mad as a frog in a sock,' said Izzy, reaching over to kiss Bridget goodbye.

Bridget laughed and kissed her back. 'Insulting me doesn't answer the question.'

Make a difference? Play small or play big? The questions confronted her like difficult clients at the Bureau. She wanted to deal with them and, at the same time, she wanted to send them away. She touched her cheek where Sean had kissed her. Her skin felt hot and sweaty now, but her hand stayed there for a while, trying to remember the feel of it.

***

Jim:	You think it's the drink that's making me paranoid, don't you? Thinking the dead boy's haunting me? Thinking Izzy's having an affair?
Therapist:	It's a possibility.
Jim:	Uncle Andy went doolally before dying of cirrhosis.
Therapist:	And your father?
Jim:	He took early retirement from his job working on the council. He was a heavy drinker, but it was the smoking that killed him. Lung cancer.
Therapist:	How old were you at the time?
Jim:	Fourteen. But mum was wonderful. She got herself a job in the Blantyre Buns factory working nights, so she was around for me during the day. Her work ethic was tremendous. She taught me a lot about the importance of graft. She liked a good drink, too, but it was never a problem.
Therapist:	What about Izzy? Does she drink?
Jim:	No, but she likes seeing me have a good time. She still laughs at my jokes. Bless

her. I met her when she came to work in the office at the garage. She was sixteen, and the most beautiful girl I'd ever seen. Tall, pale skin covered in freckles, with a mass of light brown hair. She was a natural beauty, but shy. Her parents were a lot older than mine and very strict. They made me promise to provide for her and that's what I've done. The job, bidding for the Rangers contract – it's all for her and Davy.

Therapist: Have you suspected her of having affairs before?

Jim: No and I don't know why I'm thinking it now. It's all in my head. She wasn't excited about the Rangers bid because she's exhausted. She works so hard at the Bureau and at college. What I need to do is spoil her a bit more.

Therapist: You might also consider cutting down on your drinking.

Jim: I might …

Therapist: Think about it. That's all I'm asking. Come back next week, we can talk more then.

CHAPTER 7

Izzy stood outside their mid-terrace villa. It had been their dream home when they'd bought it sixteen years ago, when Davy was a baby. Neat and squat, the grey sandstone walls sparkled in the summer light. The beech hedge had grown tall and the climbing rose now curled around the door and halfway around the back. She stood on the path and breathed in the blooms' pale perfume. Time doesn't fly, it dissolves into thin air.

Dust motes shimmered in the light that streamed from the stained-glass pane above the front door. The curtains were drawn in the big bay window, making the lounge gloomy, the atmosphere lethargic from the trapped warmth of the day. She drew the curtains apart and opened the windows. A warm flow of air filled the room. Her eye caught sight of the orchid that Bridget had bought her for Christmas. It was in pride of place on the mantelpiece, just below the picture of The Singing Butler. Bridget had said the red flowers and the black lacquer vase would match the colours in the painting, but the blooms hadn't lasted long. It had been a dead knobbly stem for months, though she hadn't had the heart to throw it out. She looked at it closely and let out a cry of surprise. Small flower buds were forming on the stem. It was a miracle. She hadn't watered it in weeks.

She closed the lounge door and turned to go upstairs. Her skin fizzed with heat. There was enough time for a cool bath before Jim and Davy got home.

'In here,' came a shout from the kitchen, followed by a crash of pans. Her heart folded in disappointment as she walked down the hallway to the kitchen. Jim was wearing his barbecue apron, with "*Get it doon yer gob*" written across it.

'I'm cooking tea tonight. Special treat. Steak and chips,' he said. His face was the colour of cooked beetroot and he looked as pleased as if he'd announced that he was taking her on a Caribbean cruise. Three slabs of red meat sat on greaseproof paper, a smearing of blood soiling the edges. The steaks were trimmed with fat, the colour of fungal nails. She could smell their flesh: warm, almost fetid, and swallowed a mouthful of saliva. 'What's the special occasion?' she asked, opening the back door to let some air in.

'Does there have to be a special occasion to spoil my lovely wife?' he asked catching her unawares in a bear hug. She thought, with dismay, that he might have sensed her initial flinch. She hugged him back, a little harder than usual, to compensate. His body felt spongy, the new floral aftershave he had taken to wearing smelt mouldy in the heat. There was a bottle of red wine on the table, half empty.

'There doesn't need to be a special occasion for you to cook tea, but as you've never done it before, you can't blame me for asking,' she said, freeing herself from his hug and sitting at the table.

'Where do you keep the chip pan?' he asked. He had hunkered down and was rummaging through the cupboard where the pots and pans were kept.

They hadn't had a chip pan for years. 'Just use any of the big pans,' she suggested. He hauled one out. It gleamed with newness. Izzy had bought it in a rare moment of extravagance at The Ideal Home Exhibition. It had been endorsed by a celebrity chef and boasted properties like radial heat and the latest non-stick technology.

'How was your day? Did you hand in your essay?' he asked. She watched with a sense of grief as Jim spooned slicks of beef dripping into the pan, wincing at the sound of the metal spoon scratching its non-stick surface. 'I don't know why you worry, Izzy. You'll be fine. You always do well.' She felt a mild throbbing begin at her temples. He was trying to be encouraging, but his careless belief in her ability had the effect of diminishing any achievement. His phone vibrated on the kitchen table and he snatched it up quickly. 'Jim Campbell here.' It was his dulcet voice, the voice he used for women. He brushed past her, as if she was invisible, and walked to the far end of the garden.

'Hiya,' shouted Davy from the front door. There was a soft scuffle, the thud of a rucksack being thrown to the floor and muted voices. He was not alone.

Six inches taller than Jim, Davy's head brushed the top of the doorway. His face had changed in recent months. His jaw and nose had lengthened and broadened. Only in the untidiness of his black hair and his guileless eyes could she see a trace of the disappearing boyhood face. She felt an acute sense of loss, as if something precious had been taken from her. His sixth form suit was shiny at the elbows and knees and his tie was loosened and askew, giving him a rebellious, cool look. Someone was standing behind him. He stepped aside and a girl came forwards, shyly. She was small, slim, with long red hair and a slender nose that some might describe as sharp, though it suited her pale, oval face. She was wearing a cotton dress and elaborate sandals, with straps that wrapped themselves around her thin ankles and calves.

'Mum, this is Cas, our lead singer.'

The girl stepped forward, uncertain of herself, her shyness adding to her beauty.

'Pleased to meet you,' said Izzy, standing up to shake her hand. It felt cool and boneless. 'Dad's cooking steak and chips, you're welcome to stay, Cas. There's plenty to go round.'

The girl's gaze drifted to the three slabs of meat. Her face paled further.

'Cas is a vegan, Mum,' said Davy. 'Anyhow, we're not staying. I just need to pick up my laptop and then we're off to Paul's.'

'What about a cup of tea,' said Izzy, 'or maybe you'd prefer something cold. It's so humid, isn't it?'

Cas looked from side to side, torn between choosing who to please. 'A glass of water would be lovely, Mrs Campbell,' she said quietly.

'I'll just get my laptop,' said Davy, bounding along the hallway at speed, as if he didn't want to leave Cas and Izzy alone for a moment longer than needed.

Izzy filled a glass with water and set it down in front of Cas. A silence descended between them. It had a fragile quality, like the girl herself. Then she remembered *The Shindig*. She reached over to her handbag and pulled the leaflet from it.

'Have you heard about this?'

Cas took the leaflet, looping a strand of titian hair behind her ear. Her ear lobe was as delicate as a sea shell. Her eyebrows, barely visible on her high forehead, knitted slightly. 'I love *Django, Django*,' she said.

'What would you say if I told you there's a chance for your band to play alongside them?'

Cas looked up in surprise.

'I would say that's ridiculous.' Cas and Izzy turned to see Davy in the doorway, laptop under his arm. 'We're not ready for a gig. We've barely got started.'

'They only want two songs. Eight minutes max,' said Izzy, handing Cas the booking slip.

'Mum,' said Davy, stepping forward, 'we don't even have a name.'

'I made something up: *No1dea*.'

'That's brilliant, Mrs Campbell,' said Cas, breaking into a wide smile. Two rows of metal braces dazzled. They didn't diminish the girl's attractiveness but, rather, held something of her beauty in reserve for later.

Davy looked agitated. 'We don't need you interfering, Mum.'

'I just thought … well, I just thought it was an opportunity, that's all.' Izzy got up to re-fill her glass with water.

'I wish my mum was as cool as yours, Davy,' said Cas.

'Don't encourage her,' said Davy, but Izzy could tell he was mellowing. He had picked up the booking slip and was examining it closely.

'I was speaking to my friend, Bridget, at college today. She thinks that too many people play small. More of us should take a few more risks. You know, play a bigger game.'

'What's this about a big game? You talking about the Hibs match on Saturday?' asked Jim, coming back into the house. He had shouldered his way into the kitchen and hadn't noticed

Cas. 'Whoa. Who have we got here?' he said loudly. He meant to be friendly, but she could see the girl shrinking from him.

'This is Cas,' said Izzy. 'She's the singer in Davy's band.'

'Well, you're a lot easier on the eye than that other bunch of scruffs,' said Jim. Cas looked as wary as a cat. 'Are you at school with Davy?'

'I'm at university, Mr Campbell. First Year. Studying law,' she said, in the guarded, dutiful manner pretty girls use when dealing with leery, middle-aged men.

Jim took a swig of wine. 'Fancy some steak and chips? You look like you could do with a decent meal,' he said.

Izzy groaned inwardly. He meant it as a joke, playing a caricature of himself, but Cas was looking at her feet, fiddling with the strap of her shoulder bag.

'We're off now,' said Davy. 'We'll talk about this other matter with the rest of the band, but I'm not promising anything.' Cas got up and stood beside him. There was a scuffle as they dithered about who should go out the door first. Davy made a show of letting Cas go before him.

'What other matter? What promise?' asked Jim.

'There's a chance for their band to play at a gig, that's all,' said Izzy, pushing *The Shindig* poster across the table to him. He barely glanced at it.

'Sense over Sectarianism? What a lot of crap,' he said, finishing off his drink in one swallow, then emptying the last of the bottle into his glass. His tone was pure contempt. No surprise there. The only surprise was how much it still had the capacity to disappoint and infuriate her. She didn't trust herself to speak.

'Anyhow, Davy won't be able to go. Rangers are playing at home that day,' he continued, as if that was the end of the discussion.

'Who were you speaking to on the phone?' she asked.

'No one you know,' he said gruffly.

'One of your girlfriends?' she said, teasingly.

He got up from the table and went to the pantry, returning with another bottle of wine. He placed it between his legs and pulled the corkscrew out with a flourish. 'That … that was none other than Mrs Mellows, secretary of Glasgow Rangers Football Club, asking if we'll need transport. You see, Izzy, Verisafe have been invited to The Chairman's Club as special guests of the Board of Directors.'

Izzy could feel her smile stiffen. There was only one possible response: 'That's fantastic, Jim.'

'This is an elite hospitality event, you know. Invitations are only extended to a small number of specially selected businesses.'

She suspected such an honour would come at a price, but she knew better than to ask. 'Sounds like it'll be a good chance for you and Bill to do some networking.'

'Bill? No. No. No. Not Bill. I want you to come with me.'

'Me? Why on earth would you want me to come with you?'

'I know you know nothing about business and you hate football, but this is really important. I need you by my side.'

She looked around at the mess in the kitchen. It all made sense to her now. This was Jim's charm offensive to persuade her to go to the Rangers event with him. He was a straightforward man. She should be thankful for that.

'What will I have to do?'

'Just be yourself. Business is about relationships, and if we make a favourable impression, we could influence the decision about the alarm contract. The new management team will all be there. The Chairman. The Directors. Most of them will bring their wives and girlfriends, too.'

He came up close to her. His moustache was damp and his top lip was moist, engorged. She stiffened, thinking he was about to kiss her, but he leaned past her and picked up his glass.

'No one's going to be interested in the likes of me,' said Izzy.

'Izzy, you're such a good listener. People tell you things they would never tell most other people. D'you remember the party the new neighbours gave? I left you for five minutes and, when I came back, the wife was telling you about her vaginal dryness. You, Izzy Campbell, are Verisafe's secret weapon,' he said.

'I think that might be overstating things,' she said, but her mind was already working on a parallel track. The universe had summoned an opportunity for her to help Sean Docherty. To play big. It was a dangerous thought, but impossible to dismiss.

'So, what d'you say, Izzy? Will you come?'

His eyes were filled with expectancy and hope, just like the time he had proposed in his mother's kitchen, at their house in Maryhill. She remembered feeling a heady mix of excitement and fear, a knot of panic and a rising tide of euphoria. His mother had come rushing back into the kitchen, before she'd had the chance to reply, and embraced them both, assuming Izzy had said yes. Izzy had laughed and returned her embrace. She hadn't minded then that her decision had been assumed. Jim still thought she was the same compliant woman, but inside she felt almost carefree with boldness. It made her feel a little short of breath.

'OK. I'll come,' she said.

'Brilliant,' said Jim, turning his back to her, his shoulders set in a confident line.

Her mind was racing. Should she call Sean now? She took a couple of deep breaths to steady herself. Better to call him tomorrow, after she had done some research about these hospitality events. After she had worked out what she would say. After her speeding heart had calmed down.

Jim had taken a potato peeler from the drawer, the old blunt one with the orange string wound round the handle. He was hacking at a potato as divots of skin fell to the floor.

'You're better off using the new one,' she said, but he dismissed her suggestion with a wave of the peeler.

'You sit down and relax. None of your tasteless oven chips tonight. Maris piper tatties fried in beef dripping,' he announced.

He lined up the roughly peeled potatoes on the work surface. Their pale flesh sparkling. She wanted to tell him to dry his hands, to slice the potato in half, to put the cut side on the chopping board to keep it from slipping, but something held her back. The potato skidded from under the blade of his knife and landed on the floor. He bent down and stumbled against the kitchen units.

'Naughty tattie. Come back to your Uncle Jim,' he crooned as he picked it up.

He sluiced it under the tap and took a smaller knife from the chopping block, the one that she always kept lethally sharp. He took another swallow of wine. It was like watching a film she had already seen. She knew what terrible thing would happen next, but she was powerless to stop it happening.

*   *   *

Therapist: What happened to your hand, Jim?

Jim: Oh, that? Nothing. Just a wee accident in the kitchen.

Therapist: Impressive bandage.

Jim: Don't look at me like that.

Therapist: Like what?

Jim: I know what you're thinking. That I was under the influence when it happened.

Therapist: Were you?

Jim: Izzy has got herself involved with that sectarian charity I was talking about. That lad's ghost is definitely haunting me. No question.

Therapist: That must be frightening.

Jim: I'm going to take your advice. To cut down on the bevvy. I've got to land this Rangers deal and it's no time for dead spirits to be fucking with my head.

Therapist: I think it would be a good idea for you to commit to seeing me on a regular basis. Say, once a week?

Jim: Aye. OK. For a short time, but I'm fine, you know. Really, I am.

CHAPTER 8

'Jim's been in hospital?'

Bridget was wearing a horizontal-striped jumper and a beret that matched her navy lipstick. She looked like a cross between a goth and a French onion seller. At breast level, she wore an SNP badge, that beneath read: "Yes."

'He cut his wrist. Badly. The doctor said we got him to hospital just in time,' added Izzy. They were sitting in the college canteen. It was quiet and their voices echoed in the space.

'How did it happen?'

'I did it,' whispered Izzy, leaning in.

'What do you mean you did it?' asked Bridget, matching her whisper.

Izzy nodded as if in a daze. 'He was making steak and chips as a special treat to butter me up into going to this Rangers function with him. He even joked, "*none of your tasteless oven chips tonight.*" Anyway, he was too pissed to be using a sharp knife. I should have taken it from him, but I didn't. I just watched as the potato slipped and the knife sliced into his wrist.'

'Oh Jesus,' said Bridget.

'He slid to the floor in a dead faint, he's always hated the sight of blood and, my God, Bridget, there was blood everywhere. Not the bright red stuff you get when you graze your knee, but rich and dark, like port wine. My mind was racing: make a tourniquet, put him in the recovery position, run to the neighbours for help, call an ambulance. The steps were as clear to me as if I was reading from a list of instructions, but I just stood there, watching him bleed all over the kitchen floor.'

'Rabbit in the headlights, Izzy. It was the shock of it,' comforted Bridget.

'After a while … I'm not sure how long … he came around. Seeing the blood, he started screaming: "*Oh my God. Oh my God. Help me. Help me.*" I grabbed a dishcloth and stemmed the bleeding as best I could, then ran next door for help. Our neighbour took us to the hospital.'

'Well, he won't be complaining about tasteless oven chips again,' said Bridget.

Izzy tried to smile but failed. 'There are times when I look at him and feel nothing. I ask myself, do I even like you?

After the Verisafe party, I fantasised about pushing him out of the car. I mean, what sort of terrible person thinks like that? It sounds crazy, Bridget, but d'you think these thoughts triggered the accident?'

'What? Like some subconscious death wish? You're right, it does sound crazy. As you said yourself, he was too drunk to be using a sharp knife.'

'His drinking has got a lot worse over the summer. I know it's his way of coping with his mum dying and the new job, but, Bridget, he's turning into a different person. Mood swings … insomnia. He told me he'd cut down after this Rangers deal is finished, but, honestly, I'll believe it when I see it.'

They didn't notice the leader of the hairdressing girls until she was standing over them.

'Excuse me. Did I leave my magazine here?' she asked.

Bridget curled her lip. Izzy looked over to the seat beside her and picked up a magazine. She glanced at the front cover. It was one of those celebrity magazines with a family photograph on the cover; a couple with their two children in stiff poses, arranged around a Rococo chaise-lounge. The headline caught her attention: "Jack Marshall, financial genius behind Rangers' buyout bid, at home with his TV presenter wife, Michelle, and their beautiful children."

'Any chance I could borrow this?' asked Izzy.

The girl took a step back, her eyebrows arching. 'Sure, if you want,' she said.

'I'll give it back tomorrow … I'm sorry, I don't know your name.'

'Eloise. No rush. I've already read it.'

'Thanks, Eloise.'

'Maybe your friend would like to read it, too? There's an article on how to get rid of facial hair,' she said, before turning and leaving. Her high ponytail swished from side to side, as if it was laughing at them.

'Cheeky bissom,' said Bridget looking uncertain. 'I haven't got any facial hair, have I, Izzy?' she asked, stroking her chin.

Izzy shook her head and turned the pages of the magazine until she got to the photo shoot of Jack Marshall's family. Michelle was gym-toned and petite. Their two children, a toddler and a baby, were dressed in elaborate outfits that made them look hot and uncomfortable.

'Why the sudden interest in minor celebrities and dodgy businessmen?' asked Bridget, peering over her shoulder. She was still stroking her chin, checking for hairs.

'Research. Jim's asked me to go to this hospitality function at Ibrox with all the senior management. This Jack Marshall character might be there, too.'

'Wow,' breathed Bridget. 'So you've decided to help Sean Docherty?'

'I'm going to a hospitality event with Jim. That's all.'

'I take it you haven't told Jim about Sean's investigation?'

'I've been thinking about what you said about being proactive. I mean, it would be terrible if Verisafe fitted all those alarms and the club didn't have the money to pay.'

'Go on, admit it. You fancy the pants off him.'

'Sorry to disappoint you, Bridget. Sean Docherty is trying to do something important, and I think I can help him. That's all there is to it.' Izzy pulled out his business card from her purse and with a steady hand, texted a message:

Been invited to meet the Rangers Board. Interested? Izzy.

She put the phone down between them. They waited in silence. She found herself holding her breath. Bridget's eyes were shining. They both flinched when the phone pinged.

Intriguing. I'll be in Glasgow week after next. When can we meet? Sean.

They exchanged a knowing look.

Thursday. I finish at the Bureau at 3 p.m.

This time, the reply was immediate:

Necropolis. John Knox. 3:30 p.m.

'He must mean the John Knox statue in the old Victorian graveyard beside the cathedral,' breathed Bridget. 'Very romantic.'

The sensible voice in Izzy's head dismissed romance as a sad fantasy of the middle-aged. She was married for a start, and he must have his pick of hundreds of London lovelies.

'It's a good choice because we're unlikely to miss each other there,' she said, yet she could feel her pulse speeding up as she replied:

Perfect.

***

Therapist: I'm glad you've decided to come every week. Have you told Izzy?

Jim: No, and I don't intend to either.

Therapist: Why not?

Jim: It would only worry her. I'm not one of those sad sickos she sees down at the Gallowgate, the ones the police find in the

	gutters of Cumbie Street on a Friday night. I'm not in that league.
Therapist:	What league are you in, then?
Jim:	No higher than the third division. I just need to cut down a wee bit, that's all.
Therapist:	I suggest you taper down your intake slowly. Aim for two or three alcohol-free days a week.
Jim:	OK. That sounds do-able.
Therapist:	And, I'd like you to consider telling Izzy you're doing this.
Jim:	Why?
Therapist:	To give her the chance to support you.
Jim:	Look, Izzy isn't bothered by my drinking. Our marriage is rock solid, but that doesn't mean I have to tell her everything.

CHAPTER 9

On the face of it, it had been an ordinary week. College, the Bureau, Jim's blustering about Verisafe and Davy's comings and goings with the band, now fuelled with a new purpose having decided to audition for *The Shindig*. Yet, for all its ordinary rhythms, Izzy's life had filled with a vibrant undercurrent. Her meeting with Sean was in seven days' time and it felt like the week before Christmas; each day a small, delightful eternity.

At first, Jim was surprised at the number of celebrity magazines appearing on the kitchen table, and her questions about security alarms. Eventually, he figured it out. All this research was a ploy for a new outfit. Izzy hadn't corrected him, pleased with her "guilty as charged" acting skills. That morning, he pressed ten twenty pound notes into her hand, and told her to shop where the directors' wives would go. There was only one proviso: '*Nothing green.*' They had both laughed at that.

Her last client had left and she had half an hour to kill before meeting Bridget to go shopping. She laid out three folders on her desk. The first was titled "WAP" ("wives and partners" was written in small letters beneath). She flicked through the images of whisked hair, high wattage smiles and luxurious settings. She had called Mrs Mellows at The Chairman's Club under the pretext of asking about the dress code, but it had been an easy job to prise out who was coming. It was an Old Firm match. The Chairman and the Directors would all be there and some of the wives were expected. She suggested Izzy wore a cocktail dress.

The second folder was titled "Verisafe". It contained details of the alarm bid and some background on their two competitors: DDT and Belmarsh Security. Moira from Finance had happily given her whatever information she had asked for – copies of company accounts and bank statements. Neither Jim nor Bill showed any interest in what she was doing, or asked her any questions. She wasn't sure how relevant Sean would find this, but she liked the idea of demonstrating thoroughness and a head for technical and financial matters.

The third folder was untitled. Although, in her mind she had begun to think of it as the *Downfall Dossier*. At first she hadn't found much in the papers about the club's financial troubles. An odd article here and there, mainly in the English press; a thread on social media; some rantings in the Celtic fanzine. But one lead had led to others, and now, the *Downfall Dossier* felt satisfyingly hefty. You didn't have to be a super sleuth to be an investigative journalist. The information was there if you were determined enough to find it.

There was no doubt about Rangers' financial shenanigans. Employee Benefit Trusts that offered loans instead of salaries had been set up for players and staff to avoid paying income tax. A similar scheme had been discredited at Leicester City three years ago and the owners had been forced to pay the tax, almost crippling the club. It looked like the practice had been going on at Rangers for much longer. They hadn't filed any accounts to the tax authorities for years. She knew she was staring into a financial abyss, and it felt strangely breathtaking.

She finished updating her system, tidied her desk, locked the cabinet and walked towards the reception area with a spring in her step. Alan's hatch was shut. She tapped on it, but it remained closed. Ever since the Mr Docherty incident, there had been tension between them. 'That's me finished for the day,' said Izzy brightly, shrugging her shoulders. He would come round in his own time.

She passed the SOS office and tried to resist the temptation to look in. Someone had stuck up a poster of Alex Salmond on the inside wall. The speech bubble said: "*As leader of the Scottish National Party, I am proud that Scotland is on a journey and the path ahead is a bright one*". Alex had an inscrutable smile. If you weren't a fan, you might think he looked smug, but today, Izzy could only see his optimism, and admired his vision. She had a sudden premonition that Bridget would one day replace his face. She could already see the speech bubble coming from her red lips: "*Scots in charge of our own destiny*".

Buchanan Street was busy with shoppers. The big retail chains were all represented, their flagship stores cleverly renovated from Victorian buildings that once housed merchant houses and banks. One version of capitalism replaced by another. Two women were walking towards her, burdened with shopping bags. They had that tell-tale mixture of exhilaration and shame, like the ones she'd seen on the faces of the shopaholics she worked with at the Bureau. The world was truly geared to encourage debt and heartache.

Her phone rang. Bridget sounded breathless. She'd had a call from the SNP Chairman inviting her to come to a selection interview and wouldn't be able to join the shopping trip. Izzy felt a stab of disappointment. Although Bridget didn't have the perfect credentials for choosing an expensive cocktail dress, she would have made the experience fun, an adventure. Izzy's first instinct was to go home, but a sense of duty made her hesitate. The dress was part of a bigger plan, a higher purpose.

The Princes Square Mall had been designed to lift the eyes upwards to the magnificent Victorian atrium, taking in an open vista of three floors of shops and restaurants. Down-lighters sparkled like stars, giving a glow to the creamy smoothness of the marble floors. A seductive potpourri of coffee, garlic and expensive perfume filled the air. Muted chatter and the tinkle from a grand piano rose from the ground floor.

The dress shop opened directly onto the lower ground concourse. Rails lined the walls, each with a tiny number of dresses hanging from them. The dresses looked exposed, as self-conscious as Izzy felt. She touched one of them; it felt soft, fragile. The price label read £785. She remembered that Sean's mum had saved for fifteen years to scrimp together £1,600 for Sean's books. Just enough to buy two dresses. It was hard not to feel a sense of hopelessness about the world.

'One of our couture range,' a soft voice murmured over Izzy's shoulder. The shop assistant was as slim as a young girl, but her face was large, her skin the colour of uncooked pastry and deeply lined, as if a fork had been raked over it. 'Was there something in particular you were looking for?'

'Something blue? Something not so couture?' suggested Izzy.

The assistant brought her two blue dresses. One was a simple shift design. She checked the price: £145. The other was in a jersey fabric with an asymmetric hem: £200. She pretended to consider them both before handing the more expensive one back.

'The tanzanite will be wonderful with your colouring,' said the assistant, pulling back the heavy curtain of the changing room. Izzy slipped on the dress. It *seemed* to fit in all the right places, but she couldn't be sure. The changing room had no mirror. She opened the curtain and the assistant's face creased into a smile. Her teeth were large and unnaturally white.

'Lovely. Now, how about some shoes to match?' she was holding out a pair of silver slingback sandals. Izzy took them, examining the construction of the heel whilst trying to find a price label. She had the impression the assistant had worked out how much money she had and was skilfully managing her to part with it.

'In our pre-season sale: fifty pounds.'

The shoes pinched the joint of her big toe and she wobbled as she stood. She allowed herself to be guided to a full-length mirror in the centre of the floor. Thankfully, the shop was deserted. At these prices, she wasn't surprised.

'Stunning,' breathed the assistant.

Izzy stared at her reflection. A sophisticated woman, an executive's wife, stared back. Moira from Finance would be thrilled. She caught a lock of hair that had sprung out of her ponytail and re-tied it.

'I could arrange an appointment with Adrian, our hairdresser. He has a three-month waiting list for new clients, but I could pull some strings. With a deep heat treatment and proper conditioning, your hair would look fabulous,' offered the assistant.

Izzy turned to the left and right, then looked over her shoulder. She tried a pouty expression and felt a giggle bubble up inside her. She had a mad thought: not an executive's wife but a glamorous spy.

The assistant clasped her hands together. 'Truly fabulous,' she sighed.

It was then that Izzy understood what many other women have always understood: the power of clothes to present a version of yourself that had nothing to do with who you were inside. 'They'll do,' she said in a matter-of-fact tone, pulling her ponytail tighter. She would have a chat with Eloise at college about the deep heat treatment.

The invitation sat on the hall table like a trophy. "Rangers Hospitality" was written in gold lettering, with a crest embossed beneath it, as if it had come from royalty. Inside was a handwritten invitation to The Chairman's Club, signed by the Chairman himself – a royalty of sorts, she supposed. The itinerary listed a champagne reception, a five-course lunch with fine wines, half-time refreshments, full-time high tea and complementary bar throughout the afternoon. Izzy thought it was a miracle they'd managed to squeeze in a football match as well, and not just any football match, an Old Firm match: Rangers versus Celtic.

She popped her head round the kitchen door. Davy and Jim were sitting side by side, hypnotised by a football match on the TV. Davy had a can of coke in front of him; Jim had a bottle of beer. Their faces were frozen like the hapless citizens of Pompeii. There was an ominous absence of cooking smells.

'Did you not think to get the tea started?' she asked, putting down her bags and filling the kettle.

Davy looked blank, as if she had spoken in a foreign language. Jim raised his bandaged wrist as if that was all the answer she needed. 'We can get a carry-out at full time,' he said. 'There's only twenty minutes of the match remaining.'

She began opening and closing cupboard doors, a little louder than was necessary. Their heads turned in unison, brows furrowed. 'I'll make omelettes,' she said, but they had turned back to the TV. She felt her irritation soften. At least they weren't arguing.

'I love the Tabasco you put in this, Mum,' said Davy as he wolfed down his food. Jim nodded. There was a contented silence as they ate. Jim reached for the bread basket and buttered two slices, then opened another bottle of beer. She couldn't help counting. This was his fifth.

'What do you think of the invitation, then?' asked Jim.

'Very impressive,' said Izzy.

'Does that look like a club in financial trouble?' Jim's voice was louder than usual.

'No, it doesn't,' agreed Izzy.

She glanced towards him, there were bits of bread churning in his mouth and a globule of egg had stuck to his moustache.

'So, did you buy a dress?' he asked.

'I had enough for shoes as well,' she said.

Jim grinned. 'You know, Davy, ever since your mum agreed to go to The Chairman's Club, she's done all this research. She'll be able to talk the hind legs off a donkey with all the big bosses.' He leaned across towards her, his mouth moist and puckered. She took his plate and side-stepped past him.

'Good for you, Mum,' said Davy, standing up from the table. 'Thanks for tea. See you guys later.'

'Don't you have homework to do?' Jim called out, but Davy had bounded down the hallway. A moment later, they heard the front door slam.

'You're too soft on that boy. He needs to get down to some serious studying,' said Jim to Izzy.

'The band's busy practising for the audition.' Izzy turned on the taps and watched as the water and soap bubbles submerged the plates. She steeled herself, expecting Jim to repeat his objections about a do-gooder concert. Instead, he came up behind her and nuzzled into the crook of her neck, his fingers pressing into her ribs. She closed her eyes and tried to relax.

'How about putting on the new dress and shoes for me. See if I approve?' his voice was thick with desire.

'I've got all these dishes to do,' she protested.

'They can wait, but I'm not sure I can,' he said. It was a mild threat, a sexy sort of urgency. She knew she had to respond.

A good wife should want to respond. She shut her eyes to expel any stirrings of dread and slowly shifted his hands from her waist.

'Let me take a quick shower. I'll be back in ten minutes.'

'Good girl,' he said, drifting back to the TV and turning up the volume to listen to the pundits discussing the match.

Standing in the shower, Izzy let the water cascade over her. Sex with Jim had become less and less frequent in recent months, and now the prospect felt unwelcome, the effort enormous. An image of his fleshy buttocks, the bucking and grunting, chilled her. She directed the shower head between her legs, the jets of water probing and stroking, until she felt the beginnings of heat swell inside her. She closed her eyes and saw Sean's face floating in front of her. Those beautiful, tallow eyes; his slim body, toned and firm. She stopped, feeling shocked and, at the same time, defiant, almost pleased with herself.

The dress fell in silky folds from the tissue wrapping. She slipped it over her bare shoulders. She was naked underneath and the material moved against her skin like a soft breeze. She ignored the sensation, concentrating instead on the task ahead, trying to detach any feelings about it. She supposed it was what all dutiful wives did.

Jim was lying on the sofa. The TV was blaring, the blue light illuminating his face. He looked peaceful as his chest moved up and down, a quiet wheeze escaping from him. She shifted the cushion under his head and he snuggled into it. 'Thank you, darling.'

She watched him sleep; his wheezing deepened into a snore. He wouldn't wake for hours. Relief wrapped itself around her, blameless and comforting; the residual warmth of her shower a delicious and private pleasure.

***

Therapist: Hello, Jim. How are you?

Jim: Ticketty-boo. I've cut right back on the booze and I'm feeling much better. No more ghosts of dead boys messing with my head.

Therapist: I'm glad to hear that.

Jim: I know Izzy's not having an affair. She's a loyal and devoted wife. I'm very lucky to have her.

Therapist: Is she pleased that you've cut down?

Jim: I've been thinking about these sessions. Maybe I don't need to come *every* week.

Therapist: (Silence)

Jim: It's been good to talk about … stuff. I certainly feel better having told someone about … well … about what happened. But now that I've decided to get the drinking under control, maybe I only need to come once in a while.

Therapist: It's very early days. I'd like you to think carefully before deciding to come less often.

Jim: Well, I haven't made my mind up for definite. Just wanted you to know that I'm feeling much better about things.

CHAPTER 10

Corkscrew curls fell about Izzy's shoulders. Eloise had impregnated her hair with warm oils for two hours and, now, instead of a wild frizz, glossy tendrils fell about her face. She had refused the blonde highlights, but agreed to have it cut to shoulder length with a side parting. The rest of the hairdressing girls had cooed around her, taking photographs on their phones as if she was a wonder of nature. She told them they were being daft, although, privately, she thought she looked lovely, but it was too heady a thought to hold on to for long, so she tucked it away in her mind, resolving to recover it occasionally, in small, careful doses.

It was 3:00 p.m.; she was meeting Sean at 3:30. She had already timed the walk from the Bureau to the Necropolis: 13 minutes. She checked the folders in her briefcase, shut down her computer, took a deep breath and walked into the reception.

'Shona asked to see you when you're finished,' mumbled Alan from his open hatch. She wanted to pretended she hadn't heard him, but it was too late. She had already stopped mid-step, as if her feet were obeying a higher authority. 'I like your hair,' he added.

She touched her head involuntarily. 'Thanks,' she said, trying to think of a complement to give him in return, but he had already shut his hatch. She knocked quietly on Shona's door. Hearing voices from within, hope stirred. Perhaps Shona would ask her to come back another time.

'Come in,' came a cheery voice.

Shona was on the phone. 'Take a seat, Izzy. I'll be with you in a sec ... listen to me, Mum. You need to take your water pills. Listen. Listen. It's important that you follow the doctor's instructions. Your heart isn't pumping as well as it should. Fluid can build up easily, especially in your legs. You don't want to go back into that wheelchair, do you?'

Izzy shifted in her seat, trying not to look at her watch.

'That mother of mine,' sighed Shona as she put down the phone, 'is driving me mad now she's out of hospital. I don't know how I'm expected to cope on my own *and* work full-time.'

Izzy would normally have taken this as a cue to empathise about the trials of nursing an elderly relative with chronic health problems, but impatience was eroding her usual tolerance.

'Sorry, Shona, but I'm in a bit of a rush to get away. Alan mentioned you wanted to see me?'

Izzy thought she had managed the right mix of friendliness and assertion, but Shona looked as if she'd been poked in the eye.

'We haven't spoken since the Mr Docherty incident. I just wanted to ask if you're OK.'

'I'm fine. Everything's good,' said Izzy, hoping her decisiveness would keep things short.

Shona returned her gaze with what seemed like an equal determination to prolong the meeting. 'No more after hours meetings with clients, then?'

'No, absolutely not,' said Izzy quickly. Too quickly. She felt the lie flame her skin.

Shona's smile was beatific. 'No need to look guilty, Izzy. I'm not suggesting you would do anything as mad as meeting clients outside office hours. Not after the last time.'

Izzy smiled, hoping to hide her dismay. She rationalised that Sean wasn't a client, that he had only pretended to be one, but anxiety was worming its way under her skin. Her blush deepened and she could feel her inner confidence unravelling like a pulled thread on a hem. Perhaps Shona knew she was meeting Sean Docherty? Although, that was unlikely, impossible even, anxiety has a knack of transforming the impossible into the possible.

'How's college?' asked Shona.

'I got an A for my Bateson essay,' replied Izzy, feeling like a child offering a parent a morsel of achievement in exchange for a quick escape.

'Wonderful. Have you had any thoughts about what you might do after you've finished your degree?'

Izzy felt a fresh blow of frustration. She put her briefcase on her lap, her hands gripping the handle. She shook her head.

'Have you heard about the Policy Research Department? It researches family welfare, work and housing matters. I think it would be right up your street.'

Izzy nodded. 'That sounds interesting.'

'Here's a paper they wrote. It'll give you an idea of the work they do.'

She handed Izzy a small brochure with the headline: *Curing the Disease, Not the Symptoms – a New Approach to Debt Management.* 'Have a think about it.'

'Thanks, I will,' said Izzy.

'Going anywhere nice?'

'Meeting a friend, that's all.'

A friend. Shona held her gaze, a knowing smile on her lips, her head tilted in anticipation of more detail. Izzy could see she was taking in her new hairstyle, the lip gloss, her agitation to get away. Seconds passed.

'OK. We'll talk later,' said Shona, returning to her papers, making a show of interest. Izzy made a mental note to schedule another meeting with her as soon as possible.

She texted Sean as soon as she left the Bureau to let him know she was running late, before breaking into a jog, only slowing as she approached the cathedral. Elderly American tourists were milling around the entrance waiting for the next guided tour to start, their chattering as carefree as children on a school trip. 'Good afternoon,' she said, in a confident voice, to a couple who were dawdling at the back. They mistook her for the guide and she had to redirect them back to the others at the church entrance.

In the late afternoon light, the Necropolis graveyard rose from behind the cathedral like a gothic film set: obelisks were scattered across the hillside like great granite fingers pointed heavenwards, and the silhouettes of crosses and tombstones outlined the incline at tipsy angles. The theatricality of the place and meeting an investigative journalist, felt surreal and faintly absurd.

She began the climb up the steep hill towards the John Knox statue. At the top, the sky seemed to open above her; her hair was swirling in the wind, giving her an unfamiliar sense of abandonment. She dithered about keeping it loose but pulled it into a ponytail. It would look more professional.

John Knox's column was a hundred yards to her left. Crows, glossy-headed with black, button eyes, hopped from tombstone to tombstone, following her. She circled round the plinth of the statue. She could hear foreign voices coming from far below, but she was alone. Perhaps he had got fed up of waiting, but, before disappointment had time to settle, she saw him standing off to her right.

He turned as if sensing her presence. 'Hey, Izzy,' he called out.

He was wearing a leather jacket and tailored trousers. She noticed his shoes: tan brogues with pointed toes. He looked every inch a famous London journalist, a friend of JK Rowling.

'Sorry I'm late,' she breathed, 'got held up at the Bureau.'

'It was me who kept you waiting last time. We're quits now,' he said.

'Gosh, I haven't been to this place since I was a kid. It's creepy, isn't it? Creepy in a good way, I mean.' Nerves were making her chatter. 'Look at that view,' she said, gazing out towards the city.

The Victorian landmarks of the city were easy to spot: the splendid façade of the City Chambers, the spire of the university, the massive bulk of the old Infirmary and, in between, patches of wilderness and derelict spaces. The tower blocks of Glasgow Tech were also visible. Even from this distance, she could see they were crumbling.

'Glasgow may be one of the poorest cities in Europe, but this graveyard is a reminder that it was once one of the richest,' he stated.

He was standing close to her and her heart stuttered. They both looked around at the Greek columns, Roman temples, Celtic crosses and massive blocks of granite. 'Victorian merchants, clergymen, philosophers, writers, entrepreneurs, explorers; they're all here,' he added.

She gazed at his profile; his straight nose and the tilt of his chin gave him a determined look. He looked a bit like a Victorian explorer himself, someone driven by a higher purpose. She felt herself becoming unhinged; could feel herself being pulled towards him.

'The Victorians claimed to value modesty, but the rich and famous couldn't resist one final stab at excess,' he continued, shrugging his shoulders, as if asking himself: what else can you expect from the rich and famous.

'I suppose we're all guilty of hypocrisy at times,' said Izzy.

He looked at her, his head tipped to one side as if her remark had physically knocked him sideways. She felt herself relax. Emboldened, she offered another view. 'I feel a bit sorry for them.'

'What aspect of these privileged, wealthy people elicits your sympathy?' he asked.

'To spend all this money to be remembered. Now, it's only foreign tourists who visit, and most of them have never heard of these Victorian people or what they achieved.'

'Maybe names don't matter. Their real legacies are their buildings, their inventions and the places they discovered.'

'Yes, and the people they knew and loved.' Davy was the best legacy she could think to leave the world. She felt sure that Sean's mother would say the same about him.

'John Knox said ideas were the only legacy that mattered.' They both looked up at the column, squinting to make out the details of the statue on top. Sean read the inscription out loud:

'There lieth he who never feared the face of man: who was often threatened with clay and dagger yet hath ended his days in peace and honour.'

There was a break in his voice and his head was lowered. This could be his own epitaph and Izzy felt a new resolve to do whatever she could to help him.

'Macho bollocks,' he declared, smiling. His grin was like a schoolboy who had booted a ball through a kitchen window, and was proud of his aim. 'It's normal – human – to feel fear. Admitting vulnerability is a strength in my opinion, not a weakness.'

She felt her face light up. How unpredictable he was. One minute a brooding intensity, the next, as playful as a child.

115

She felt her connection with him deepen. Not a connection in the sense of familiarity, but in how each of his edges gave her small darts of pleasure, drawing her towards him.

'Are you frightened of Rangers' management?' she asked.

'If you spit in their soup, you must expect them to get angry and make threats.'

'I suppose they might be scared, too. I see people facing financial meltdown every day at the Bureau. It's terrible to feel responsible for the breakdown of a business or a family. To think it was your fault. It makes people do desperate things.'

'Do you always do that?'

He looked at her with such attention that she felt her heart flip. 'Do what?'

'See things from other people's point of view?' He didn't give her a chance to reply. 'Look, I believe the new management started off with the club's best interests at heart, but then they made mistakes, took bad decisions. Now, the only way they deal with someone like me asking questions, is to insult and threaten them.'

Izzy thought about her *Downfall Dossier* and wondered if now would be a good moment to show it to him. She felt excited, confident he would be impressed. They sat on the bench beside the monument. He turned towards her, fixing her with a level gaze. 'So, Izzy, I was intrigued when I got your text. What's this about you meeting the Rangers Board?'

He looked impossibly attractive. She hesitated, reluctant to bring Jim into their conversation.

'Jim Campbell, my husband, is the Managing Director at Verisafe, an alarm company based in Glasgow,' she began.

Sean nodded, his face had taken on the attentiveness of professional curiosity. She wouldn't have been surprised if he pulled a notebook from his jacket pocket and began taking notes.

'Your husband's the big Rangers fan, isn't he?' asked Sean.

'Yes, well remembered. His company is bidding to upgrade the club's alarm system. He's been invited, well, we've both been invited to The Chairman's Club at the end of the month.'

She expected a start of recognition at the mention of The Chairman's Club, but his expression was clouded, puzzled. Her breath shortened, suddenly unsure whether her plan would pass muster.

'Never heard of it. What is it?'

She felt her confidence begin to trickle away, but there was no going back. 'It's an elite hospitality event at the next Old Firm game at Ibrox. The Chairman and the Directors will be there, along with some of the wives and girlfriends.'

'Wives and girlfriends, too?' he repeated, incredulously.

This wasn't going as well as she expected, but she soldiered on. 'I remember you saying that you were finding it hard to get people in the club to talk to you. I thought this might be an opportunity? That I could ask some questions? Find out some information for you perhaps?'

He exhaled slowly and looked up to the sky, screwing up his eyes as if in pain. She waited for the blow to fall. 'It won't work.' His verdict was delivered with the casual insensitivity of a stranger. She felt stunned, unable to speak, to ask why.

'These hospitality events are a way to flatter businessmen out of money. They're told the top brass will be there, so they pay a fortune for tickets, but more often than not, no one shows up.'

'You mean Jim won't meet anyone from the Board? Surely not.'

'One or two might drift by so the punters can say they met someone important, but they won't stay for long. As for wives and girlfriends … the nearest they'll get to Ibrox is the Princes Mall on Buchanan Street.'

Izzy felt the stir of a small kernel of defiance. 'I spoke to Mrs Mellows from the Hospitality Department and asked her who, from management, would be attending. She assured me that everyone from the Board would be there. Admittedly, though, she wasn't so sure about the wives and girlfriends.' Her chin was set in a confident line. Inside she was dissolving.

'An assurance from Rangers? I'd be more inclined to believe the exact opposite.'

She felt like she had lost her footing, as if she'd just stepped off a roundabout, unprepared for the ground not to be moving. The weight of her briefcase seemed ridiculous. Her folders of information as useless as a child's scrapbook. Tears pricked her eyes as she rummaged in her bag for a tissue.

He looked contrite. 'Sorry, that came out harsher than I intended. OK, let's assume I'm wrong and some of the Directors do turn up. What would you ask them?'

She wished he wasn't humouring her. She dabbed at her eyes with a used, paper handkerchief she found at the bottom of her bag. 'I don't know, maybe mention that I'd heard about possible financial difficulties, and see what they had to say for themselves?'

'They would palm you off with their usual assurances. If you were to probe, alarm bells would ring and they would make their polite farewells and leave. You'd have achieved nothing, except arousing suspicion that you're a Rangers hater. I don't think your husband would be pleased with that, do you?'

The implausibility of her plan was now obvious. The excitement and anticipation, the preparation, the certainty that she could help, had all evaporated. She felt the strength drain from her legs.

'I'm sorry, Izzy. I've had a tough day. I shouldn't be taking that out on you,' he said, rubbing the bridge of his nose.

She felt a pulse of hope. A comforting voice inside her head assured her that, perhaps, she hadn't made a complete fool of herself.

'I had a meeting with the BBC at lunchtime. I've a lead on a potential ticketing scam the club is running, involving advance season tickets. I thought they'd bite my hand off to run a feature on it, but no, not interested. I'm gutted. Totally gutted.'

'I thought you looked smart,' she said, looking at his clothes. It was a ridiculous thing to say, but his face softened and he gave her a wry smile.

'You've done something different to your hair?' Her heart bounced. Her hand flew to her ponytail. She wanted to loosen it, like untying a present.

'What I need is an interview,' he said, returning to his usual seriousness. 'Where I can put the allegations to someone directly. If the BBC had agreed to some air time, I'd have asked one of Rangers' management to take part. That was my best hope, and now it looks like that's gone.'

She looked down at her lap. Ridiculously, only twenty minutes ago, she had thought she was his best hope. She felt a jag of failure in her throat, as sharp and painful as a fish bone.

'But, hey, thanks for thinking of me. For wanting to help. You're a good person, Izzy. Sometimes I forget there are good people out there.'

They stood up. The wind was whipping at her face and the scudding clouds had turned the colour of slate. 'I'm sorry it wasn't as good an idea as I hoped,' she said weakly.

He touched her lightly on the shoulder and kissed her cheek. It was another of his meaningless London kisses yet she felt herself gasp inside. She touched his sleeve and offered him the other cheek, breathing in the leather of his jacket. He was freshly shaved and his skin smelt like a sea breeze.

She was unlikely to see him again. The thought flooded her with such regret that she sat on the bench, watching him as he walked away, his tall figure outlined against the fading light of the afternoon. Then, an idea popped into her head with such clarity, with such completeness, that she leapt to her feet and almost cried out. He turned round at that precise moment, as if she had. He waved and she waved back. A pair of crows flew skywards, calling raucously.

***

Therapist: Jim? Just wondered if you were coming in
                  for your appointment today?

Jim: What time is it? Shit! I totally forgot. Sorry.

Therapist:	No problem. Just wanted to make sure you're OK?
Jim:	I'm fine. Just very busy.
Therapist:	Would you like to reschedule?
Jim:	Aye, sure thing.
Therapist:	I can see you tomorrow morning.
Jim:	On a Saturday? I'm going to the match in Dunfermline. Kick-off's at 4 p.m.
Therapist:	No problem. I've a Saturday morning clinic. Shall we say ten?

CHAPTER 11

Izzy woke with an intention to act. The idea that had hit her with such certainty at the Necropolis had persisted, grown and strengthened. It was now as insistent as the shaft of light that lasered through the gap in the bedroom curtains. She smoothed the tangle of sheets that had gathered at Jim's side of the bed and plumped up his two pillows. He had left early for a business meeting and was going straight to the match at Dunfermline afterwards. He would be gone all day. Davy had stayed over at Cas's. The day stretched ahead of her, like an adventure waiting to unfold.

Saturday morning on a sunny September day and the Bellevue Golf Club was busy. She was lucky to find a parking space between the low-slung art deco clubhouse and the practice putting green. The air of privilege and wealth around her was palpable. Row upon row of parked cars, expensive and new, sat patiently in the sun, as if reconciled to the hours it would take for their owners to play a round, which included an extended stay at the nineteenth hole. Golf. What a pointless waste of time and money.

A men's foursome walked out to the first tee, dapper in their bright sweaters and two-tone shoes. They were chatting and pulling their golf carts behind them as absentmindedly as suitcases, the wheels bumping over the perfectly tended grass of the fairways. The club was notorious for being the last golf club in Glasgow to admit women members. Although, as Izzy looked about her, there was no evidence of any of those rare creatures, apart from herself.

She picked up the *Downfall Dossier* that lay on the passenger seat and checked that the article from the morning paper was inside; the Lord Justice had said that he believed the club had the potential to be declared insolvent. The weight of evidence was building. Her breathing was steady and she felt calm, resolute about what she needed to do.

Bill's Jaguar slid into the car park and he parked six feet from her. He was wearing a tweed flat cap and sat hunched in the driver's seat, as if working up the energy to make a move. She knocked on his passenger window. 'Hi, it's me,' she said, waving her arm.

He reached over and opened the passenger door. 'Izzy, love. I didn't recognise you, sorry.' He reached over and gave her a clumsy peck on the cheek. 'I wish women wouldn't change their hairstyle, it doesn't make it easy for old codgers like me.'

She could smell stale alcohol and bacterial breath and wondered if he had forgotten to brush his teeth. He was wearing a cream jumper that had the shadow of scum at the back of the neck. She felt a surge of maternal affection at the sight of these small signs of neglect.

'The new hairdo is for The Chairman's Club,' she said. 'I've got keep up with all those glamorous Director's wives. You do remember we're going, don't you?'

'Of course I remember. The price of those tickets isn't something I'd forget, but I don't understand why Jim thinks you need to change your hair. It's more a case of how can those other wives can keep up with you.'

'That's very sweet of you, Bill.'

He was examining her closely, as if inspecting her for other changes he hadn't yet noticed. 'I didn't know you were a member here.'

'I'm not. I just wanted a quiet word with you, that's all.' Her voice sounded bright, almost brittle.

Bill settled back into the seat, looking worried. He took off his flat cap. His hair was matted beneath it. 'Is everything OK? Jim all right?'

'Jim's fine,' she said breezily, 'but I wondered if you'd read this?'

She passed him the article quoting the Lord Justice. He glanced at it briefly. 'Yes.'

'And? Does it concern you?' she asked, trying to keep her voice neutral.

Bill's eyes were hooded with fatigue. He glanced around, as if worried he might be overheard. 'Of course it does. I told Jim we should play it canny, maybe even back off. But no. He wants to offer "invoice after installation", on condition they give us the contract.'

'And they've agreed?'

'They'd be daft not to consider it. Most of the other bids will want big, upfront deposits. I thought the bank would turn us down flat, but Jim told me yesterday that he's expecting a loan of three hundred thousand. No problemo.'

In the past it would have been a comfort to Izzy that the bank's judgement was in line with Jim's, but now she felt herself go numb. 'Rangers are heading for a financial meltdown,' she stated.

Bill shrugged. 'Then we'll have to hope that the new management keep their promise to bail them out.'

'I've a journalist friend who's working on a documentary about Rangers for the BBC. He thinks someone in the new management team should give an interview. Deny all these bankruptcy rumours.'

'Nae chance. None of them trust the media, apparently. Who can blame them?'

'But, not saying anything makes it look like got they've got something to hide.'

'The problem is, Izzy, no one's interested in finances. The team have been top of the Championship for the past two seasons. Two years of beating Celtic makes it awfy easy to turn a blind eye.'

'So we do nothing but hope for the best?' she asked.

'I've had a word with Jack Marshall, and he's confident the club will be able to ride out this rough patch.'

'Jack Marshall, the guy behind the buyout?'

Bill looked at her in surprise.

'I've been doing some research,' she explained.

'I've known Jack for years. He helped me finance Verisafe's first big expansion and we've been friends ever since. He's always been a big Rangers supporter. He brokered the deal between the old owners and this new consortium, so he knows what he's talking about when it comes to the club's finances.'

'Could you ask Jack Marshall if he'll talk to my friend at the BBC? If Rangers' management won't give an interview, maybe he will?'

'Jack loves publicity so he might be persuaded to make a comment or two.'

Bill opened his car door and walked round to the back of the car, lifting his golf clubs out of the boot. 'I take it Jim doesn't know you're here?'

'No,' she said, reaching in and helping him pull out his golf cart. The folding mechanism reminded her of the buggy from Davy's baby days.

'Don't worry, I won't tell him,' said Bill. 'He doesn't take kindly to people interfering. I should know. He's happy for me to be on the golf course, out of his way, while he runs the show.'

He clipped his golf bag onto the trolley, which had a grubby flannel hung from its side. Three woods poked out the top, covered with toy tiger heads. Izzy stroked the soft fur of their ears.

'You might not believe it, Izzy, but I was a tiger once,' said Bill. His watery eyes lifted to hers.

'That tiger's still in there, Bill. You just need to let him out from time to time.'

He looked at her carefully, as if weighing up his options. 'Jack's been talking about having me round to his house in Bearsden. He's got some old footage of the European Cup game in 1967 that we could watch. I'll have a word with him then … *If* the moment's right.' He hesitated for a moment, a concentrated look on his face, as if trying to remember an important message, 'Tell your friend at the BBC to be careful, Izzy. These are powerful people we're talking about.'

***

Therapist:	I'm glad you could make it, Jim. How are you?
Jim:	Fine. Looking forward to the match. We're going to give them a battering.
Therapist:	You sounded very busy on the phone. How are you managing with the tapering down? It can be a challenge when there's a lot on.
Jim:	I had a big meeting with the bank this week. Well, you know what bankers are like. I'd lose my credibility if I didn't have a drink with them, so we all got hammered. If I'm being honest, I'm a tad disappointed in myself. When I commit to something, I usually follow through.
Therapist:	It's important not to catastrophise these setbacks. You can get back on the wagon anytime you choose to.
Jim:	I'm going through to Dunfermline on the supporters' bus this afternoon. Not exactly an ideal time to stay on the lemonade.
Therapist:	Perhaps we could discuss some strategies to help you manage these situations?

Jim: Perhaps we can agree that I'll start over again on Monday?

CHAPTER 12

Izzy suspected that real spies went about their work with meticulous planning. Yet, sometimes it was necessary to improvise, respond to events. Her instincts told her that Bill was unlikely to speak with Jack Marshall any time soon. She empathised with him not wanting to raise his head above the parapet; she had been the same once, but his reluctance to act meant she had no option but to take matters into her own hands.

Jack Marshall lived in Bearsden, according to Bill, and she knew from the magazine article that Michelle ran a Lifestyle business called Yin Yan Time. It had been easy to check the company's address online. It was listed at 6A Russell Drive, slap bang in the middle of Bearsden. She felt pleased with her investigative abilities but, as she drove down Russell Drive, doubt began to bubble inside her.

The houses were huge. Intimidatingly huge. Built in the 'thirties on vast plots, there had been plenty of opportunity for subsequent owners to extend, then extend further. Trees lined both sides of the road and bright light filtered through the leaves. Estate agents would use words like "prestigious" and "exclusive" to describe the neighbourhood. Her anxiety deepened. Her ten-year-old car would stand out amongst all the expensive models parked in the driveways; people might be watching her, suspicious about why she was there.

6A was one of six modern semi-detached houses that had been squeezed into a single plot at the end of the road. She felt herself relax, thankful there was no gate or fancy intercom to navigate her way through. The houses were the sort that you would find in any modern housing estate, yet the aspirational address would make them expensive; you could get something twice as big in Scotstoun for the half the price. What sort of people would buy them? Daft, vain people she concluded, and then corrected herself. Everyone was entitled to do what they liked with their money, even if it defied common sense. It was just another sad truth about the world they lived in.

She turned out of Russell Drive and onto the main road towards Bearsden Cross. Parked cars lined the road – she wouldn't be noticed if she waited here. There was a space, ideally situated, where she would have a clear view of the front door of 6A. She sighed deeply and quietly thanked the universe.

She pulled the "WAP" folder from her bag and had another look at the four-page spread of Jack Marshall, Michelle and their children. They were shown off in a succession of stylised poses, some in rooms filled with overstuffed and gilded furniture, others in lavish gardens with banks of flowering azaleas. Wherever the pictures had been taken, it was not 6A Russell Drive. More sham. More nonsense.

Jack was described as one of Glasgow's most successful businessmen, having made his fortune in venture capital. He was quoted as saying how unbelievably happy he was that he and Michelle had married, following a difficult divorce. She looked again at his modest house. Clearly, the new marriage had been a drain on Jack Marshall's resources. She studied his stiff posture in the photographs. His belly was sucked in and his face was a mixture of pride and pressure. Michelle, once a popular presenter on Scottish TV, had recently launched an exciting lifestyle and fitness business. Behind her glossy smile and sparkly eyes, there was a shadow of exhaustion. For all their claims, they didn't look very happy.

Out of the corner of her eye, Izzy caught the movement of a silver car. It reversed and drove away with practised speed. She couldn't be sure if the car had come from Jack and Michelle's house. There was a white Mini still parked in their driveway but she couldn't remember if there had been one or two cars when she first arrived. She banged her palm against the steering wheel, frustrated with her lack of concentration.

There was no point in waiting any longer. She was going to knock on the door. Her pulse quickened as she took a deep breath, closed her eyes and visualised a successful outcome. Jack Marshall would open the door and she would introduce herself as the wife of Jim, the MD of Verisafe, a close friend of Bill, the Chairman. She would ask him directly if the club was in financial difficulty. He would reassure her and she would show relief. He wouldn't expect the punch until after she landed it. As there was no problem, he must take the opportunity to go on TV and give an interview, publicly denying the rumours. If he didn't, Izzy would go to the media herself and tell them that Jack was hiding the truth from the club's suppliers.

She pulled down the sun visor and checked herself in the mirror. She licked a fingertip, smoothed both eyebrows and pursed her lips. Her eyes were clear, her breathing steady and a faint blush coloured her cheeks. She was ready. She walked calmly towards the house, though her heart had begun to pump unnaturally. The doorbell chimed noisily. The Marshalls' door was half panelled in wood and frosted glass. She resisted the temptation to press her nose against the glass and peer through.

Michelle Marshall was immediately recognisable. Her short bob was highlighted in different hues of caramel, her breasts jacked up and pointed out, disproportionately large to the rest of her tiny body. She was wearing neon leggings and a sleeveless sweatshirt that hung in flattering swags from her muscled shoulders. The scent of citrus and coconut drifted from her silky limbs.

'No thanks,' said Michelle, slamming the door shut.

Izzy stared at the shut door. Indignant. She rang the doorbell, again. And again. Michelle re-appeared. On her hip was a baby; plump, dewy-eyed, with a pink bandanna wrapped around her bald head. The baby stared impassively at Izzy, chewing on her fat fingers. Izzy remembered her name from the file. Esme.

'What do you want?' Michelle's accent had a touch of Bearsden breeding, but the flat vowels of the East End were unmistakable. Her eyebrows on her high forehead were wrinkling in irritation.

'Is Jack in?' asked Izzy, casually.

'He's not here,' she replied and turned to shut the door. Izzy pushed her foot in the doorway. Michelle spun round, the baby's eyes widened in shock at the suddenness of her movement.

'Who the hell are you? What do you want?' Her accent was now pure East End. The baby arched her back and began to struggle and thrash. There was a loud crash from the kitchen, then a heartbeat of a pause before a loud wail erupted.

'I'm sorry. I didn't mean to alarm you. I'm a friend of Bill's …' began Izzy, but Michelle was looking behind her. The crying from inside the house was becoming frantic.

'Shit,' cried Michelle. 'I'm sorry. You'll have to come back later,' she said, turning and pushing the door shut with the back of her heel. She was shouting: 'I'm coming, Crawford. Mummy's coming.'

The door hadn't closed properly. It took the lightest of touches to push it open. Izzy had a clear view of the corridor

135

and the kitchen at the back. She stepped inside. Her heart was thudding; she half expected someone to pounce on her at any moment. The back door was open. Michelle was in the garden, hauling a toddler to his feet. Esme was lunging forwards to grab her brother's hair.

'Hello there,' said Izzy as she reached the back door. She waved in what she hoped would be a friendly greeting.

'What the hell are you still doing here?' snapped Michelle, walking towards her. The children were staring at Izzy, their eyes wide, fearful.

'You left the front door open. You dropped this,' said Izzy, holding out a soother she had picked up from the kitchen table.

'Right. Sorry. Shit. It's been one of those mornings,' Michelle replied as she pulled a reluctant Crawford into the house.

'Can I help?' asked Izzy. Michelle stared at her as if assessing the risk. Izzy smiled reassuringly. Before she knew it, Esme was being pressed against her chest. The baby's eyes were creasing into the preamble of a major strop.

'Is it OK to give her one of these?' asked Izzy, taking a rusk from a packet on the kitchen counter. The baby snatched it from her before Michelle could reply.

'Mummy told you not to go running off like that,' said Michelle examining Crawford for broken bones. He was looking past his mother, his eyes glued to the rusk packet.

'They've already had their mid-morning piece of fruit but, what the heck, you can give him one.' Michelle pushed her hair out of her eyes. Crawford took the biscuit from Izzy carefully, examining it as if it might be contaminated.

The two children fixed their mother and Izzy with wide-eyed curiosity as they sucked and munched. Izzy put Esme in her high chair and Michelle strapped Crawford into his booster seat. Peace descended.

Izzy was beginning to enjoy herself. A current of adrenalin pulsed pleasantly through her. 'I'm sorry to turn up on your doorstep like this. I'm a friend of Bill, the Chairman of Verisafe Alarms. He's a good friend of Jack's.'

'Is he the old guy whose wife died a few years ago? Crawford was due on the day of the funeral. Jack went, needless to say. Lucky for him, Crawford decided to wait another week before making his appearance.' Michelle slumped down onto a chair.

'Can I get you anything?' asked Izzy.

'Double espresso would be great,' said Michelle. 'The machine's over there. Help yourself to anything you want.'

The coffee machine was the sort that looked complicated but only required a capsule and pressing buttons.

'Jack's buggered off to golf, even though I told him I was running a yoga class this morning. I had to rush around to find a replacement teacher. Then he's going straight to Dunfermline for the match. It's our nephew's birthday party this afternoon but he said it can't be helped. The club comes first. My sister's going to be furious. It's going to be horrendous.' She rolled her r's like the quiet growl of a lioness.

'It's tough to do all that on your own,' agreed Izzy, handing her a coffee.

'His first wife popped out four boys as easily as shelling peas. He's forever saying she had twice the work but made half the fuss.'

Izzy made a clucking noise. 'What do men know about raising small children?'

'They've no idea, do they?' Michelle sat for a moment, sipping her coffee. Izzy found two lidded cups on the draining board and filled them up with water. The children took them soundlessly.

'Sorry, I think I asked you this, but why do you want to speak to Jack?' asked Michelle.

Izzy felt temporarily stunned. She hadn't planned what to say if Michelle opened the door. She wiped Esme's rusk encrusted mouth. 'I'm worried about all these stories in the papers about the club. They say it's going bankrupt,' she said, keeping her tone mild.

Michelle laughed. 'God, don't pay any attention to those stories. The club's always in the news.'

'Jim, my husband, is the Managing Director of Verisafe Alarms. He's bidding for a big contract with the club and thinks the world of Rangers. He'd be furious if he knew I was here.'

Michelle gave her a knowing nod. 'I won't say anything.'

'The thing is, Michelle, I wanted to ask Jack directly if there was any truth to these rumours. I've got a child and I'm worried about our future.'

'I totally understand that. There's a lot of Rangers haters out there scaremongering, but you've got nothing to worry about. Believe me, nothing will ever happen to Rangers,' said Michelle.

The biscuits were finished. Crawford slid off his booster chair and was heading towards the open back door. Michelle turned to catch him but he wriggled out of her grasp like a slippery fish.

'That's why I was going to ask Jack if he could give an interview to the media. You know, publicly reassure everyone. It seems Rangers haters have got the upper hand. It's all you read about.'

Michelle narrowed her eyes. Izzy felt a rise of panic. Perhaps she had gone too far. She smiled, hoping to soften any suspicion but Michelle was staring at her, hard. Izzy felt her mouth go dry and her tongue thicken. Michelle's eyes flicked over to the kitchen counter where her handbag lay. Her phone was probably inside it.

Crawford, sensing a lapse in his mother's concentration, ran to the back door. The baby began to shout in her high chair, her arms raised upwards like a hungry chick. Michelle turned to Izzy. 'I promise you, Rangers is a very successful club. If your husband has business with them, you should be grateful.'

The danger had passed as quickly as it appeared. 'That means a lot coming from you,' said Izzy, pleased that she sounded grateful, sincere. Michelle hooked Esme out of her high chair and trotted after Crawford, who was running towards the back door.

'I'll let myself out,' shouted Izzy, but she wasn't sure Michelle had heard her. She was too busy running down the garden, chasing her son.

Her footfall was silent on the hall carpet. There was an open tread stairway to her right, a lounge on her left, and a study adjacent to the lounge. The door to the study was open, so she peeked in. It was a small room, dominated by a large desk and a computer screen. She could hear Esme crying in the garden and Crawford yelling: 'It's not fair.'

She slipped inside the office. Adrenaline rushed through her like electricity and her eyes cast about wildly. Papers, envelopes and books littered the desk as if they had been flung on top of each other. A folder lying on top caught her eye: *GET ME IN. Advanced Ticket Financial Report*. She slipped it into her bag and rearranged some papers to cover up its absence. The desk was a shambles anyway and she doubted it would be missed.

She peeped outside the study door. The hallway was empty. Her legs felt like lead. She opened the front door and stepped outside. A gust of wind caught it, slamming it shut behind her with a bang. She quickened her step, convinced that Michelle would come running after her, catch her by her sleeve, and demand to see what was in her bag. But no one followed. The road was quiet, as sleepy as before.

Sitting in her car, she felt a moment of numbness and her head fell back on the headrest. Then joy flowered inside until it escaped out of her in a burst of happiness. 'I did it,' she laughed.

She drove into the city and parked on a side street. She sat quietly for a moment to compose herself, and then made the call. Sean sounded wary on hearing her voice. She ignored the brief winding of disappointment and read out the title of the folder in a clear voice: *GET ME IN. Advanced Ticket Financial Report.* It struck her then that she hadn't even looked inside it. Perhaps it was worthless but before that thought had time to form, he was telling her to come to an address in the West End. Right away.

***

Therapist: What makes you think that, if you wait until Monday to get back on the wagon, it will be any easier? You've already told me you're under a lot of pressure at work.

Jim:	The pressure with this Rangers deal is temporary. I should hear in the next couple of weeks. If we land it, I'll make enough cash to buy us a house in Bearsden.
Therapist:	That must be quite a deal.
Jim:	There's nothing wrong in wanting to better yourself, is there?
Therapist:	Not at all. If that's what you and Izzy want.
Jim:	It's my dream to give Izzy a lovely home in Bearsden. She deserves a bit of luxury.
Therapist:	I wonder if she worries about you? If she sees the stress you're under?
Jim:	It's my job to look after my family. I've never shirked from my duty. I keep telling you I'm fine.
Therapist:	I'm sorry to disagree, Jim, but I'm not so sure.

CHAPTER 13

Izzy parked in a public car park a short distance from the address Sean had given her. She was deep within the fashionable West End. Glasgow University towered over the district, its great gothic tower announcing itself as one of the oldest universities in the country. Impatience gripped her; her heart hadn't stopped pounding since their call.

Coffee bars and bistros were filled with students and stylish men and women cradling massive cappuccinos. Swathes of pedestrians crossed Byres Road with little regard for the pedestrian lights. They could dictate their own terms due to their sheer numbers and the inner confidence that comes from educated people. Glasgow Tech would be looked down upon around here, but she felt strangely powerful and drew herself up to her full height as she ignored the red man and crossed the road with the rest of them.

The nearer she got to the flat, the more she wanted to break into a run. Her bag, with the file inside, bumped against her thigh. She had only one thought. She needed to show Sean this folder as soon as possible.

The flat was in a sandstone tenement that had been recently cleaned from soot-blackened to russet red. She had a passing thought that it had been built in the same period as Connor's house in the Gallowgate and yet, although only five miles apart, they might as well have been on different planets. Here, millions had been invested to restore the building back to its Victorian splendour, whereas in the Gallowgate, they were taking the cheaper option and knocking the whole lot down.

Her heart tightened as she rang the doorbell. It tightened a little further when he opened it. He was dressed in jeans and a T-shirt and slippers, the slip-on kind in dark leather. She felt herself blushing, as if he'd come to the door in his pyjamas. 'Come in,' he said, gesturing for her to enter. His tone was polite, measured. There was no London kissing of cheeks.

It was an effort to match his casual attitude. 'Thank you,' she said, offering him a small smile.

She followed him down the hallway, her eyes darting from side to side. They passed an open door where she glimpsed a double bed. The bed was un-made with its sheets and bedding strewn across the mattress. It struck her as intimate rather than untidy and she felt her face burning.

He led her into the kitchen, a large square room with high ceilings. There were farmhouse style kitchen units and a large table that had been scrubbed to faded wood.

Instinct made her look up. The Victorian cornicing was an elaborate moulding of swags of flowers and fruit. Someone had spent weeks stripping it back to its original state. A jam jar of wild flowers sat in the centre of the table. A woman's touch. She didn't know why, but the thought had a sobering effect.

'Nice flat,' she said.

'It belongs to a friend who lets me stay here when I'm in Glasgow,' he said. He emphasised the word *friend* as if he wanted her know it was a woman. He held up a coffee pot to her. It was one of those aluminium Italian ones that Izzy had seen but had never known how to use. 'Coffee?' he asked.

'No thanks. I'd rather we get down to business.'

'I see,' he said, leaning back against the sink, his arms crossed, his expression calculating. The coolness of his gaze was disconcerting and a hot thought poked at her. Did he think she was stalking him?

'Here's the information I was telling you about,' she said, pulling the file from her bag and placing it on the table. He looked at the cover and read the title out loud before sitting down opposite her. Putting on his glasses, he began to read. He had a way of holding his head so that it appeared to be perfectly still. Light poured in from the large sash windows, bathing him in a warm glow. She allowed herself the smallest moment of admiration.

'How did you get this?' he said, looking at her with surprise.

She felt a pulse of delight but kept a neutral face. 'I went to see Bill, Verisafe's Chairman, to ask him to persuade Jack Marshall, the businessman behind the management buyout, to give you an interview. Bill said he'd think about it but I knew that wasn't going to happen, so I went to Jack's house myself. Things sort of spiralled from there.'

She expected to be given a gold star, or at least a "well done", but his expression was inscrutable as he flicked through the pages. 'It looks like a record of Rangers' dealings with the ticketing agency, Get Me In. My sources tell me they've raised over twenty million against the sale of future season tickets, but there's never been any proof,' he said.

She remembered Jim telling her he had bought two years' worth of season tickets for him and Davy. It had the sad ring of truth. 'Is that illegal?' she asked.

'No. But they might be using this money to finance the club's debts. The fans think the new management team has plenty of cash. They don't realise that it could be coming from their own pockets,' he explained.

He was watching her carefully. She couldn't tell whether he was admiring or admonishing her. He took off his glasses. His eyes were as beautiful and as complicated as a cat's. She had a premonition, of danger, of excitement, she couldn't tell which.

'So, this is good isn't it? It's the proof you need,' she said, smiling broadly.

His expression hardened. 'I've learned to be suspicious, Izzy. To question everything. Everyone. There's something about all this that seems … a bit too good to be true.'

She looked at him uncomprehendingly.

'You walk into Jack Marshall's house and steal a file. Not just any file either. One that contains incriminating evidence that would expose the management's fraudulent claims to have enough money to save the club.'

Her brain felt stiff. 'I don't understand. What exactly are you saying?'

'How do I know this isn't some kind of sting? You give me information that looks legitimate but is, in fact, total bullshit. If published, it would result in me being sued for slander, my reputation ruined.'

'That's ridiculous,' she managed to say, but couldn't control the sense of fury that was building inside her. 'That's more than ridiculous. That's insulting.'

'Insulting to whom? To you, or to me? You appear out of the blue, offering to help. You're married to a fanatical Rangers supporter on the cusp of winning a huge business deal with the club. How much more convenient would it be for you if I was shut up for good.'

'I can't believe you'd think I'd do that,' she said.

'Why not? You expect me to believe that you're so fired up with social injustice that you're prepared to expose the club's mismanagement and likely wreck your husband's business deal in the bargain? I don't think so.'

'I think I should leave,' she said, getting up from the table.

He said nothing. His look was flinty, defensive. The surge of anger and disappointment coursing through her felt unstoppable as she walked towards the door.

'Don't forget to take this,' he said, offering her the file.

'Keep it. If what you say is true, it won't take long for a lawyer to verify the contents aren't some rubbish that I've secretly concocted to discredit your reputation. Goodbye, Sean. And don't worry, I won't bother you again,' she said, thinking calmly: *I'm walking out of here and will never see him again.*

He caught her by the arm. 'Izzy. Sit down.' She felt the heat transferring from his body to hers. 'Please, Izzy. Sit down. I'm sorry. I know you're not working for Rangers.'

She sat down. 'I don't understand. What made you think I was some kind of double agent?'

'I never really thought you were. No one experienced in undercover work would do what you've done, in the way you did it.'

'They wouldn't?' she asked.

'They wouldn't steal the file. They would take pictures of it. They'll find out eventually that it's missing and it will be obvious as to who stole it.'

'Is that your way of saying I'm an idiot?'

'No, not an idiot. Impulsive, maybe. Inexperienced ...' he said, sounding like a doctor stating a diagnosis. 'But it still leaves me with a question.' He leaned forward, smiling, one eyebrow raised suggestively. 'Why is a lovely lady like you so keen to help me?'

Irritation flared again. His parody of flirting felt more painful than his accusal of betrayal. 'Has anyone ever told you that you're an arsehole?' she replied. It was out of her mouth before she could stop it.

Sean's smile broadened. 'Many times,' he acknowledged, happily.

There was a dimple in his cheek that she hadn't noticed before. She wondered how she could have missed something so charming. Irritation melted and she found herself laughing. 'Go on, then, if you're so smart, tell me why I'm here,' she said.

He shrugged. 'We've discounted double agent and fanatical Rangers football fan. How about bored wife looking for a bit of adventure?'

She laughed. It came out more as a splutter. 'Don't flatter yourself. You're not the only person who cares about exposing corruption and exploitation, who thinks the interests of ordinary people might, for once, matter.'

The atmosphere between them became serious. He was looking at her kindly. 'There's more to it though, isn't there?' he said.

She drew a deep breath, 'Bill, the Chairman, told me my husband's about to borrow £300,000 to finance this Rangers deal. You and I both know they won't be able to pay him back. It'll ruin the business and it'll probably ruin my family,' she said quietly.

Sean looked as shocked as if she had slapped him. 'Shit.'

She tucked a lock of hair behind her ear and silently promised herself she wouldn't cry.

'I'm sorry for being flippant about your motives. I can see why this is important to you.' He leaned over and touched her hand. Desire flared inside her like a flame being lit.

'Apology accepted,' she said quietly. She didn't trust herself to meet his eyes. 'This isn't a game for me, you know.'

'It's not a game for me either,' he said. His hand was still on hers. She lifted her head and the look that passed between them was as serious as a pledge.

Sean got up quickly and went towards the sink. She hoped he was going to offer her that coffee again. 'What you've done is potentially brilliant. If we return the file before they discover it missing, no one will know it was taken in the first place.'

Her mouth felt parched. The thought of going back to the Marshall house filled her with dread, like a murderer returning to the scene of the crime. She swallowed hard. 'Michelle and the children are going to a birthday party this afternoon. Jack's gone to Dunfermline for the match,' she said, sounding like a pupil anxious to please the teacher.

'Good. We'll do it now,' he said, ducking under the sink, bringing out a small cardboard box. Latex gloves, the fingers the colour of dead skin, poked from it. He pulled on a pair and wiped the folder with a damp cloth. He began taking pictures of each page with his phone. His movements were neat, clinical, practised. All her previous excitement drained away, the start of a headache throbbing in her temple. 'Don't look so worried,' he said, 'breaking into a Bearsden semi is well within my repertoire.'

She tried to smile but her face was rigid. She told him she wasn't playing a game, but she wished she felt braver, more careless. The vision of them getting caught and arrested was so vivid, it felt like it had already happened.

'Have you something to tie your hair back?' he asked, looking at her with such care that she felt temporarily lost to him. She took the elastic band that she wore on her wrist and gathered her hair into a ponytail. 'Wear these,' he said, holding out a pair of sunglasses. He came a little closer and put them on her face; a gesture that felt playful, almost flirtatious. She could hear a roaring in her ears as he leaned towards her, whispering against her hair. 'Trust me. Everything will be fine.'

***

Therapist: Of course you can decide to give up drinking any time you want, but I think you're putting yourself under more pressure than you need to by keeping all this to yourself.

Jim: You think I should tell Izzy I'm seeing you, don't you?

Therapist: I think you should tell her everything.

Jim: She would be worried sick if I told her about seeing that boy in the alleyway. She's the most law-abiding person you could ever hope to meet. The only person I know that hasn't so much as stolen a sweetie from the pick 'n mix.

Therapist: She may find out anyway, now she's involved with the boy's mother and her charity work. Wouldn't you rather tell her yourself, than let her find out from someone else?

Jim: She may find out I was at the match on the day he was killed but I'll deny seeing anything. Sometimes honesty isn't the best policy.

CHAPTER 14

Bearsden Road was busy with Saturday afternoon shoppers. They sat, unnoticed, in Sean's car, watching the Marshalls' house. Michelle's white Mini was still in the driveway. Sean was working his way through the photographs of the GET ME IN file on his phone with the concentration of someone threading a needle.

Her phone rang, making her jump. Davy. His audition for *The Shindig* would be starting soon. She wanted to pick up but couldn't risk arousing any suspicion. She let it go to voicemail. Almost immediately, she doubted her decision. What if there was a problem with the audition? Perhaps he needed help? Should she call him back? Her right leg began to tremble. She put her hand on it to stop it.

She tried to remember who she was: mother, wife, part-time student and volunteer at the Bureau. An honest member of society. A responsible person. A law-abiding citizen. Breathe: four counts in, four counts out. Almost before realising it, she found herself falling into a state of relaxation. Thoughts flew in and out of her mind, like the cars passing by outside. She watched them come and go but felt no need to think about them. Sean was leaning against the window, his head cradled in his palm. She wondered if he had dozed off. The atmosphere between them was easy now, like old friends. Then a crazy thought: like a married couple. They might be about to break into a house, but it was beginning to feel as workaday as waiting for the shops to open.

Then, as if on cue, the front door opened. Immediately, they sat up. Michelle was carrying Esme in her car seat, Crawford was dawdling behind her. He wandered out, close to the road, and Michelle said something sharp and pulled him back onto the driveway. She clipped Esme's car seat in the front and Crawford clambered into his booster seat, flailing at his mother's hands as she tried to help him with his seatbelt. Michelle was wearing a midnight blue fitted dress with high-heeled shoes. Izzy had to admire her style; both she and the children looked lovely. She returned to the house, finally emerging with a bag with lots of compartments and a birthday present crammed on top. The car reversed at speed out of the driveway and then it was quiet, save for the drone of a hedge cutter and the rumble of traffic from the main road.

Izzy's heart began beating painfully in her chest. She pulled her ponytail tighter and adjusted her sunglasses. Nerves were making her want to giggle like one of those hapless housewife spies in Hollywood films.

'We'll wait a few minutes. She may come back. Easy to forget things when you've got all that paraphernalia to think about,' said Sean. He smiled reassuringly and put on his gloves. She settled back into her seat and tried to empty her mind, waiting for Sean's instructions to fill it. 'Did you notice if there was an alarm?' he asked, leaning forward to get a better view of the eaves under the roof.

'I can see a box,' replied Izzy, spotting a white cube tucked under the guttering above the front door. It had the Verisafe logo on it. She suppressed a small cry, a combination of horror and laughter. The irony of it.

'Let's hope it's fake.'

'And if it isn't?'

'I'll cut through the telephone cable at the front to disarm it. If I do that, we'll have to make it look like a proper break-in though.'

'You mean steal stuff? Mess the place up a bit?' asked Izzy, matching Sean's even tone.

'Hopefully it won't come to that,' he said.

They waited a while longer. A few leaves rustled along the pavement and spits of rain spotted the windscreen. Izzy felt suspended in time, each moment tinged with an edge that felt both sharp and dreamy at the same time. There was no sign of Michelle returning. Sean looked across at her and smiled. She felt herself give way to him again: his calmness, his confidence in what he was doing. 'OK,' he said, 'time to go. First, I'll deal with the alarm. Then I'll go to the back door and pick the lock. Wait in the car until you see me open the front door. Then walk up the driveway, put the file back where you found it, and then we leave.'

She felt a sharp rush of panic and took another deep intake of breath: four counts in, four counts out.

'Put your gloves on and wait for me to open the front door.' He was speaking gently, as a parent might to a child. He pressed the car keys into her hand. It was the smallest of touches but it burned long after his hand had left hers. 'Lock the car when you leave.'

He walked towards the house. From the back, he had a boyish slimness to his hips. At the house, he stood a couple of paces back from the front door and looked up at the alarm box. Then he walked past the garage and down the side path to the back door. The alarm must be fake. Thank goodness. She hadn't been aware that she was holding her breath until she released it. She put on the latex gloves, picked up the GET ME IN folder and readied herself.

She walked steadily, her eyes fixed on the front door. It was still closed; she had left the car too soon. What was she thinking? He'd told her to wait until he'd opened the front door before getting out the car. He was probably still at the back door, breaking in. Maybe it was proving trickier than he expected. Fear flooded into her. She couldn't loiter about in case someone was watching her and she couldn't return to the car in case she missed him. She walked up the front path, slowly, willing the door to open. But it remained shut. She rang the doorbell and waited, looking down at her feet and then, cautiously, around her. The street was deserted. She rang the doorbell again. Her heart was clattering. Then a shadow appeared behind the frosted glass and the door opened.

The scent of lemons, baby powder and something less savoury filled the air. Her eyes met Sean's. She wondered if he could see that she was panicking, but his face was calm, focused. She walked in and pointed towards the study door and he pushed it open. She laid the folder on top of the pile of papers on Jack's desk, exactly where she had found it that morning. Given the mess, Jack would hardly notice the other papers she'd shuffled about that morning.

The sound of an engine approaching felt as loud as an aeroplane's. A car was on the driveway. She fought the overwhelming urge to run. Sean pulled her towards him and they stood pressed together in the hallway. His head was turned in the direction of the front door. His face was so close she could see the pores in his skin, feel the hardness of his body; so different from the soft pillow feel of Jim's.

The engine coughed then stopped. She felt Sean's gloved hand on her wrist, pulling her in the direction of the back door. For a moment, her feet were stuck. He gave her a gentle tug and she moved, half stumbling towards the kitchen. They stopped by the back door, straining to hear, expecting the front door to open. Instead, the stillness deepened. A fly buzzed lazily. The work surfaces of the kitchen were pristine and two lidded cups sat upended on the draining board.

Sean pushed his sunglasses on top of his head. His expression was composed. He put a finger to his lips. She felt incapable of speaking, even if she wanted to. He opened the back door carefully, waved for her to follow him, then shut the door with the quietest of clicks.

They pressed themselves flat against the garage wall as they made their way down the side passage. She felt sure he could hear her heart beating. She herself half expected to look down and see it pulsing against her sweater. A woman's voice sailed over: 'I'll put the kettle on.'

The voice was coming from next door. Izzy closed her eyes and let relief wash over her. She heard a car door shutting, a rattle of keys in a lock then a front door opening and closing. She leaned against Sean, their arms touching. She didn't want to move. She wanted to stand like this forever, pressed together as if their bodies were joined.

***

Jim: I should go. The bus to Dunfermline will be leaving soon.

Therapist: Before you go, I'd like us to agree on what your next steps will be.

Jim: Well, I'm having a drink tonight. But nothing too heavy.

Therapist: OK.

Jim: On Monday, I'll talk to Izzy about coming
                to see you and about being serious about
                cutting back. Happy?

Therapist: Just one more thing I'd like to say before
                you go.

CHAPTER 15

Izzy pressed her trembling leg down, but it continued to twitch as if connected to an electricity supply. She dug her thumbs into her thighs to loosen the tightness of the muscles and rolled her head in a circular motion to ease the tension in her neck and shoulders. The fingers of their latex gloves lay tangled together in the compartment between the car seats. She felt an odd affection towards them, a symbol of their crime.

Sean was driving towards the city centre, although they hadn't discussed where they were going next. His expression was tense, and there was a faint twitch in his jaw muscle. It was an effort for her not to lean over and smooth his hair, to touch his cheek, to reassure him. 'You OK?' she asked.

He nodded. 'You did well.'

She let the compliment warm her. 'Thanks, but I left the car too soon.'

'You rang the doorbell and stayed calm. Not easy to do under the circumstances,' he said.

The trees by the side of the road were bending in a brisk breeze and clouds raced across the sky. 'I don't want to go home,' she said suddenly. 'Not yet.'

He lifted an eyebrow, a half-smile on his lips. 'What about a walk? I know just the place,' he said, indicating left and leaving the dual carriageway, heading west and out of the city.

Her mind began to roam in delicious ways. She caught herself looking at his hands, those elegant fingers on the steering wheel. Her body relaxing at the thought of them stroking her skin. He shifted gear with the palm of his hand, then placed it by his side, millimetres from hers. Sunlight was filtering into the car and she tilted her head backwards against the headrest. They had got away with it; they were going for a walk together. Happiness eddied around her. His hand, so close to hers, radiated energy.

He drove through Knightswood, Drumchapel and then onto the Boulevard heading north. It was the same route her parents had taken on their annual holiday to The Trossachs. A ribbon of flowers on the central reservation waved in the wind and she felt that wonderful holiday feeling of anticipation and escape. At Balloch, he turned onto a minor road and stopped in a deserted lay-by. Izzy guessed they must be somewhere on the east side of Loch Lomond, but she had lost her bearings miles back.

'Have you been here before?' he asked.

'I don't think so.'

'Then you're in for a treat.'

She turned her face into the wind, feeling it blow against her face. She undid her ponytail and shook her hair loose as Sean watched. She wanted him to watch her. She felt happy and a little foolhardy.

'There's a path to the top of the hill. It's quite steep in places, but I promise you, it'll be worth the effort,' he said. She barely hesitated at the daunting prospect of climbing up a hill. The power of his presence would pull her upwards. The ground was thickly overgrown with ferns and brambles. Almost immediately, her feet felt damp. Her pumps might be good footwear for a burglary, but they were hopeless for hill walking. Sean made no allowances for either her shoes or her state of fitness as he bounded up ahead of her. For a moment, she lost sight of him and the path seemed to disappear. At that moment, she slipped on a stone hidden beneath the heather and felt her ankle twist awkwardly. A bolt of pain travelled up her leg.

'Izzy,' his voice carried in the clear air, 'over here.'

She looked up. The hill was unrelentingly steep. She wanted to shout back, to ask him to slow down, but a knot of stubbornness prevented her. She started scrambling, grabbing on to roots of broom and bracken, barely aware of her legs aching, her lungs burning. After a few minutes, the path flattened and she could see him standing on a small outcrop above her, a hundred metres ahead. It didn't take her long to haul herself up beside him.

The vista of Loch Lomond was laid out before them, so spectacularly beautiful, it demanded a round of applause. The water was the colour of her new dress: tanzanite. A string of small islands fringed the shoreline following the line of the ridge on the right and mountains, as bright as clouds, clustered at the top end of the loch.

They were standing close together, their hands almost touching. An intensity fizzed between them, which shouldn't have been there. He turned his head and they kissed, a light brushing of lips that transformed everything into a magical awakening. Her heart flew open. She couldn't help it.

He broke off, looking stricken. 'I'm sorry, Izzy, that wasn't meant to happen.'

An awkward silence, as solid as a fence, lay between them. She shrugged her shoulders. 'Don't worry about it,' she said lightly, but the magic of the moment was spoiled. Her smile stuck to her face as she looked out at the view, the romantic beauty of Loch Lomond mocking her.

He pointed towards the mountains. 'That's Ben Lomond at the front and, beyond it, the Arrocher Alps,' he said, keeping his eyes locked firmly ahead. He was speaking a little too quickly.

'Have you climbed all of those mountains?' she asked.

'Many times. I would come up to Glasgow during the school holidays and Dad would take me and Connor hill walking. My favourite is Ben Lui.'

His voice had recovered its usual confidence.

'Is your dad still alive?'

'He died when I was eighteen,' he said in a matter-of-fact way, though she heard an echo of sadness in his voice.

'I've never climbed a hill before,' said Izzy, looking down at her sodden shoes, 'I'm ashamed to say. Hard to believe I've missed out on so much beauty when it's on my doorstep.'

'Sometimes it takes an outsider to make you see the things you've taken for granted in a different light,' said Sean.

She wanted to tell him that it was more than hills he was making her see differently. She wanted to tell him that everything was suddenly new and interesting. The effort of keeping that inside was almost painful. They sat down on a small wall that had been built alongside the summit cairn. There wasn't much room and they had to squeeze together. It felt as breathtaking as the view.

'The BBC must give the programme the go ahead now,' he said, 'and if they don't, I'll try Channel Four or STV. Someone will want me to tell the story.'

They settled into the curve of the wall. His arm was touching hers. Izzy sat motionless, her nerves pitched so tight, she thought they might snap.

'Would you like me to speak to your husband? I'll tell him about my concerns about the club's finances. It might make him think twice about taking out a loan to finance the deal.'

She looked away, brushing the hair out of her eyes. 'I'm afraid he wouldn't listen.'

'No. I don't suppose he would. Not from the likes of me, anyhow.'

She bit her lip and blushed. 'Jim's family ingrained a deep and abiding distrust of catholics in him. It disgusts me. Rangers disgusts me. Football disgusts me.' Tears were forming in her eyes. Angry tears. 'I'm not a timid person, Sean, but I've never challenged how things were before. I suppose I've been too content.'

'Well, you're certainly challenging things now.'

She lifted her face to the sun. 'When I was at school, you were ambitious if you wanted to become a nurse or a secretary, never mind a doctor or an engineer. We were all so passive, accepting. Volunteering at the Bureau, going to Glasgow Tech, it's changed all that for me.'

'They say education doesn't form character. It reveals it,' he said.

She felt a start of pleasure at his insight. 'Did Cambridge change you? Your relationship with your family or your old friends from school?'

'How do you know I went to Cambridge?'

'I read the article you wrote about single parents.'

He shook his head. 'I can see I've underestimated you, Izzy. Yes, on one level, going to Cambridge changed me. Profoundly. I was one of the few students from a working-class background. I was determined not to become a middle-class ponce like everybody else but, in the end, it was inevitable that my interests, tastes and ideas developed in different ways than if I'd stayed. But I've never forgotten where I come from. I'd like to think that I have the same politics and values that I've always had, but I know my life is very different to that of many of my old school friends. A lot of them still live locally and are married with kids.'

'You've never married?'

She expected to see his guarded look descend but he looked at her frankly. 'Work makes relationships difficult. The travelling, the hours, the commitment needed for a major investigation ... it's hard to maintain anything serious.'

'Maybe you just haven't met the right girl?'

He was looking at her carefully, as if calculating how much of himself to reveal. 'There was someone once. There still is in a way, but it's complicated. I wish it wasn't, but I haven't worked out how to simplify it,' he admitted. He frowned. She wanted to smooth the lines on his brow with her fingertips.

'I'd like to keep helping you,' she said, looking down at her wet shoes. The dampness had seeped into her socks and her feet were starting to chill.

'I'd like that, too, as long as you understand the risks,' he cautioned.

'What risks?' she asked.

'When this goes public, I'm expecting Rangers' management to hit me with everything they've got: lawsuits, character defamation, insults on social media, hate mail and threats. Believe me, even when you're used to it, it's horrible. It's not just me they'll target. They'll go after my family and friends, too.'

Izzy remembered Davy being bullied in his first year of secondary school. Those terrible emails, the nightmares and the bed-wetting. The memory made her shiver.

'So, if you want to help me, you can't tell anyone. Not your husband, your family or your friends,' he warned. 'If there's nothing to connect you to me, you'll be spared that nightmare.'

She felt a pinch of dismay at leaving Bridget in the dark. 'I understand,' she said.

'Good. You'll also be of more help to me if no one knows about our collaboration. I've been banned from Ibrox, but you haven't.'

'You mean The Chairman's Club event? I thought you said no one important turns up?'

'They don't, but it's not the management I'm interested in. I want you to spend time hanging around the place. Immerse yourself. Watch. Listen. Chat with the staff. Information can come from the unlikeliest of sources.'

'I can do that,' she said.

Sean looked up to the sky, as if considering the vastness of the space. 'You're a kind person, Izzy. The poet, Joyce Carol Oates, says kindness gives us an interior light,' he quoted. 'You have a luminous soul.' She felt moved, almost stricken by the compliment.

He threaded his fingers through hers and they both stood up facing the loch. The wind ruffled the water into creamy spumes. The air was clear and boundless. It felt like they were alone in the world, the astonishing vista belonging only to them. She closed her eyes, feeling the pressure and heat of his hand in hers, and resolved to lock the memory of this precious moment in her mind forever.

'Be careful when you go to Ibrox, Izzy. Nothing rash or impulsive this time,' he said. She leaned into him and punched his arm in a playful gesture. He laughed and put his arm round her shoulders. It was too late for caution. She was caught in a hopeless infatuation. They stood for a few minutes more, watching a drift of low cloud float along the mountain ridge, until the shadows of the late afternoon moved across the water like the closing of a scene.

***

Therapist: The last thing I wanted to say, Jim, is, after you tell Izzy about seeing me, please tell her she's welcome to join us. Or, if you both prefer, she can come on her own.

Jim: Izzy doesn't need to talk to a therapist. She's the sanest, most sensible person I know.

Therapist: I'd just like her to know the offer's there, if she wants it.

CHAPTER 16

The Curry House was busy with families out for their Saturday night treat, and youngsters lining their stomachs in readiness for a night on the razz. Izzy looked at her watch. Davy and Cas would arrive soon. Jim wouldn't be long after. He said he would come straight to the restaurant as soon as the supporters' bus returned to Glasgow. She licked her lips, smoothed down her blouse and rehearsed her usual smile.

Once she started smiling, she found she couldn't stop. She was in a daze of happiness. She turned and caught her reflection in the mirrored panel behind her head. It was an unfamiliar version of herself, both a young girl and a middle-aged woman. A small fern had stuck to her hair. It was brown and wispy, a perfect filigree of frond and stem. She picked it off as gently as she could and put it in her pocket, even though she knew it was likely to crumble to dust. Bits of mud and grass had also stuck to her shoes. If anyone asked, she would say she had taken a short cut over Glasgow Green. She suppressed a giggle. The secrecy and pretence were all part of her new, thrilling inner life.

She hadn't thought about Davy's *Shindig* audition all day and she had forgotten where Jim had gone to see Rangers playing. She felt giddy with recklessness. She took a sip of water and waited for its sobering effect.

'How are you tonight, Mrs Campbell?' The waiter was young, tall and loose limbed. 'Shall I bring you some poppadums and onion bhajis whilst you're waiting?'

The food arrived immediately and she realised she was starving. She gave the stack of poppadums a karate chop, feeling powerful as they splintered into fragments. Three onion bhajis sat in a frill of lettuce. The scent of coriander and cumin burst from their hot, smoky interior as she cut into them. She ate quickly, barely pausing between mouthfuls. She stared at the empty plate, amazed at her capacity to eat like she had done. She touched her lips, remembering their kiss, then slowly wiped her mouth clean with a napkin, saying a silent, tender farewell to him. Time to return to her family, to normal life.

They came through the door in a flurry. Davy's T-shirt hung about his hips and his black curls had worked up into a wild nest. His eyes dazzled as he leaned over and brushed his cheek against hers, his familiar smell catching her breath.

Cas was wearing a pink chiffon dress. It floated around her skinny knees and reminded Izzy of a nightie. Her black bra and knickers were mistily outlined beneath the sheer fabric. She gave Izzy a hot and musky hug. Izzy wasn't sure if she was smelling her perfume or her perspiration. They were a fabulous couple. Young, beautiful and full of a sexual chemistry, something she understood so clearly, it gave her a sharp pull of envy.

'Well? How did the audition go?' she asked, but she had already guessed the answer.

'We must have called you four times or more. Where have you been?' asked Davy.

Izzy felt a nudge of guilt. Her phone had been switched to silent all day. 'Sorry, love. It's been a busy day,' she said.

'Oh yeah. All that shopping must have run you off your feet,' he teased.

Cas looked at him, her eyes flaming. 'Your mum was probably in the college library studying.'

Izzy smiled weakly. Laughter was bubbling in her chest and she had to cough to keep it suppressed.

'It was just a joke, Cas,' said Davy. His eyes widened in mock innocence.

'Don't do that,' said Cas.

'Do what?'

'Belittle people, and then, if they have the balls to challenge you, tell them it was just a joke. Or worse, tell them to stop being sensitive,' said Cas.

'OK. OK,' said Davy, putting his hands up as if she'd pulled a gun on him.

Izzy felt an old instinct to change the subject to avoid an argument, but something made her hesitate. She could learn a lot from Cas, like, how to stand her ground and not allow others put you down. Davy was looking at her, his eyes pleading for some support.

'We're in,' said Cas. 'We've got a fifteen-minute slot as part of the warm-up.'

'That's wonderful. Wonderful,' said Izzy, feeling that the day had acquired a magical invincible quality. Cas was smiling, her metal teeth were brilliant. Davy held her hand and they turned and kissed each other. A big, happy, public kiss.

'When's Dad coming?' asked Davy.

She felt a small clouding over at the mention of Jim, but she summoned a smile. 'He's on the supporters' bus. He should be here soon,' she said brightly.

'It's just that there's a party by the Sense Over Sectarianism organisers,' said Davy.

'*Django Django* might be dropping by,' chipped in Cas. She looked as eager to go as a foal getting to its feet for the first time. Izzy felt dismayed. She knew it was ridiculous; young people were always changing their plans at the last moment, yet the thought of them leaving made her feel as if she was being abandoned. She wondered if they would let her join them.

'Carol Docherty invited us. She's the head of SOS,' added Davy.

Izzy's face ignited at the mention of Sean's sister-in-law. The possibility of Sean being at the party made her feel a little faint. 'I know who she is, but I've never met her. What's she like?'

'Amazing. Totally together person,' said Cas eagerly.

'The party's at her flat,' said Davy, showing Izzy his phone with the address on it.

Not the Gallowgate address, but the same flat she had met Sean at that morning. Carol and Sean. Their names in a single breath sent her mind burling. Pieces of a terrible jigsaw were falling into place. Sean had told her that Carol and Connor were separated. The *friend* who owned the flat was clearly female. There was someone in his life, but it was complicated. An affair with your sister-in-law? It doesn't get more complicated than that.

Davy and Cas were looking at her strangely. Her mouth felt parched, words trapped in her throat. 'You go on. I'll be fine here waiting for Dad,' she said, surprised she had managed to speak and sound normal.

'Are you sure, Mum? You look a bit upset.'

'Off you go,' she said, shooing them away.

She stared, dry-eyed, towards the door, expecting Jim to come through it at any moment. The voice of common sense in her head was telling her it was good that she knew about Sean and Carol. She was in danger of getting carried away with herself. She took a sip of water and a wave of sadness washed over her. She rummaged in her bag for her phone. There were several texts from Jim. The latest one saying he was getting the late bus back and that he wouldn't get into Glasgow until after 11, and she wasn't to wait up. She let out a sigh of gratitude, of relief.

'Are you ready to order?' asked the waiter.

'I'm sorry, there's been a change of plan. I have to go,' she said, her voice sounding strange and small.

The westerly wind was laden with moisture, the atmosphere dull and heavy. It was getting dark and it had begun to rain. People hurried past her with umbrellas up and hoods pulled around their faces. Drawing her coat around her, she stepped out onto the street, and straight into a puddle. Looking down at her sodden shoes, the mud and grass from her hill walk with Sean had been washed away. It was a sign from the Universe; to wash away any thoughts about romance.

A well-behaved queue of buses was lined up on Cathedral Road, waiting for their parking bay at Buchanan Street Station. The drivers had opened their doors early and the Saturday night crowd was streaming off, skittering and skipping around puddles, huddling under umbrellas and laughing. She felt sorry for them. After the excitement of their Saturday night on the town, life, with all its mundane details and obligations, was waiting for them on Monday morning.

She walked past the bus station and up the hill towards The Hungry Tum. She peered through the window. It was dark and she could barely make out the table in the far corner where she and Sean had sat. She remembered the title of her Bateson essay: Why do things get in a muddle? Well, she knew the answer now. Things get in a muddle when you allow them to get into a muddle.

She turned to head back to the West End where she had left her car earlier in the day. The rain had stopped and the cool air brought with it a moment of clarity. She and Sean were collaborators and colleagues. The Rangers project was important to both of them. She felt a pulse of hope: perhaps they'd become friends ... good friends.

'Izzy.' His voice carried in the wind towards her.

'Jim?' Her surprise was enough to snuff out all thoughts of Sean.

'Izzy. Why didn't you reply to my texts? I was worried. Cadged a lift back early,' said Jim hugging her. His breath was lethal.

'You look nice,' he said, nuzzling into her ear.

There was a slur in his voice and his eyes were glazed. His face was the colour of a skinned tomato. Her soul began to shrivel. 'You've just missed Davy and Cas. They've gone to a party to celebrate. The band's playing at *The Shindig*,' she said.

Jim shrugged. 'Good for them,' he said carelessly. He put his arm through hers. 'So, it's just you and me for a curry then?'

His clutch on her arm felt too tight. She shook her arm free. 'I think you need to get home.'

'No problemo. We can get a carry-out and watch the replay on Sportscene. We blootered them three nil. The last goal was a cracker,' he said, swaggering along the pavement in front of her, pretending to score. She stood in silence, her arms crossed.

'C'mon, Izzy, lighten up. It's Saturday night. Rangers won. Look, it's even stopped raining,' he said, holding his arms out, palms up.

'You're drunk,' she said.

'I'm allowed a wee bevvy at the weekend, surely.'

She felt anger, frustration and a deep sense of sadness building inside her at the sight of him. And something much worse ... disgust. A deep pervading sense of disgust. 'Look at the state of you.'

'Christ, Izzy. These days you've become such a ...'

'Such a what?'

'… Such a fucking bore.'

She felt fury rise and take hold of her. 'And you've become a fucking drunk.'

He was breathing heavily, sucking in air. His bloodshot eyes stared at her in astonishment. He shook his head as if he couldn't work out what amazed him more, her swearing or her calling him a drunk.

'What did you say?'

This was the moment when she was to say sorry, to take his arm and walk back home together. She wanted to do that but, at the same time, it was as if all her wanting had turned into vapour, disappearing into the damp sky like a dying breath.

'You're got a drink problem, Jim. You need help.'

He lowered his head, still shaking it from side to side as if what she was saying was beyond belief. He looked at her with a mixture of defiance and anguish before she turned and walked away.

***

Therapist:	Hello, Jim. I wasn't expecting you to call me on a Sunday. Everything OK?
Jim:	I've fucked up big time.
Therapist:	What happened?
Jim:	I've let you down. I've let Izzy down. I've let everyone down. Christ, I can't believe I could be such an eejit. (Begins crying) And I can't believe I'm crying down the phone like a lassie.
Therapist:	It's OK. Take your time.
Jim:	Izzy and I had a slanging match in the middle of Buchanan Street. I told her she was a fucking bore. I was pissed. I was right out of order. She's not speaking to me. (Crying starts again) I've promised to stop drinking for the next month. D'you think she'll forgive me?
Therapist:	If you keep your promise, she might.
Jim:	We're going to this hospitality "do" next weekend at Rangers. There's a free bar the whole day.
Therapist:	Can't you cancel? Don't make things harder for yourself than they need to be.

Jim: Izzy wasn't keen to go in the first place.
                God love her, she's done all this research
                about the Directors and the club to help
                me win the bid, but she'd be delighted if I
                said we weren't going.

Therapist: Actions speak louder than words, Jim.

Jim: The tickets cost a fortune mind … It would
                be a shame for them to go to waste.

Therapist: As I said, actions speak louder than words.

CHAPTER 17

'You go first.'

'No, you go first.'

'If we keep this up, it'll be time for the first lecture and we'll be none the wiser about either of our weekends,' said Bridget, tetchily. She was dressed head to toe in black and her cropped hair was a shade darker than usual. Her scarlet lipstick looked gory against her pale complexion. She looked to be in mourning and Izzy felt an echo of the same mood.

'I heard back from the SNP selection committee,' said Bridget. Her face had sagged. Izzy steeled herself for the worst.

'You're looking at the SNP candidate for the next seat that becomes available,' Bridget announced quietly. She took off her glasses and began cleaning her lenses in short, impatient swipes. Her eyes looked small and naked.

'I would say congratulations, but you don't seem very happy about it,' observed Izzy.

'Of course I am. Well, some of the time. Oh, I don't know how I feel about it. I've to give a speech next month at a conference in front of hundreds. I've not slept all weekend worrying about it. Maybe they should choose someone else.'

She looked forlorn, her skin pouchy and haggard.

'I don't understand,' said Izzy, 'you were so passionate about being part of a resurgence of Scottish nationalism.'

'Talk is cheap. Now it's happening, I don't know if I've got what it takes. I'm terrified.'

'Owning up to vulnerability is not a weakness. It's a strength.' Izzy realised she was repeating Sean's words at the John Knox statue. A punch of wistfulness threatened to wind her.

'You're right, dear friend,' said Bridget, putting on her glasses and giving herself a shake, as if waking herself up. 'I may well start my speech with those very words.'

Izzy felt a stab of admiration for her resilience and courage.

'Now your turn. I'm dying to hear about your meeting with Sean Docherty. I want the details. *All* the details.'

'He said no one important turns up to these hospitality events and, even if they did, all I would do is arouse suspicion if I asked too many questions. He's got some confidential information about a ticketing scam and he's hoping to persuade the BBC to make a documentary. So, no, he wasn't impressed with my offer of help.'

She felt pleased with her story. She hadn't lied, but rather had offered fragments of the truth stitched together in such a way that bore little resemblance to what actually happened.

'So, that's it? End? Finito?' asked Bridget. 'Not even a wee bit of flirting?'

'He's got a girlfriend and, in case you've forgotten, I've got a husband,' Izzy stated. She might have added that any infatuation on her part would be, frankly, pathetic, but she couldn't bring herself to say that out loud.

'I don't know why I was expecting a bit of scandal from Mrs-Happily-Married-Ever-After,' Bridget joked.

Tears swam in Izzy's eyes and she blinked to keep them back, but they rolled down her face, unchecked.

'Jesus, Izzy. What's the matter?'

'Jim and I had a big row on Saturday night. I told him he was a drunk and left him on the street. He came back in the early hours, hammered, and we had another row before I packed him off to the spare room. The next day, he was full of apologies. Offering to grant me any wish.'

'I've met that genie many times. Three rubs of a whisky bottle and out he pops.'

'He said he'll stay off the booze for the next month. I told him he was staying in the spare room until then, too,' added Izzy.

'Good for you,' said Bridget, coming to sit beside her, putting her arms round Izzy's shoulder.

'Don't be nice to me, Bridget, or I'll start crying again and never stop.'

'I knew Jim liked a drink. Well, let's face it, in Glasgow, it's more unusual for someone not to like a drink,' said Bridget.

'Maybe I'm over-reacting. He's under a lot of pressure with this Rangers deal. But bless him, he even offered to cancel going to The Chairman's Club this weekend.'

'At least he's trying,' said Bridget.

'I didn't have the heart to let him cancel. He's paid a fortune for the tickets and this Rangers deal means everything to him. So, I told him we should go, and he could have the odd drink as long as he took it steady.'

Izzy felt herself flush and her palms were sweaty. She wasn't very good at lying; she'd had so little practice.

'You're so supportive, Izzy. It's probably why your marriage has lasted twenty years and mine didn't. Jim's a lucky man. I hope he knows that.'

***

Therapist: You look well, Jim.

Jim: I'm much better, thanks. Izzy and I have had a good chat. She was amazed when I offered not to go to The Chairman's Club. It made her realise how serious I was about cutting down on the drinking.

Therapist: Good.

Jim: She insisted we go. She even gave me a free pass for the day if I took it easy. Christ, she's a wonderful person. I don't deserve her.

Therapist: Is it possible for you to take it easy when there's a free bar all day? I worry it's asking too much of yourself.

Jim: No one else is worried, so why should you be?

CHAPTER 18

Ibrox reared up from the wastelands of Govan, looking more like a massive Victorian factory than a football stadium. Izzy felt a flutter of excitement, like a child arriving at a funfair. Sean had texted her that morning to wish her luck and asked her to call him afterwards. He had followed the text with a smiling face emoji. It was going to be a good day.

Jim was smiling and walking with a slight swagger. She decided to grasp the slim prospect that she and Sean were wrong about the club's financial problems and took Jim's hand, squeezing it tight. He squeezed it back in three short bursts: I. Love. You.

It was hours before the match, and stalls were being set up around the concourse to sell food and team memorabilia. Chimneys from fast food campervans had begun to smoke. Union Jacks ruffled in the stiff breeze at every vantage point while small knots of Rangers supporters milled around with cans of lager in their hands. They looked glum, as if they were going to the dentist. Old Firm matches were clearly serious affairs.

'Let's buy a scarf,' she suggested. 'It'll get us into the mood.'

Jim shook his head, 'No team colours allowed inside The Chairman's Club,' he said kindly. 'Anyway, it would spoil your outfit. You look smashing,' he breathed.

'You don't look so bad yourself,' she said, pinching his cheek. He was wearing a navy pinstripe suit with a blue silk handkerchief folded neatly in the top pocket. His hair and moustache shone. Her blue dress flashed beneath her coat as she walked towards the main entrance.

A doorman inside the vestibule asked for their invitations before allowing them into a wood-panelled hall. Team pictures covered every inch of wall space. Izzy could smell a combination of lentil soup and floor polish. It reminded her of school. A group of men milled around at the bottom of the stairs, dressed in identical dark suits and blue ties. Their jackets had embossed pockets with lavish crests. They looked like a cluster of prefects.

'Past players,' whispered Jim.

Her eyes met those of a man in his sixties. He was fit but looked ill at ease in his suit and tie. He would be more at home on the pitch or, perhaps these days, at the Bellevue Golf Club.

The Chairman's Club was like a bar in an exclusive hotel. Glittering chandeliers caught the light that sparkled off the optics and bottles, casting a nicotine-coloured glow. People were standing in line to pick up their drinks, jostling each other as if at the start of a race. Flutes of champagne and crystal tumblers of whisky had been laid out on a long table and the waiting staff were dispensing them at speed. Izzy asked for a glass of water. The waitress seemed puzzled, as if she had come to the wrong event.

Izzy looked around, feeling like her brain was on steroids, trying to take everything in. Sean had asked her to watch and listen, but watch and listen for what?

The men were mostly stocky, with razor haircuts and ruddy complexions. It struck her that, if Martians landed, they would think all Scottish men looked as if they spent all day in the pub. Women stood in small groups, leaning in to each other to hear above the noise. On closer inspection, she could see the effort most of the guests had made to match the luxury of their surroundings, but their watches had too much gold and their jewellery had too many diamonds to be real. She recognised the signs of nerves: the flickering eyes, the stroking of glass stems and the talking a little too loudly. Jim stood next to her with a champagne flute in his hand. It was already half empty.

'Take it easy, Jim. Remember?' said Izzy, pointing to the glass.

Jim smiled and patted her arm. 'Don't you worry, love,' he said and before she could tell him that she was counting, even if he wasn't, he was already halfway to the crowd at the bar. She watched his disappearing back and felt her faith in him gently slipping away.

A waiter appeared at her side. 'If you're interested in a tour of the trophy room, now's a good time to go, before lunch is served,' he told her.

The trophy room was small, with three huge glass cabinets dominating the space. Each was filled with cups, trophies, pennants and plaques stuffed inside in a haphazard way. There was a tang of silver polish and pine-scented room freshener in the air but she didn't notice the small man sitting in the corner until she was almost upon him.

His eyes blinked open with the speed of a reptile. 'Come for the tour?' he asked. "Tour" was a grand description for a walk about this modest-sized room.

'Yes please.' His small face creased into a thousand wrinkles and he took her to the first cabinet, already embarking on his commentary. It was as highly polished as the silverware surrounding them.

'The European Cup Winners' Cup,' he stated, pointing at an outsized trophy. 'It was an epic game against Dynamo Moscow. We hung on to an early lead for an emphatic 3-2 victory.' His eyes were full of reminiscing. Izzy realised her presence was only required to give him an excuse to re-live a glorious memory. The cup was dated 1972; thirty-nine years ago. She wanted to ask if the club had won anything as important since then, but she worried that that might come across as critical.

'It's very impressive. Is this the actual trophy?' she said, admiringly.

190

'It's a replica. You only get to keep the real one if you win three finals.'

'Are the rest of them replicas, too?' she asked, looking around.

He flinched as if she had poked him with a sharp stick. 'Of course not. What a daft idea.' He said quickly. Too quickly. She felt her heart speed up; her antennae on alert.

'Sorry. I don't know much about football,' she said quietly. Her guide's expression softened.

'Here's my favourite,' he said, pointing to the middle cabinet. 'The Katowice Vase. Carved from a solid piece of coal. It was presented to us in 1988, after we beat Katowice 5-2 on aggregate.'

Izzy peered at the tiny black vase. 'It's beautiful. Why is it your favourite?'

'It was handmade by Polish miners, true craftsmen,' he said. 'Things don't have to be big and shiny to be impressive.' Izzy wondered if that had become a mantra for him personally; he barely reached her shoulder. The final cabinet was almost empty. Izzy looked at him questioningly.

'They're being cleaned,' he said. He was blinking furiously like a small boy giving a bad excuse.

'It's wonderful that you take such good care of them,' she said, keeping her voice light, inconsequential.

He leaned forward and whispered: 'These trophies are our history.'

'Your proud history,' she added.

'They're like my bairns,' he said in a tremulous voice.

'And it's your job to make sure no harm comes to them,' she said.

They exchanged a knowing glance. 'Dead right. The taxman isn't getting near them,' he said under his breath, his tone venomous. There was a small disturbance as the door opened and more people from The Chairman's Club made a noisy entrance.

'Excuse me,' he said formally, as if he'd realised he'd said too much. 'I need to see to my new visitors.'

Thoughts were flying around in her head. He had all but told her they were replicating their trophies. It made sense. They would need to be sold against their debts if the club was declared bankrupt. She felt a sudden warmth towards this man who loved his cups like children and hoped his plan to save them would be successful. At the same time, she felt elated at what she had discovered. It felt like she had scored an early goal.

A wiry woman, with the demeanour and energy of a small terrier, greeted her at the door of the dining room. Her name badge read "Betty". Lifting a pair of huge, purple glasses onto her forehead, she consulted the guest list before flicking her forefinger at a young waiter, who guided Izzy to a large circular table. There were handwritten place cards at each setting, like a wedding reception. She sat down and looked around for Jim, hoping he wasn't still at the bar. A weary voice told her not to be so naïve. Where else would he be?

Betting slips were scattered on the table and people were already filling them in with the concentration of an examination. The waiter told her they were offering odds of 3-2 for a Rangers win. She felt her happy mood slipping and a sense of disquiet taking its place. The price of the tickets for this hospitality event was eye watering and now the club was asking their guests for even more of their hard-earned cash. She scrunched up her betting slip and put it in her handbag. Then she took the slip at Jim's place and did the same.

Jim bustled in and sat down beside her. His face was flushed. He patted her hand, as if she was a docile dog, and placed a glass of red wine on the table. His lips had turned the colour and texture of liver. A compère was tapping a microphone. One, two, three; one, two, three … Izzy was grateful for the distraction. She didn't trust herself to speak to Jim in a civil manner.

'Good afternoon, Ladies and Gentlemen. I'm delighted to welcome you to Ibrox.'

She leaned forward in her chair, listening carefully, reminding herself about her task. Watch. Listen. Become invisible.

'Today, we've a special guest: the famous businessman and special friend to the club, Mr Jack Marshall.'

There was a polite round of applause. Jim turned and winked at Izzy as Jack Marshall strode onto the stage. He was shorter and stockier than his photo in her WAP file, but he had the same stiff look about him.

'Old Firm matches are always special, but today we're looking forward to our eighth consecutive win over our old rivals, Celtic,' Jack started. There was loud cheering.

'Our newest signing from Arsenal, Johnny Binooti, is here with us today. Johnny, come on up and meet some of our great supporters.' Jack stretched his arm towards a tall, skinny youngster waiting by the kitchen door, who loped toward the microphone. The difference in their physiques was almost comical.

'How important is it that Rangers win today?' asked Jack.

'Very important,' said Johnny, gamely.

'Have you received a friendly welcome since joining the club?'

'Yes. Very friendly,' replied Johnny.

'And if you score, will you remember which end to run to?' asked Jack.

That brought a howl of laughter from the crowd. Johnny frowned. 'It's been a long time since I played for Celtic Youth,' he said.

Jack slapped him on the back. 'And we're delighted you've decided to play for the right side this time. A' the best for the match today.'

The young player bounded away as fast as a greyhound out of a trap. Jim nudged Izzy in the ribs. 'I told you important people will be here. Oh, look, there's his missus and the weans.'

Michelle and the children were now standing beside Jack. Esme was on her mother's hip; Crawford was wriggling by her side. Michelle was wearing a skin-tight sheath dress and the brightest of smiles. 'Michelle, Crawford and Esme, say hello to all these lovely people. Crawford already shows great talent with a football. Unfortunately, he favours his left foot.'

There was another roar of laughter from the crowd. Jack had them eating out of his hand. She felt faintly nauseous about their underhand, anti-Catholic comments, as well as the possibility of Michelle coming over and greeting her like an old friend. Her only thought was to escape.

'Just off to the ladies,' she whispered.

After the luxury of The Chairman's Club, the toilets were a disappointment. The floor tiles were cracked wood chip and the walls looked like they hadn't been painted since the 70s.

The soap dispenser needed several pumps before a dribble was produced. She felt a sense of injustice, the neglected state of the toilets seemed to reflect the value the club placed on women. She washed her hands slowly; she was in no rush to return to watch Jim knock back another drink and listen to Jack Marshall's snide bigotry.

A labyrinth of corridors fanned out from the foyer outside the toilet. She wandered down the first one. Off to the left was the kitchen. At the end of the corridor was another door with a window. She looked through it and could see Jack Marshall and Michelle with their backs to her, still speaking to the room.

'This is for staff only.' Betty, the dining room hostess, was looking at her suspiciously. Her eyes were like bright brown pebbles behind her purple glasses.

'Sorry,' said Izzy. 'I got lost.'

Betty shrugged her shoulders as if it was of no concern to her if Izzy wanted to stand at the employee entrance rather than sit at a table in the main dining room. Betty was holding a glass filled with a clear liquid, ice cubes and lemon slices were floating on the surface.

Izzy turned to peep through the window again. 'Does Jack Marshall often come to these events?'

'He's been around this club for as long as I have. Thirty years,' replied Betty proudly, taking a dainty sip from her glass.

'You must have seen a lot of change in that time.'

'The stories I could tell you,' agreed Betty.

'I'd love to hear them,' said Izzy.

Betty looked at her coldly, suddenly suspicious. 'No one's interested in what I've got to say,' she said bitterly.

'I bet your stories are a lot more interesting than Jack Marshall's. I hate football,' said Izzy.

Betty laughed, the hard, asthmatic laugh of a heavy smoker. 'The club's changed a lot. And not for the better, I might add.'

Izzy nodded her head. 'I heard something about financial problems but it's good the new management will sort everything out.'

Betty gave a loud harrumph. 'Don't believe a bloody word of it. Not that the likes of Jack Marshall will suffer. It's always the workers who suffer.'

'That's so true,' agreed Izzy.

'Thirty years of loyal service and what d'you get? Nothing. The likes of me will be the first ones out the door when the shit hits the fan.'

Betty drained her glass. She had a distant, unfocused expression on her face. 'Those new-fangled contracts. I should have known better. But what can you do?' And, as if remembering where she was, she gave a small shake of her head and turned back down the corridor.

Izzy's gaze hardened as she watched the animated back of Jack Marshall working the crowd. She blazed with anger. The new-fangled contract was probably the Employee Benefit Trust the club had offered the players and staff, to avoid paying income tax. These loyal workers deserved so much better. She itched to go home and do some further research on it.

The dining room had undergone a transformation in the ten minutes she had been gone. The volume of conversation and laughter had been turned up, ties were loosened and jackets hung over the backs of chairs. Three of the men on the far side of her table had abandoned their glasses and were swigging beer direct from the bottle. There was a shrimp cocktail in a tall glass at her place. The Marie Rose sauce had formed a skin, the crust at the edge was red and sore looking. Jim was deep in conversation with a man on his left. His glass of wine was full to the brim. She was about to sit down when she saw Michelle coming towards her. Her eyes fixed on Izzy like a target.

'Won't be a minute,' she said to Jim, though she wasn't sure he heard or cared. She skirted round the tables towards the bar. Michelle followed her.

'Hello, Lizzie. I was hoping you might be here,' said Michelle, hooking her arm with hers as if they were best friends. It wasn't worth correcting her name.

'I don't want my husband to know we've already met,' said Izzy.

Michelle took a moment to process this. 'Oh, yes. Sorry, I forgot you didn't want him to know about you coming to see me.'

'He'd be furious if he thought I was interfering. Anyhow, how are you? I saw the children earlier.'

'My mother-in-law's taken them home. I'm leaving as soon as the match starts. Jack's given me his gold card to do some shopping. It's the least I deserve for coming to this.'

For a moment, Izzy thought Michelle might invite her to join her shopping. For a moment, she thought she would accept.

'Lovely dress, by the way. Anna Brown?'

'I think so,' said Izzy. 'My only instruction was that it had to be blue.'

Michelle's bright laugh tinkled above the clinking of the glasses. Jim looked up. A great grin spread across his face as he gave Izzy a thumbs-up.

'Anyhow, the thing is, Lizzie, I wanted to talk to you about the day you came to the house.'

'You do?' asked Izzy. Alarm bells were going *ding dong* in her head. Had Michelle noticed the file was missing? Had the neighbours seen her or Sean later in the day?

'I should have been more sympathetic,' she continued.

'Oh, no. Reassuring me about the club's finances was very helpful,' said Izzy as relief flowed through her. 'In fact, seeing all this here today, I feel daft about thinking the club was ever in trouble.'

Michelle leaned in close. 'Shall I tell you a secret? I hate Rangers Football Club.'

'Surely not,' said Izzy in surprise. She could smell pear drops on her breath. Her jaw was working as if it had become unhinged. *Cocaine.* She was almost certain.

'But let me tell you another secret, Jack hates Rangers, too,' added Michelle.

Izzy looked across at where Jack was sitting. He was surrounded by admirers, like a king holding court. 'I find that hard to believe.'

Michelle looked agitated. 'We've got a plan.'

'A plan?' Izzy repeated.

'We're getting out. I can't tell you the details, obviously. But, what I can tell you is that your husband's going to be just fine. I asked Jack about his company. Verisafe, right? And he told me that Verisafe's got the job.'

Izzy's heart plummeted. Jack Marshall was now sitting next

to Jim, both deep in animated conversation. Her head was swimming and all she wanted to do was weep.

'So, you see, you've nothing to worry about,' said Michelle happily.

'You know, Michelle, I don't think I'll stay for the match either,' she said, walking back to where Jim was sitting. He was grinning uncontrollably. 'This is the missus,' he said, introducing her to Jack as she picked up her bag. 'You're not leaving?' asked Jim.

'Stay,' commanded Jack, patting the empty seat beside him. His features were leery, loose.

'No thanks. I'll leave you boys to it,' she said pleasantly.

They both nodded slowly in unison. She fixed Jim with a stare. She wasn't mistaken. He was relieved she was leaving.

***

Therapist: Jim? Is everything OK?

Jim: Sorry to be calling you on a Saturday, but I wanted to tell you that Jack Marshall just told me we've got the contract. It's not official yet, though. The Rangers Board will be making a formal announcement to the press tomorrow, but I just had to tell someone.

Therapist:	That's wonderful, Jim. Congratulations.
Jim:	It means job security for at least two years. Thirty-seven members of staff depend on me for their living, you know.
Therapist:	That's quite a responsibility, Jim.
Jim:	It's a huge relief, I can tell you. A bloody, huge relief. You can probably tell I've had a few but I think I can be forgiven, eh?
Therapist:	I thought you'd promised Izzy to take it steady?
Jim:	Sorry. I have to go. Jack's taking me out to dinner. I'll tell you all about it when I see you next week.

CHAPTER 19

The cold air slapped her in the face as she stepped outside the club. The wide concourse was now filled with thousands of supporters pouring through the turnstiles, mainly men and boys wearing navy anoraks brightened by blue, red and white scarves. She walked into the crowd and the press of bodies swept her along. It was almost frightening. She could feel the heat and smell a mix of body odour, beer and damp wool. Someone close by started singing *"Follow, we will follow. For there's not a team like Glasgow Rangers."* Others joined in, their faces a mask of ecstasy and aggression. A vision of Highlanders going to the Battle of Culloden formed in her head, the men wrapped up in their invincibility; delirious and doomed.

Two mounted policemen moved in and about them, herding them gently to the Rangers-only gates. The horses were wearing day-glow blankets draped over their haunches and sashayed through the crowds good-naturedly. Izzy felt like she was being herded to the edge of a cliff.

She took her chance of an opening to turn against the flow. A few looked at her in confusion as she brushed by them. She wanted to shout: "*No. Don't follow. You're going the wrong way.*" She kept walking; the breeze in her face was making her eyes water, so she put her head down and picked up her speed towards the exit.

She walked into a small park opposite the stadium. A light rain was falling and families were packing up to go home. Her dress was getting wet where her coat had fallen open. Her feet were pinching in the silver sandals and her glossy curls were slowly turning to frizz. She sat on a bench, unable to summon the energy to go home. A sandy-coloured dog sniffed at her legs. She bent down to stroke him but he ignored her, moving on to the next bench in the hope of scavenging something to eat.

The news that Jim had won the contract was playing over and over in her head. Remembering the drunk joy on his face, a hot feeling of panic at their certain doom; her mind fast-forwarded to the future: Verisafe finished with all its employees made redundant and Jim declared bankrupt followed by his rapid decline into alcoholism. She closed her eyes and summoned some calmness. She had a nest egg of £10,000, inherited from her parents. It would be enough for a deposit to buy a small flat. She would persuade Jim to go on a rehab programme. She would get a job in the Social Research Department after she graduated. They would survive, somehow.

She looked up to the sky, the clouds were low and thick; the rain was set in for the night. She should go home. There was just one more thing she needed to do. She dialled his number.

'Hey, Izzy,' he said.

She felt a furious heat in her face, her neck and her arms. 'Hey, Sean.'

'Enjoying your day with the Ibrox faithful?'

'Great. I left early,' she said.

He laughed. She found herself laughing with him. A quiet joy had begun to radiate inside her.

'Pick up anything useful?'

'Something odd is going on in the trophy room and the staff are worried about their contracts,' she said.

Ding Dong. A tannoy announcement interrupted them.

'Sorry, Izzy, didn't catch that last bit. I'm at the airport.'

Her world stopped. Airport. He was leaving Glasgow.

'I'm off to London for a few days,' he explained.

'I was saying some of the employees are worried about the special contracts they'd signed. Never mind. It was probably nothing,' she said, twisting a coil of hair around her finger.

'Are you kidding? This is good stuff, Izzy. Honestly, I want to hear all the details. I've got a meeting with my editor to agree the programme, and then, all being well, I'll be back in Glasgow for filming in a week or so.'

A week or so? It was all taking too long. Sean wasn't going to save them.

'Jim's won the Rangers bid,' she said quietly.

'Shit,' said Sean.

'Yes. Shit,' agreed Izzy. She looked down at her hands, her palms were damp, her fingers felt numb.

'Look, don't panic. I hear HMRC are going to lodge a case against the club for non-payment of taxes tomorrow. It's going to be headline news. That might be enough for him to think twice,' said Sean.

'It might,' said Izzy hopefully.

'You've got to speak to him. Tell him to hold off,' he said.

'I'll try …'

'There's a lot happening, Izzy. Momentum against the club is building. It won't be long till the truth is out there.'

A quiet determination bubbled inside her. 'Don't worry. I'm not giving up.'

'That's my girl. Call me tomorrow. Tell me how it went

with Jim,' he said.

'OK,' she replied. Her heart was swelling, dangerously close to bursting.

***

Jim: I'm sorry. I know it's a Sunday morning. I didn't know who else to call.

Therapist: It's fine. I've told you, you can call anytime. Is something the matter?

Jim: Jack Marshall took me out to dinner last night.

Therapist: To celebrate winning the contract?

Jim: I could hardly say no.

Therapist: I understand alcohol plays a big part in your business relationships.

Jim: This is Glasgow, pal. I'm a lightweight compared to someone like Jack Marshall.

Therapist: How drunk did you get?

Jim: Let me say, right off the bat, I'm not proud of what happened next.

CHAPTER 20

A dull thud woke her. Izzy's eyes snapped open, adjusting to the dark almost instantly. She strained to listen but could only hear the usual sounds of the house sleeping: the creak of wood expanding and contracting, and the hum of the boiler on night mode. Then another thud. She held her breath, the glacial stillness of the night answered back with an even deeper silence. She snuggled back under the covers and closed her eyes, but every part of her was alert, poised. She heard the next sound almost before it had been made. A scuffle in the hallway. It was unmistakeable. Someone was downstairs. She reached over to wake Jim, but his side of the bed was empty.

The neon numerals of the alarm clock read 3:40 a.m. and she felt the first stirrings of resentment. She pushed the covers aside and lay for a moment, allowing the night air to numb her legs. She opened the door carefully to avoid the squeaking of its hinges. Davy's bedroom door was closed. He had come in hours ago. She crept to the top of the landing and looked down.

'Aw, fucking hell,' said Jim as he made his unsteady progress towards the kitchen. More thuds and bumps. It sounded like he was opening and closing kitchen cupboards. Rage flowered inside her. She thought about confronting him, but couldn't face the prospect of his incoherent mumbling and pathetic excuses. She turned back to her bedroom, locked the door and lay in bed, her body rigid with unspent anger.

She slept fitfully and woke when the alarm clock buzzed, surprised she had slept at all. She pulled back the curtains. Rain battered the window. The sky was glowering and a damp chill had seeped into the house. She rested her forehead against the cold glass and summoned her resilient self.

'8 a.m.,' she called, knocking on Davy's door. He had asked her to give him an early shout. She heard him stirring, mumbling something she couldn't make out.

The spare bedroom door was closed. She put her ear to it, but heard nothing. Jim was too drunk to even snore. She predicted his defence: Verisafe had won the contract. It was only fair for him to celebrate. It was Sunday and he had a day to recover for work on Monday. Then he'd promise her that he would go on the wagon for the rest of the month. She told herself she would wait for him to wake up, and then, staying calm, allow his excuses, his promises and his stale smell to bounce off her. She would make him a black coffee and a bacon sandwich and then they would sit down and talk.

The kitchen door was closed. Strange. It was never shut. She walked towards it, feeling a terrible sense of dread. She tried to push it open but it wouldn't move. She tried again, but it was stuck. Her mind floundered, trying to make sense of how the door could be locked from the inside. Davy bounded down the stairs, two at a time.

'Here,' he said, pushing her gently aside, 'let me have a go.'

'The wood's probably warped in this damp weather,' said Izzy, as Davy put his shoulder against it. The door shifted slightly, with just enough room for them to squeeze inside.

The kitchen looked just as she had left it. The work surfaces were tidy. The kettle was filled, ready to be boiled. Her handbag was on the table. There was a sparrow feeding on the windowsill where she had left some breadcrumbs the night before.

'Mum,' said Davy. She turned. Jim's body was squashed against the back of the door, his back to them, curled in a foetal position. One arm was outstretched, his fingers swollen and mottled. He still had his coat on. Terror fired through her. He looked like a bloated corpse.

'Help me, Davy. Help me turn him over.' She was pulling at Jim's shoulder but couldn't move him. Panic was beginning to grip her.

'Is he dead?'

'Of course not,' said Izzy crossly, though she did wonder the same thing. She touched his purple fingers. They were warm.

Davy bent down beside her and they pulled him onto his back. His mouth was slack, his body like a boneless sack. A sonorous snore vibrated through his body. She felt a moment of relief and then she smelt it. It filled the room; a rich, acrid, and sweet smell. She gagged, covering her mouth and nose with her hands.

'What the hell …' cried Davy.

Davy opened the back door and stood outside, his back turned, arms folded. 'Unbelievable,' he said. She went and stood beside him. They were both shivering, half with shock, half with cold. The beech hedge was turning bronze and there was a hint of sleet in the rain that was blowing in from the garden. 'We can't leave him on his back. If he's sick, he could choke to death,' she said.

Davy stood impassively and gave her his "so-what?" look.

'Help me roll him onto his side so I can put him in the recovery position,' she said. Her common sense voice was back in charge, as impassive as a nurse tending to the sick.

They returned to Jim's spread-eagled body. Spittle had crusted on his moustache. Shame and pity suffused her as they muscled him over onto his side, shifting his leg to a right angle so his body was supported. His face was squashed and misshapen, his nose wattled, his mouth open, his lips wet. She pulled his coat over his body to cover the stain around his crotch.

'Get your coat, Davy, we're leaving,' Izzy commanded.

'You're leaving him here?' asked Davy. There was a hint of admiration in his voice.

'He can clean up his own mess when he wakes up,' she said marching towards the door.

Rain was falling steadily, muting everything to grey. The granite houses on Crow Road, the cement coloured sky, and even the air they breathed felt thick and drab in her mouth. They walked side by side in silence. There was no need for words. Jim was in a bad way and now Davy knew it, too.

The Brunch Bar was empty and they had their pick of the tables. Davy ordered a hot chocolate and a pancake stuffed with blueberries. The smell of sugar and coffee filled the air. She closed her eyes, savouring the sweetness of it.

'This is really good, Mum, you should have some,' he offered as he poured more maple syrup over a towering pile of pancakes.

Davy's appetite astonished her. She felt grateful for it; it offered her a moment of normality, a hope that he hadn't been too traumatised.

'No, thanks,' She sipped her coffee instead, gazing out at the howling rain, sadness seeping into her skin, through every pore.

'Are you going to leave him?' asked Davy.

She gave him a small smile. 'Your dad needs help. Alcoholism is an illness.'

'A self-induced illness, you mean.'

'No one chooses to have a drink problem. He's a good man, Davy. A good provider for the family,' she said. The hollowness of that statement felt even more crushing today.

Davy looked unconvinced. 'I would totally understand if you left him. You don't have to waste your life on that guy.'

'That guy? We're talking about your dad, Davy.'

'I know who we're talking about,' he said, taking one of the Sunday papers from the rack behind him and starting to read. 'And I don't want to waste another second talking about him.'

She couldn't blame him. She was finding it easier to think of Jim as one of the Bureau's clients: someone who needed help, not judgement. She realised, with a small start of recognition, what she was experiencing: emotional detachment. Shona would be proud.

'Your pal, Bridget, is in the papers,' remarked Davy, pushing the newspaper towards her. There was a photograph of her on the front page. The headline read: '*Bridget Lafferty – bringing a breath of fresh air to Scottish politics.*' Izzy traced the shape of that familiar face with her finger – her dark hair, the ruby lips and that steely stare that pierced you from behind her glasses – and felt a flash of love and pride.

'She looks like a ballbreaker,' said Davy.

Izzy gave him a withering look. 'You wouldn't say that if Cas was here and I'll thank you not to say it to me, either.'

'Sorry, Mum. I'm sure she's a very nice person, but the SNP will never overturn Labour.'

'The Party gained a lot of seats at the last election. I wouldn't underestimate Bridget. She's very talented.'

'So are you. I don't want Dad to drag you down. You need to be tough with him. Give him an ultimatum. Sober up or he ships out,' he said.

She wanted to hug him for his support. 'Ultimatums don't work,' she said sadly. 'If they did, there wouldn't be any alcoholics. Dad's got to decide to do something about it himself. Maybe when he wakes up, he'll realise that.'

'You may be Mother Theresa, but I'm not. Text me when the house is in a fit state for human habitation. I'll be at Cas's,' he said pushing his empty plate aside.

She ordered another coffee and watched it as it cooled, a skin wrinkling the surface. She felt exhausted, the effort to pick up her phone almost beyond her.

'Hey, Sean,' she said.

'Hey, Izzy. You OK?'

'It's a driech, Glasgow day,' she said quietly.

'Not much better here in London. Some bad news, I'm afraid. The tax case got dropped at the last minute. The club's got a stay of execution but it's only a stalling tactic.'

'Do the good guys always win, Sean?' she asked sadly.

'In the end, yes, I believe they do. But it's a tough road. Look, if you've had enough and want to bail on me, I'd understand.'

'That's what they want, isn't it? To wear people down, to expect that we'll give up.'

'And it works ... a lot of the time ...'

'... But not with you?' Her voice had recovered its strength, she felt herself begin to re-inflate with determination.

'Of course, I have my doubts from time to time. But, no. I'm not going to let the bastards grind me down.'

'And neither am I,' she replied.

'Good. Write down all the stuff you found out at the Chairman's Club and email it to me. I'm planning to be in Glasgow the week after next. We can talk about it then.'

'The week after next? That's the week of *The Shindig*,' she said.

'Yes. Carol would never allow me to miss that. She and Connor are talking about going on holiday straight afterwards, so I'll have the flat to myself.'

'Carol and Connor going on holiday? I thought they were separated?'

'Another attempt at reconciliation. I hope this one goes better than the last one.'

Sean and Carol weren't a couple. Her heart lifted and the clouds outside seemed to brighten.

'I haven't asked you how it went with Jim. Have you managed to talk some sense into him?'

A queue was forming, waiting for an empty table. A couple hovered nearby, eyeing her untouched coffee and the empty chair beside her, as if she was committing a crime.

'I'll tell you about it when I see you,' she said, picking up her bag and coat. She felt rejuvenated, ready for her conversation with Jim, suddenly clear about what she needed to say.

'OK. See you at *The Shindig*,' he said.

***

Jim:	It was like I stepped onto a busy road for the thrill of not getting hit, but then I got hit, and kept getting hit some more. I couldn't stop drinking until I was annihilated. Totally annihilated. I've no idea how I got home. I woke up in a pile of my own shite on the kitchen floor this morning.
Therapist:	It was expecting a lot of yourself to keep it to one or two when there was free drink all day.
Jim:	Is that your way of saying I told you so?
Therapist:	(Silence)
Jim:	I think I've got a problem and I can't seem to fix it myself.
Therapist:	That's a sign of real progress, Jim. To admit you've got a problem and that maybe you need help.
Jim:	Progress? I'm not sure Izzy or Davy would agree with you.
Therapist:	You need to be completely honest with them. Tell them what you've told me.
Jim:	They've gone out. I don't know when they'll be back. I don't know *if* they'll be back.

CHAPTER 21

Izzy let herself into the house and hung her raincoat over the banister. The heating was on and the dampness of her coat mixed with the smell of Davy's shower gel. The kitchen door was open. There was no one inside and the floor had been cleaned. She caught a waft of disinfectant and one of her scented candles had been lit. The washing machine quietly chugged and churned, a swirl of fabric agitating a froth of suds and foam. Then she heard the gurgle and clunk of the upstairs shower as it powered into life. She felt detached from her body, looking down at herself, a solitary figure sitting at the kitchen table, waiting and dreading Jim's arrival.

Jim looked refreshed, as if returning from a jog around the block. He filled the kettle, careful not to spill any water, then rummaged in the bread bin and placed a slice in the toaster. He slid the toaster button down with a shade too much force. She could hear him whistling softly under his breath.

'Do we have any bacon?' he asked, looking at her for the first time. His eyes were bloodshot, the whites yellowed. His stare had a mixture of defiance and shame, like a boy who had been caught stealing apples but was ready to defend his crime because they were windfalls and there was no likelihood of the owner ever eating them. Her heart hardened.

'Davy and I found you on the kitchen floor this morning, lying in your own excrement,' she said, as if stating the most mundane of observations.

'I'm sorry, Izzy. So sorry. That was out of order. Totally out of order,' he said, looking up to the ceiling and smoothing his hair with both his hands. 'Is Davy here? I need to apologise to him as well.'

'I think we're beyond apologies, Jim.'

He sat down heavily, spreading his hands out on the table. 'I know it's no excuse but, Izzy, we've won the Rangers contract. You can't blame me for celebrating.'

She could see a tremor in his hands and the way his wedding ring had become embedded in the flesh of his fingers. She couldn't face him, concentrating instead on the sugar bowl, taking off the lid and stirring the granules around with a spoon.

'And you had your part to play. I saw you chatting with Michelle Marshall. You were quite a hit. Izzy Campbell: Verisafe's secret weapon.'

She winced and put the lid back on the sugar bowl.

'Christ, Izzy. Say something. I've said I'm sorry. What more do you want? I'm back on the wagon as of today. I won't drink for the rest of the month. That's a solemn promise.'

'It's not only the drinking, Jim. I'm worried this Rangers deal will bankrupt the business and us along with it.'

Jim held his head in his hands. 'Christ, you don't give up, do you?'

'Tell me, Jim. Tell me honestly. How much did the deal cost you to win it?'

Jim looked stricken. 'On my mother's grave, I swear there's nothing like that going on.'

'And you're certain the club's got the cash to pay you?'

'Of course I am,' he said.

'So why did you take out a loan for three hundred thousand?' Jim looked up in surprise. 'Bill told me about it,' she explained.

'It's for back up, in case we have cash flow problems,' he said quietly.

'Give it back,' she demanded.

'Izzy … be reasonable.'

'Give it back,' she repeated.

'You're worrying over nothing. I can assure you …'

'If you don't give it back, Jim, it will be the end of us,' she warned.

He sat hunched over, lost in a trance of misery. 'Are you going to leave me, Izzy?'

He began to cry. Messy, childish sobs that shook his big body. 'Izzy, come here,' he implored, reaching out his arms to her. She found herself walking towards him, enfolding in his warmth and size. There was still a trace of comfort in that big embrace. 'Please don't leave me,' he sobbed. She patted his back, as if winding a baby. 'I won't touch the money if that's what you want. I know I've got a problem with the drink,' he mumbled. 'I've been trying to do something about it. I've been seeing a counsellor for the past couple of months.'

She jerked away. 'A counsellor?'

Jim blew his nose loudly. His ruddy cheeks shone with tears. 'I didn't tell you before. I didn't want you thinking I was like one of your down and outs at the Gallowgate.'

'Oh, Jim,' she sighed.

'Please say you won't leave me,' he said. The crying started up again and she reached over to hold his hand.

'I'm not going to leave you,' she said, knowing in that moment, it was true. The thought of leaving Jim to struggle alone with his demons felt cruel, as seismic as abandoning an ill child.

His crying subsided into ragged sobs. 'Davy must be very angry with me. I need to make it up to him,' he said.

She had no clue what to suggest.

'Maybe I should go to this *Shindig* concert? Show some interest in his band?' he said, looking at her like a hopeful puppy.

She felt a start of guilt. Jim turning up would spoil her meeting with Sean.

'The problem is, it's on the Sunday we're playing Hibs. It's a big match,' added Jim.

She felt her guilt deepen. How easy it would be to agree with him. To suggest there would be another time, another way to rebuild things with Davy.

'I haven't been much of a dad recently, have I? We haven't been to the football together for months.'

'It's normal for lads his age to not to want spend time with their mum and dad.'

'You both mean everything to me.'

'You've made an important step, Jim. To get help with the drinking. I'm proud of you.'

'Proud of me? Christ, Izzy. Don't use that Bureau voice with me. You don't trust me to run my business and I only have to look at your face to know you don't believe me about giving up the drink.'

She closed her eyes. She could see the road ahead; mood swings, unreasonable behaviour and almost certain transgressions. She summoned the last of her resolve and took an intake of breath. 'I'm glad you're talking to a professional, Jim. Davy will be glad, too.'

'I'm going to prove to you both I can stay off the drink,' he said. His eyes were shining.

She wanted to weep. He didn't need to prove anything to her or Davy; he needed to prove it to himself.

***

Jim:	Good morning. I'm sorry about calling you early yesterday. I was feeling very low.
Therapist:	You can call me anytime, Jim.
Jim:	I've told Izzy about seeing you. She was pleased. It went a lot better than I thought it would. She's a forgiving soul. I just wish I knew why I drink. Why I can't seem to control it.
Therapist:	Maybe it doesn't matter why. Maybe the most important thing is how can you move on in life without it.

Jim: Without it? You mean total abstinence?

Therapist: I think it's the only way forward.

Jim: That's like saying I'm an alcoholic?

Therapist: Yes, it is. To accept that you'll always be addicted to alcohol.

Jim: You mean there's no cure?

Therapist: Think of it like someone who has lost an arm. It'll never grow back.

Jim: You mean, I'll never be able to drink again? Not even the odd one?

Therapist: Yes.

Jim: D'you not think you're being overly dramatic?

CHAPTER 22

Izzy stood on tiptoes, craning her neck. *The Shindig* stage was fifteen feet above her. The boys were fiddling with amplifiers and tuning their guitars. Cas was wearing her nice pink chiffon dress and adjusting the height of the microphone. Her hair was falling over her face, which she kept pushing away in small, impatient flicks. Izzy could sense their nervousness, their anticipation. She felt it too.

They were due to start in fifteen minutes, but there was hardly anyone about. Davy had explained that their set was part of the warm-up and that they weren't expecting people to arrive in numbers until the main acts, later in the afternoon. Still, she couldn't help feeling disappointed at the poor turnout.

Jim appeared, carrying two cans of coke with straws that bobbed from the ring pull at jaunty angles. 'You'll never guess what they charged me for these,' he said.

'All for a good cause,' she said brightly. 'C'mon let's go into the marquee and see if we can hustle up some audience for the band,' she suggested, taking him by the arm. He hadn't touched alcohol in the two weeks since The Chairman's Club event. The purple flush on his cheeks and neck was fading and his eyes were clear. She was glad, but it felt too early to relax. Maybe she would never be able to relax when it came to Jim and drinking.

They drifted towards the large tent, which was selling everything from green tea to Greenpeace membership. Flags with peace symbols fluttered in a light breeze around the perimeter fence. They were wearing hippie clothes. It had been Jim's suggestion to dress up and she had gone along with it, pleased to take part in something fun together. It was October but forecasted to be as hot as a summer's day. She was wearing a maxi dress, bought four years ago for a summer party, but never worn since. It had spaghetti straps, a deep V-neckline, in a bold red and green print. She had given herself a side parting so that her shiny curls fell across her face like a 1930s Hollywood actress. Just before leaving, though, she had had an attack of nerves and decided to wear a cardigan. She pulled it across her chest to hide the low cut of the dress.

Jim was wearing a Hawaiian shirt. It was meant to be loose-fitting, but it stretched across his belly. Three buttons were undone and she could see a sprout of grey chest hair. He walked with an easy confidence; you would have thought he wore clothes like this every day.

'Who'd have believed Jim Campbell would be at an anti-sectarian festival, eh?' he said, proudly. He squeezed Izzy's arm and gave her one of his small boy looks of contrition. The same one he gave her each night as he made his way to the spare room. It would take more than two weeks of good behaviour to let him back in. Sometimes she wondered if she would ever be ready to let him back in …

She had texted Sean to warn him that Jim was coming. He replied saying no problem; to act normally; he would find her. A nub of excitement, stubborn and bright, burned inside her. The thrill of meeting right under Jim's nose made her almost dizzy with her daring. More people were now milling around the marquee. She wondered whether Sean was already here: watching, waiting for the right moment to speak to her. She felt her insides relax and shook her hair, feeling it brush softly against her neck.

Jim was in a stall selling cheesecloth clothes and beads. 'These'll match your frock,' said Jim, hanging a string of red beads around her neck. The plastic felt clammy against her skin, the red an unflattering colour against her pale skin but Jim was handing over money before she had time to protest. He was beaming.

'Thanks, Jim. They're lovely.'

The far side of the tent was taken over by a display for the SOS charity. There was a large banner headline: *Bye Bye Bigotry*. Izzy recognised the girl she had met at the SOS offices. She was pinning up photographs and broke out into a dazzling smile when she saw her. 'I remember you. Your son's band signed up for the audition? *No1dea*, right?'

227

'They're called *The Undiscovered* now,' replied Izzy.

'Not for long, I hope,' said the girl, with what seemed like genuine enthusiasm.

'What's this about?' asked Jim, looking at the montage of photos.

'People send photographs telling us why they love football. Larry Benson, the famous photographer, is coming later to judge them.'

There was a photograph of a man in full Rangers regalia with his arm around a teenager in a Celtic strip. Both were smiling directly into the camera. Underneath, there was a caption, *Lifelong Rangers fan, Mike, is 100% proud of his Celtic playing son.* Izzy felt a lump in her throat.

'Very nice,' said Jim.

On the right-hand board, there was a pictorial history of the charity. Across the top was a newspaper headline: *Street violence following Old Firm match ends in tragedy* and, underneath, a photo of hundreds of fans, faces squashed together, mouths open, their arms raised. The article said that a record crowd had watched the 4-2 defeat of Celtic and, despite extra police presence, trouble had erupted, with one fatality and several serious injuries. Underneath was a school photo of a teenage boy with olive skin and eyes that captivated you with their gentleness: Mark Docherty. Died 31st March 2011.

'Jim,' Izzy called out, beckoning him over, 'look at this.'

'We should be getting back. The band's about to start.'

'You were at this match, weren't you?' she asked.

Jim shrugged. 'Yes, along with sixty-five thousand others.'

'Did you see any of the trouble?'

'The Celtic fans were raging after being beaten. I'm sorry the lad died but I doubt he was an innocent bystander.'

'How do you know that?' she asked.

'Educated guess,' said Jim.

He was having difficulty meeting her eye and began to nibble at his pinkie nail. 'Did you see something?' she pressed.

'I thought we were here to support peace and reconciliation, not bring up the past. C'mon, we don't want to miss the band,' he said, moving towards the exit.

'Did they find Mark's killer? Was anyone prosecuted?' asked Izzy, but Jim had already gone. She turned back to the boards, held by the drama of the pictures.

'Three boys pleaded guilty,' said a voice at her elbow. She recognised the diminutive figure of Carol Docherty from the photograph in the SOS pamphlet. She was wearing black jeans and a white T-shirt that could have been bought from a children's department. Izzy's maxi dress felt like a tent in comparison.

'They were sentenced to ten years in a juvenile detention centre. With good behaviour, they'll be out in half that time,' added Carol.

Her black hair was scraped back into a tight, shiny bun. She, too, had an olive complexion and deep-set eyes, the colour of cocoa powder. It was a frail sort of beauty, and the lines round her eyes and mouth were etched with suffering. The resemblance to Mark's school photo was heart-breaking.

'Ten years for murder?' asked Izzy.

'They pleaded guilty to aggravated assault. The prosecution produced several witnesses, who all claimed that Mark was in a gang of Celtic fans fighting with Rangers supporters, but he didn't drink, and was never involved in violence. Unfortunately, we were unable to provide any witnesses to prove it was an unprovoked attack.'

Izzy had to quell the sickening feeling in her stomach. 'That must have felt like terrible injustice.'

'For my husband, Connor, it still does. But, look around you. This is testament that good things can come out of bad.'

She felt a stir of admiration at this woman's courage, and shame that she had once harboured feelings of jealousy towards her. 'I'm sorry. I didn't introduce myself: Izzy Campbell, Davy's mum.' She searched Carol's face for any sign that Sean might have mentioned her, but she could see none. Carol's handshake was firm and light.

'Hiya,' said Davy. Jim and Cas were by his side.

'Hi Carol, I'm Davy's dad. Thanks for giving the band a chance,' said Jim.

'I'm looking forward to hearing them again,' said Carol pleasantly. A scream of feedback zipped above their heads, so loud it stopped all conversation. 'I'm afraid we've got a problem with the sound system. We're going to be late getting started. I'd better go and check what's happening,' said Carol, walking towards the exit.

'Carol seems very nice,' said Jim. Davy looked pained, unimpressed by Jim's assessment. 'We've got time for an ice cream,' suggested Jim. 'There's a van at the bottom of the park.'

Davy scowled. 'That would be lovely, Mr Campbell,' said Cas. 'They do dairy-free smoothies, you know. You should try one,' she added, skipping round to Jim's side and putting her arm through his. Izzy watched as the three of them walked towards the long queue that had formed in front of the ice cream van at the bottom of the hill. She felt a wave of happiness at seeing them together, it felt like progress.

'Hey, Izzy,' said a voice behind her.

She blushed furiously. Her legs wanted to buckle. She turned to face him, her heart softly exploding.

'It's going to take them at least half an hour to fix the PA system. Let's go somewhere quieter,' said Sean, leading her behind the stage towards a back entrance. She felt like she was the plain girl who'd been picked to go behind the bike shed by the most attractive boy in class: reckless and lucky. They sat on the stone steps on the far side of Nelson's Column, out of sight of the festivalgoers. The throttle of a helicopter overhead vibrated in the air, but the only thing she was aware of was the proximity of his thigh and the heat that passed between them.

'So, that was Jim and Davy?'

'And Davy's girlfriend, Cas,' she added.

'Jim's got into the spirit of things,' he said.

She felt her face flush. Jim's Hawaiian shirt was no match to Sean's simple sophistication. 'Jim enjoys getting dressed up. He loves a party.'

'That's what's great about Glasgow. People know how to enjoy themselves.'

'Sometimes a little too much,' Izzy couldn't resist adding.

Sean nodded, looking serious. She frowned, hoping he didn't think she was referring to Connor's drinking.

'Carol's very inspirational,' she said.

'Yes and a pain in the backside, too,' said Sean affectionately. 'Did I mention she and Connor are going on holiday next week?'

'Yes. What about the documentary? Are you starting filming, too? Exciting,' she said.

'Small problem. The script needs more work. My editor was interested in what you found out at the Chairman's Club though. He thinks we need more of a human angle.'

A small flame of delight ignited in her.

'The stuff about the Employee Benefit Trusts is brilliant. Do you know Betty's surname? D'you think she might be willing to give us an interview?'

Their eyes locked. He took both her hands. 'You did really well, Izzy. Thank you. Thank you for not giving up on this.'

Her heart was beating furiously in her chest; she looked down and could see that her cardigan had fallen open. She made no attempt to cover herself.

'Could you come to the flat tomorrow night? To go through things properly?' he asked.

'I can come after college,' she said as casually as she could muster.

'Good. I'll see you then,' he said helping her to her feet. He leaned forward to kiss her cheek. She closed her eyes, her head floating. He kissed the other cheek. 'Your dress is lovely by the way,' he said, whispering into her hair.

She looked down and smoothed her dress. 'It's just an old thing I found in the cupboard.'

He smiled at her in open admiration. 'But the loveliest thing about you, Izzy, is that you have no idea how lovely you are.'

Gratitude, affection and desire bubbled inside her. It was such a heady mixture, she didn't know whether to laugh or cry but he was already walking away, his tall silhouette moving quickly across the park.

She drew her cardigan across her chest, hugging herself. He liked her, he found her attractive and he had invited her to the flat. She lifted her hair and let the air cool her neck. Bass notes, followed by the high pitch of a woman singing, sailed over towards her. The music was getting louder, as if calling her back to the festival. She began to walk back, her body moving effortlessly through the air.

Jim was carrying two tubs of ice cream piled on top of each other in an unsteady tower. He broke into a grin at the sight of her. It was a smile so loving, so familiar, she felt a painful mix of guilt and tenderness.

'They're about to start,' he said.

A big crowd had gathered in front of the stage. Cas was standing behind the microphone, still but poised. She caught Izzy's eye and they both exchanged a nervous smile.

***

Therapist: How are things, Jim? It's been, what? Two weeks since your last drink?

Jim: Two weeks, two days and three hours.

Therapist: How are you feeling?

Jim: Magic. I heard my son, Davy, playing in his band at the weekend at the anti-sectarian charity. It was schoolboy standard but he was pleased I was there. It'll take time, but I think he'll come round to forgiving me.

Therapist: And Izzy?

Jim: We got dressed up like a pair of old hippies. It was just like old times.

Therapist: I'm glad.

Jim: There was a big display about the boy's killing at this concert.

Therapist: Did you tell Izzy what you witnessed?

Jim: What do you think? She doesn't suspect a thing. Things are going well for us. I'm a lucky bugger and I've no intention of stirring up any more trouble between us.

CHAPTER 23

Davy was hunched over his laptop with an expression that was both vacant and concentrated. 'Carol told me that the whole of *The Shindig* was being uploaded to YouTube, but we're not here.'

Izzy looked over his shoulder. She could see the number of views was 12,450, along with a list of comments using abbreviations and acronyms that were hard to translate. 'That's a lot more people than were there on the day.'

'I know we were part of the warm-up, but they promised they'd upload it.'

'Never mind. Dad and I were there. You were great.' She wanted to ruffle his hair, to give him a hug. It was an effort to resist.

Davy turned his attention back to the computer, his head down, rapt. 'It's so unfair,' he blurted. His lower lip was pouting – he looked like he might cry.

'Did you see the photo of Mark Docherty in the SOS tent? Carol's son, who was killed?' she asked, thinking it would help to change the subject. 'It made me realise how lucky I am. It could have been you.' This time she couldn't resist the impulse to hug his shoulder.

'I'm sorry he died but he was one of those guys who love aggro, who think having a fight is the best part of the day. I run a mile if any of that stuff happens near me.'

'What makes you think Mark was a fighter?'

'Dad told me he saw him fighting against a gang of Rangers supporters on his way home.'

'When did he tell you this?'

'When he got home from the match. He took me into a corner and said he'd seen a young Celtic fan getting slashed in a fight. He made me promise to walk away from any trouble. The next day, I read about Mark in the papers and showed Dad the photo. He recognised him right away.'

'But I asked your dad if he'd seen Mark that afternoon and he said he hadn't.'

'All I know is what he told me,' said Davy, going back to his computer screen.

Jim opened the door with a flourish. 'Good morning, family,' he said brightly. Izzy felt herself stiffen. He was in one of his dangerously good moods. It was like watching a rollercoaster cranking itself up and up to the top of the curve. It was only a matter of time before his mood plummeted. Davy flipped down the lid of his laptop and made a move to leave.

'Why don't you stay and chat, son?' asked Jim.

'What about?' asked Davy.

'How's school going?' asked Jim. Davy groaned, opened his laptop and turned his attention back to the screen. Jim glared at Izzy, as if expecting her to do something. She shrugged.

'OK,' said Jim. 'Maybe your mum will talk to me. What's on at college today, Izzy?'

She cleared her throat but her mind had frozen. Her only thought was that she was going to Sean Docherty's flat tonight. She walked over to the pantry, found a packet of Jim's Cornflakes, and brought it back to the table. 'I've got an extra tutorial after college so I'll be home late,' she said. 'There's a lasagne in the fridge. Thirty-five minutes at 170 degrees.' Her heart was slamming against her chest.

'And what about you, Davy? Are you coming home tonight or do you have a better offer, too?'

Davy closed his laptop and stared at them both, running his hands through his hair. 'I've got something to tell you both.' A faint blush crept across his cheeks. His mouth, full and ripe, still had a petulant look. Izzy held her breath. 'I'm taking a gap year. To concentrate on the band,' he announced.

'What? You're not going to university?' asked Izzy.

'I'll defer starting until the year after, assuming we don't make it big in the meantime.'

'And assuming you get the grades you need this year,' added Jim. His face had darkened. The atmosphere had chilled.

'How will you finance this?' asked Izzy, thinking it best to keep to practical matters.

'Granny's money. I'll get it next summer, when I'm eighteen,' said Davy.

Jim's eyes had not left Davy's face. 'My mother left that money for you to go to university. It was her dying wish.'

'If Davy gets his Highers, there's no harm in taking a year off. Anyhow, he won't need much money if he's living at home,' she said, trying to cool the heat that was building between them.

'Cas and I are going to London.'

'London?' chorused Jim and Izzy.

'You're not bloody well going to London, and that's the end of it,' said Jim.

'I'm eighteen in summer, and there's nothing you can do or say to stop me.'

'I'll not allow you to squander your inheritance,' said Jim, raising his voice.

Davy stood up to his full height and looked down on Jim. 'What right d'you have to tell me how to live my life? Sort out your own crap first.'

'Davy, sit down,' ordered Jim.

'What do you know about having ambitions and dreams, Dad? You can't see further than the bottom of a wine glass,' said Davy, gathering up his computer.

Jim caught him by the sleeve. 'Of course I understand about ambitions and dreams. I had to do it the hard way, but you've got the chance of an education. A university education. I won't stand by and let you screw up your life.'

'Well, you know a lot about screwing up, don't you, Dad? You've got a fucking A+ on that subject.' He tore himself away from Jim's grasp and bundled out the door.

Jim stood stunned, chewing furiously on some gum.

'He'll apologise later. When he's had time to calm down,' she said quietly.

'The more I try to reach out to him, the more he pushes me away,' said Jim angrily. He thumped the table in frustration. 'He's an ungrateful little sod. You've been too soft on him, Izzy.'

She took a dishcloth from the sink and wiped down the table in short, resentful swipes. There was no point arguing with him while he was in this mood. Her heart slowed and a cold curiosity took hold. 'Davy told me you saw Mark Docherty on the day he was killed,' she said.

'Who's Mark Docherty?' asked Jim, pouring himself a large glass of orange juice and draining it in one swallow.

'Carol Docherty's son. The boy who was killed on the day of the Old Firm match, back in March.'

Jim gave her a mystified look and then a slight shake of the head. 'I don't know what you're talking about.'

'Oh, I think you do,' she said.

'Why are we talking about this? We should be discussing Davy.'

'Jim, I need to know what you saw.'

He looked stricken, his mouth still chewing the gum as if working up the energy to speak. He looked at her, a fleeting plea for mercy in his eyes. She dried her hands on the tea towel and sat down. 'I'm listening.'

'OK. OK. Yes, I saw Mark Docherty on the day he died. He was walking, alone, down an alleyway towards me. There'd been a bit of trouble earlier on, but Mark wasn't involved in that. He was just in the wrong place at the wrong time.'

'What happened?'

'He was about fifty yards in front of me when three or four Rangers supporters attacked him from behind. They were older, armed with broken bottles. Mark didn't put up any resistance. It was over in seconds.'

'What did you do?'

'I asked him if he was OK. He looked shocked but said he was fine. I tried to get him to his feet but then I saw blood running from his thigh.'

'Did you make a tourniquet?'

'You know I faint at the sight of blood.'

'So you did nothing? You left him alone to die?'

'I didn't have a phone so I ran across the road and asked a woman to call for an ambulance. I heard sirens almost immediately. Professional help would have been with him in a matter of minutes.'

'What? So, you left him? Left a boy the same age as your own son to die in a dark alleyway on his own?'

'It wasn't like that, Izzy. He didn't seem that bad. Anyhow, I had touched the broken bottle. I could have been implicated.'

'You mean you were more worried about yourself than what might happen to him?'

'I did my best for him, but in the end, I did what most people would do: I put the interests of my family first. I couldn't have changed the outcome for him in any way.'

Carol's face swam into view; her sense of injustice that her son would be forever branded as a common thug. 'You're wrong, Jim. If you tell the police, Mark's name will be cleared; everyone would know he was innocent. And those boys may get a longer sentence for murder.'

'What good would that do? Except to deny those lads a chance to make something of their lives, grow up and have families of their own?'

'You're the first one to complain the justice system is too soft on criminals these days. Admit it, you won't go to the police because Mark Docherty's a Celtic supporter, a catholic.'

'Of course it's because he's a Celtic supporter. It's how things work in this city. What world are you living in?'

She couldn't speak. It felt like ice was running through her veins, shutting down her system.

'If I went to the police, the Rangers supporters would think I'm a traitor for grassing on those lads. Rangers might even cancel the alarm contract. Oh, and don't think the Celtic fans would thank me, either. They're still angry about what happened. It wouldn't take much for them to come after me, you and Davy. Mark's dead. Nothing will bring him back. Carol's moved on with her life. We should do the same,' he said, taking hold of both her hands.

Her pale, freckly fingers looked small in his paw of a hand. She quietly withdrew them and placed them on her lap. Jim gripped her arm, his fingers digging into her flesh. 'Why d'you care so much? Why would I risk everything for the sake of a lad we don't know? Why?'

'Because it's the right thing to do, Jim,' she said, shaking her arm free of him. More reasons tumbled inside her head: because he isn't a nameless person, he's Sean's nephew and Carol's son; because his death has had terrible consequences for their family; because, if you don't go forward with this information, it will live forever between us, growing like a cancer.

'The right thing to do for my family, for my club, for my business, is to let sleeping dogs lie.' He wet his lips. His eyes had a haunted look about them and his fingers began to drum against the edge of the table. He looked like he would have killed for a drink at this moment.

'Let sleeping dogs lie,' she echoed, wondering then what right she had to criticise him. She had no intention of telling him about Sean or the work she was doing to discredit the club's management.

'I need you to back me up on this, Izzy,' he said, fixing her with an urgent look.

She found it hard to meet his desperate gaze.

'Let's talk about this over dinner tonight. When we've both had time to calm down,' he suggested.

'I've told you, I'm at college tonight.'

'You can skip the class, surely,' he said. His face had sagged. His eyes pleaded. 'I thought, for once, you might put me, *put us*, before your damn college course.'

'No. I can't,' she said. Her voice was quiet and clear. 'But I promise to say nothing about Mark Docherty, although, I hope one day you'll think differently about what you're doing.'

He shook his head from side to side, as if he was in great pain. 'I'm sorry, Izzy. I don't think you and I live in the same world anymore.'

***

Jim: I told Izzy about witnessing the young lad's murder. I thought about what you said. That it's best not have secrets between us.

Therapist: I think it's good you've been open with her.

246

Jim:	She wanted me to grass on those Rangers lads. Thought it was the right thing to do.
Therapist:	Could you see her point of view?
Jim:	She's become very idealistic these days: all that volunteering she does at the Bureau and now this anti-sectarian charity. As for the Rangers bid, she never asks about it. That's what's putting bread on the table, not her high-minded principles.
Therapist:	I'm sorry to hear that.
Jim:	Davy and I argued as well. Kids these days … there isn't the same respect we had for our parents, is there? I was sorely tempted to have a drink, I can tell you.
Therapist:	Let's talk about strategies to avoid temptation when under stress.
Jim:	I went to the office and worked late.
Therapist:	That's one way, but have you considered meditation?
Jim:	I think you've got the wrong idea about me. Just because I dressed up as a hippie to go to that music festival, doesn't mean I'm into all that stuff.

CHAPTER 24

The canteen at college was busy. Bridget had done well to bag them two seats. She was reading the paper and Izzy took a moment to observe her. A red bandana was knotted on her head and she was wearing matching red glasses. A wave of love washed over her.

'Great news. Muir McIntyre's in a hospice,' said Bridget, not looking up.

'That doesn't sound like good news for Muir McIntyre,' said Izzy, sitting down beside her.

'He's the Scottish Member of Parliament for Blantyre East. When he dies, there'll be a by-election. Scary or what?'

They sat in silence, taking in the magnitude of the news.

'It's been a Labour stronghold forever, but the good people of Blantyre East might be prepared to take a risk on me,' said Bridget.

'When does campaigning start?'

'We'll start canvassing door to door in the next couple of days,' said Bridget.

'But he's not dead yet,' said Izzy, aghast.

'The Labour Party started last week,' said Bridget.

'I'd like to help you,' said Izzy. The offer was out of her mouth before she had time to think about it properly.

'Since when have you been interested in politics?'

'I'm not. At least not politics with a capital P. But I'm interested in people. I realised at *The Shindig*, sectarian violence doesn't only affect the families directly involved. It affects us all. There's so much wrong about our society these days. I want to do something.'

'This Sean Docherty has a lot to answer for. Did you see him at *The Shindig*?'

'I'm going to his flat tonight.'

Bridget's head jerked up and her eyes narrowed. 'I knew there was more going on between you two than you were letting on.'

'It's not what you think. I've got my report from The Chairman's Club to go through with him. I shouldn't even be telling you this. I promised I would keep our collaboration a secret.'

'I get it. If you tell me, you'll have to kill me.'

'Bridget, I'm being serious.'

Bridget threw her head back and laughed. 'Look at yourself. Your eyes are sparkling, you're wearing your new navy blazer. You've even got lip gloss on. You might as well be shouting out of a megaphone "*I fancy the pants off Sean Docherty.*"'

'Wheesht,' hissed Izzy looking around, but no one had turned their heads in their direction.

'Well, good for you, girl. You deserve to be happy,' Bridget stated brightly.

'You don't think I'm crazy, then?' asked Izzy.

'Of course I think you're crazy. This has got heartbreak written all over it, but I don't suppose that'll stop you. Just promise me you'll be careful.'

'I've been careful all my life,' said Izzy.

Concern and excitement shone from Bridget's eyes. Their lives seemed to be transforming in front of them. Izzy wanted to say good luck but, in the end, neither of them said anything. They stood up and hugged each other hard. It was all the words they needed.

***

Therapist:	You seem a bit down this week, Jim.
Jim:	Modern life's complicated, isn't it? When we first got married, I was the breadwinner. Izzy was at home looking after Davy. It worked. We were very happy. Now she's talking about getting a job after she graduates. Davy wants to go London as soon as he can. Everything's changing and I don't like it.
Therapist:	Things change. People change. You can't control that. But you can control your responses to those changes. Are there any positive things about Izzy wanting to get a job?
Jim:	None that I can think of.
Therapist:	(Silence)
Jim:	Oh, there's one thing. She's taken good care of herself. Kept her figure. I saw her going to college this morning. She was wearing a smart jacket and fitted jeans. She looked amazing. I mean she looked really good. Christ, I love her so much.

CHAPTER 25

Izzy stood outside Carol's flat, feeling the weight of her briefcase. Even now, it was not too late to walk away. To go home. To heat up the lasagne. To repair the atmosphere between herself and Jim. She straightened the lapels of her blazer and brushed the sleeves of her jacket. She allowed a calm resolve to claim her, and then rang the bell.

Sean hugged her briefly. He was wearing a charcoal sweater with a roll neck, the sort that would look ridiculous on Jim, but looked stylish on him. The cashmere felt heart-meltingly soft.

'Drink?' he asked, leading her towards the kitchen.

'A cup of tea would be lovely,' she replied. He looked at her questioningly. Perhaps he had expected her to ask for a martini or a glass of prosecco. She was disappointing him and felt a flash of irritation. Perhaps, when you anticipate something so much, an anti-climax is inevitable.

The kitchen was in semi-darkness, but the curtains were open and the sparkly light from the street lamps drifted into the room. There were two candles standing in wooden holders on the kitchen table. Their wicks were new, rigid and ready to be lit. If his intentions were romantic, he would light them. He switched on the central light and it ravaged the room.

'Does Carol know about me being here? Helping you?' she asked.

He looked briefly puzzled and then his expression cleared. 'I promise you, Izzy, she'll never know. I keep all my sources totally confidential.'

She smiled weakly, feeling a twist of guilt that she had blabbed so easily about him to Bridget.

'Has she lived here for long?' she asked politely.

He was filling the kettle, busying himself with finding cups and getting milk from the fridge. 'She rented it after she and Connor first separated. That was a year before Mark was killed. They've had several reconciliation attempts since, but Connor refuses to leave the Gallowgate flat. Mark's bedroom has been kept just as it was when he was alive. He's not ready to let that go. In all honesty, I'm not sure any of us are.'

'Were you and Mark close?' asked Izzy.

'I'd rather not talk about it,' said Sean. He looked as heartbroken as a child and she felt a sick grief building inside her.

She touched the sleeve of his sweater. 'It's not good to bottle feelings up, you know,' she said gently.

He folded his arms across his chest. 'I'm familiar with the theory,' he said curtly. His tone felt as sharp as a rap on her knuckles. 'The only way I can deal with it at the moment, is by focusing on giving practical support. Sorting out Connor's financial mess and helping Carol whenever I can.'

Something trembled in her heart. She wanted to tell him that she knew something important about Mark's death. She wished she hadn't promised Jim to keep quiet, but seeing the effort he was making to keep his feelings suppressed, perhaps it wasn't the right time. Perhaps Jim was right after all: best to let sleeping dogs lie.

'If you change your mind about wanting to talk about Mark, you'll find me a good listener,' she offered.

'Thanks, Izzy. For now, though, I'm the one wanting to do the listening. I've got a lot of questions about your Ibrox adventure.'

He took their mugs of tea through to the lounge. It was spacious with a large bay window and a coffee-coloured carpet. Modern art lined the walls in vibrant, unsettled colours. Two squashy sofas in cream, with cushions in shades of taupe and grey, had been pushed back against the walls to make room for the piles of paper that were laid out on the floor.

'This is a lot of paper,' she said, threading her way through the stacks.

'I've organised it into two sections. The ticketing scam stuff is over by the window; the tax avoidance schemes by the door.'

'You're well-organised,' she murmured.

'I thought about you all afternoon that day at The Chairman's Club. Wished I could have been a fly on the wall.'

She felt her face colour. They sat down together on one of the sofas. The cushions sagged, bringing them closer than she intended. She suppressed an urge to touch the soft cashmere of his sweater and shifted a few centimetres away from him.

'So, what would you like to ask me?' she said, sipping her tea.

He reached over for his glasses and was skimming the pages of her report. 'Looks like they're battening down the hatches by replicating their silverware. Did you find out the name of the company they're using? We need to do a deep dive into which staff members might be recipients of the Employee Benefit Trusts. We might find some names listed on the club's website. Have you been online to check?' He looked up, smiling, knowing he'd fired off a barrage of questions. His glasses had slid down the bridge of his nose and he pushed them back up. Tenderness filled her.

'Well, that's enough for me to get started on. Anything else you want me to do?' she asked. Her heart was beating rapidly and her free will was in near total collapse. She would agree to anything he wanted. Anything.

A small frown passed over his forehead. 'I've got a file somewhere on Employee Benefit Trust test cases from HMRC. Could you go through it and see if there's anything significant? It's over there by the door.' Disappointment returned her heartbeat to normal as she walked over to the pile of papers.

They worked for a while in companionable silence. Izzy on the floor, Sean on the sofa, his laptop on a cushion on his lap. She heard the grumble of traffic outside, the soft tap tap of his keyboard, an occasional intake of breath or the soft exhaling of a sigh that could have come from either of them. She looked up once or twice, seeing his head bent in concentration and felt temporarily distracted by happiness at working together.

'How are you doing?' he asked, coming to sit beside her on the floor, cross-legged in a yoga pose. Izzy pulled her hair back from her face, she could feel his breath on her neck.

'HMRC have requested meetings with Rangers, but I don't think any have taken place,' she said, trying to keep her voice steady.

'I've been following up on the ticketing scam. It looks like all the money has gone through a London ticketing organisation, which, in turn, has transferred the money to a Bahamas-based company, whose director just happens to be …' Their heads were so close they were almost touching.

'Jack Marshall,' she said.

Her hand was trembling. He caught her wrist to still it.

'I'm glad you came,' he said, 'I know it's selfish of me …'

'Stop,' she said, turning to face him, 'stop right there.'

He pulled her towards him. The proximity of his body was overwhelming. A thin film of heat radiated from her centre. They kissed, collapsing backwards, the paper crackling beneath them as she felt his weight press her to the floor.

His phone rang. It reverberated between them like a guilty conscience. He sat up and pulled it from his back pocket. 'Shit. Sorry. It's my editor, Matt,' Sean said as he scrambled to his feet and walked towards the kitchen.

She got up and smoothed down her hair and clothes. Her heart was soaring, she felt radiant. She could hear him talking in an animated voice in the kitchen, but couldn't make out what he was saying. She began to tidy the papers that had scattered across the carpet.

He returned to the lounge, his eyes cast downwards.

'What?' she asked. Concern prickled her skin. 'Bad news?'

He blinked, his tallow eyes were sparkling. 'We've got the go-ahead to present a revised script at the end of the week.'

She was beginning to feel reckless. His eyes were indescribably beautiful. 'That's great,' she said moving towards him. He caught her in an embrace. Desire flamed and burned inside her.

'Can you come again tomorrow night?' he asked, pushing her hair from her face and stroking her cheek.

'Yes,' she said. There was no teetering on the brink. They didn't kiss. There was no need. It was as if everything had already been agreed between them.

***

Therapist:	So, how long has it been now?
Jim:	Just over a month. It's the longest I've ever been without a drink.
Therapist:	I'm delighted.
Jim:	I don't stop to think about how much I miss it. I just keep myself busy. Things at work are magic. The buzz is unbelievable.
Therapist:	And at home?
Jim:	Not so good. Izzy's collected another new lame duck project. Helping her pal Bridget's doomed SNP campaign. She going to be out every evening this week. It

	feels like we're drifting apart. What I need is a grand gesture.
Therapist:	Like what?
Jim:	A holiday. Australia and New Zealand. In May next year, after her finals. What d'you think?
Therapist:	Sounds like the trip of a lifetime.
Jim:	Business class flights. No expense spared. It'll be good for us. You know, time to talk. Just the two of us.
Therapist:	You don't have to go all the way to Australia to talk.
Jim:	Maybe not, but it feels like that's the only way it's going to happen at the moment.

CHAPTER 26

A great happiness inflated Izzy as she walked towards the Bureau. She found herself replaying, in obsessive detail, the events of the night before: Sean's suppressed grief for Mark; a tantalising glimpse into the mysterious well of his sensitivity; the intensity of his gaze, and their naked, mutual attraction. She was wearing her new jeans and felt radiant, beautiful and a little foolhardy.

An untidy queue had formed outside the Bureau, waiting for it to open. The expressions on the people's faces were a mixture of defiance, defeat and boredom. The man at the head of the queue was clutching a plastic bag to his chest. Izzy guessed it was full of unopened bills. It was going to be a busy day. Reluctantly, she put Sean Docherty to the back of her mind and pressed the entry phone buzzer. Alan's voice barked back. 'It's no nine yet.'

'It's me,' she said. There was a short pause, as if he needed to carefully consider whether to let her in.

Izzy found Shona and Alan in the reception area, bent over the coffee table, reading a newspaper.

'Unemployment up eight percent since summer. We're in the grip of a crisis but no one seems to have noticed,' Shona was saying.

'Oh, they've noticed all right, but they don't care. We're a long way away from Westminster,' said Alan.

'Sorry, folks, but I'm going to have to ask you if you can do a few more hours for the next couple of weeks. I've asked for more volunteers, but recruitment's dried up. People can't afford to volunteer, even if they wanted to,' replied Shona.

'It's scandalous that we're dependent on volunteers and whatever handouts the council, the lottery and any other worthy institutions decide they can spare,' added Alan.

'I can work an extra day if that helps,' offered Izzy.

'Make that two of us,' added Alan.

Shona looked exhausted. 'I don't know what I'd do without you guys.'

Izzy was glad to be busy. It helped keep her thoughts about Sean and the evening ahead under control, though on the odd occasion when he burst into her consciousness, she felt herself blushing furiously. She had told Jim she was helping Bridget with her campaigning and would be needed every night this week. He had barely registered she had spoken, happily informing her that he, too, was in demand, and would be working late most nights from now on.

Lunch hour was squeezed into fifteen minutes. Shona was quiet and pale. Alan was reading the paper with his usual air of incredulity. 'I hate those fucking Tories,' he said, tearing an angry piece out of his ham roll.

'Technically, we're not governed by the Tories. We've got a coalition government,' said Izzy. Her knowledge of politics had rocketed since she had known Bridget.

'I hate the fucking coalition, too,' added Alan.

Shona and Izzy exchanged weary smiles.

'The Scottish Labour Party isn't any better. A bunch of old has-beens resting on their laurels,' commented Alan.

'My friend, Bridget Lafferty, is the SNP candidate for the Blantyre East by-election.'

Alan looked at her with a new interest. 'That's my constituency.'

'D'you think she has a chance of winning?'

'I hope so, though it won't be easy,' admitted Alan. 'But we need to take control of our own destiny,' he said, leaning forward. His belly was resting on his thighs. 'I mean, when you get paid at the end of the month, you don't give your payslip to your next-door neighbour and let them decide how you spend it, do you?'

Her last client of the day was a lad a year or two older than Davy. Fixed Odds Betting Terminals had got him into a serious money tangle that would blight his life if he didn't curb the habit. She hated those FOBT machines. The people responsible for them must know their promise of quick wins was as addictive and destructive as heroin, but the boy seemed oblivious to the dangers. He finally admitted that he had kept his appointment at the Bureau because his mum had promised to give him a tenner if he did. They all knew what he would spend it on. She said a silent prayer of gratitude that Davy had never been tempted by those machines. It was the sort of thing that could happen to any family.

By the time Izzy arrived at Carol's flat, dusk had fallen. Any guilt about lying to Jim, frustration about cuts to the Bureau's funding or anger about FOBTs had melted away. She felt carefree, daring. Sean opened the door and, for a moment, they stood awkwardly. He leaned forward and kissed her gently on the lips and then, putting his arm round her, walked down the corridor. A hazy kind of euphoria settled over her, aware only of the physical sensation of his closeness. Her hip bone tucked in perfectly below his.

He leaned over to light the two candles on the kitchen table. She felt skittish and bold, and reached over to kiss him on his cheek. His skin felt like fine sandpaper.

He grinned. 'Hope you're hungry.'

There was no sign of any food. The cooker was off. The work surfaces tidy. 'Smells delicious,' she said.

'Very funny,' he said, bringing a bowl from the fridge. 'Three bean quinoa salad with spinach and toasted pine nuts in a sesame oil dressing,' he announced, 'and some rye bread.' Then, with boyish enthusiasm, added: 'From the artisan baker in Byres Road. Maybe you know it?'

Izzy shook her head. She felt like an explorer being offered the hospitality of a strange culture and wondered if this supper was for her benefit, or if he always ate like this. He tossed the salad with a pair of wooden salad servers shaped like hands using careful, practised flicks. She could see a blue vein pulsing on his forearm. He buttered a slice of the rye bread and offered it to her. She tipped her head back and opened her mouth to receive it, amazed by her wantonness. He laughed and popped it into her mouth.

'Delicious. Did you learn about this food at Cambridge?' she asked.

'God, no. I only ate junk back then. I was diagnosed with gluten intolerance ten years ago. I thought it was a life sentence of eating rabbit food, but I discovered there was plenty I could eat, I just needed to learn more about it,' he said, handing her a plate of salad.

Izzy took a mouthful. A complexity of flavours burst into her mouth, surprising and entertaining. 'This is amazing,' she said, scooping another mouthful into her mouth. She must look like a savage who hadn't eaten for days, but he was smiling broadly. She felt a passing shot of disloyalty, remembering her special suppers of lasagne and apple pie, and wondered if she would ever cook them again. It felt like she was dropping old friends in favour of someone new and exciting, but she didn't care. This was new. This was exciting.

'Is it easy to buy the ingredients in Glasgow?' she asked.

He laughed. A full-bodied laugh. 'You're living in one of the most amazing cities for food shopping. Selina loved Great Western Road for the Indian markets.'

He continued eating, oblivious to the hand grenade he'd lobbed into their conversation. Selina. She let some space form around her name and waited.

'Selina was my fiancée,' he explained. 'She died when she was twenty-nine, ten years ago. She woke up one morning with a headache that never went away. Meningitis.'

Izzy's mouth went dry. She wondered if she had enough saliva to swallow her food. 'That's terrible. I'm so sorry, Sean.'

He rubbed the bridge of his nose where his glasses had left a mark. 'It happened a long time ago.'

She could feel the effort it was taking for him to contain his emotions. They seemed tied up inside him, as tight and twisted together as the roots of a pot plant.

'People told me that I'd get over it in time. As if it was some hurdle you figured out how to jump over. But, for me, my life as I knew it ended that day.'

'I can imagine,' said Izzy, flinching at her insensitivity. That sort of loss was beyond anyone's imagination.

'Work became a massive thing for me. Maybe too massive but I love my job. It makes me slightly less of a miserable bastard. But, as for long-term relationships ...'

'Not on the menu,' finished Izzy.

He smiled, visibly relaxing. 'Correct.'

Her immediate thought was: *what a waste.* 'Understood,' she said, gathering the plates and taking them to the sink.

'The revised script is due at the end of the week. That's all the time we have. Then we'll be finished,' he said.

It was clear what he was offering: an adventure for the next four days, with no ties and no future. The clarity of it struck her as sophisticated, straightforward, ideal. Sean didn't want a serious relationship and she had no plans to leave Jim.

'I don't expect you to do the dishes,' he said, coming up to stand behind her, his arms stroking hers. She leaned back into his chest as he started kissing the side of her neck. His mouth had reached the tender curve of her shoulder. 'So, are you available to help?' His request sounded as straightforward as if he was asking for an appointment at the Bureau.

'Yes,' she whispered back.

He drew her towards him, stroking the inside of her arm. Her flesh stung with heat. They kissed. She had no control over the boldness of her longing. Her body demanded his attention. Twenty odd years of fidelity disappeared in moments. Goodbye, Jim. Goodbye, faithful wife.

*****

Therapist: How are you today, Jim?

Jim: Tip top.

Therapist: You look tired.

Jim: (Shrugs)

Therapist: How are Izzy and Davy?

Jim: Haven't seen either of them of them much this week. If I didn't know better, I would think they're avoiding me.

Therapist: Last time, we talked about you spending more time with Izzy. Maybe going on holiday.

Jim: Aye well, I don't see that happening
                anytime soon. It's full on at work. In
                fact, Jack Marshall's invited me to a Press
                Association dinner at Ibrox tomorrow
                night.

Therapist: You can't avoid social occasions forever,
                Jim, but I wouldn't advise it just yet.

Jim: I thought you might say that.

CHAPTER 27

Sometimes, during those four days, Izzy caught her reflection in a shop window and challenged herself to confront the unfaithful wife, the shameless adulteress who stared back at her, but she found it hard to muster any shame or regret. Instead, a bubble of happiness would pop inside her.

Bridget had agreed to provide an alibi for her each evening, but lying was barely required. Jim was working most nights and Davy was living, more or less permanently, at Cas's. They were like three boats in a harbour that had slipped their moorings, gently drifting out to sea. She comforted herself with the fact there would be time after Sean returned to London to work to bring the three of them back together. So much time, in fact, that she felt the first stirrings of despair.

It was her last evening with Sean. She brushed her hair in short quick tugs, reminding herself that she was not going to be one of those pathetic souls who cried and moped. She would be grown up and gracious in their farewell. Absolutely no tears. After he was gone, she would re-invent herself, be a stronger, better and more capable person because of him. Get a job. Rescue her crumbling family.

She leaned into her bedroom mirror, her freckles seemed more prominent than usual. Sean had spent the last evening trying to count them, kissing each one as he counted. It was a jokey gesture, but it had moved her in a way that had felt frightening. She was in danger of being overwhelmed by him; like a swimmer stepping into the sea, not realising how strong the undertow would be. Well, after tonight, she was heading back to shore, to dry land and the safety of her old life. She should be thankful that she had experienced such a lover, but she didn't feel thankful. Instead, wishful thoughts crowded her mind: forlorn and foolish.

It was a beautiful autumn evening; the trees lining Sean's street were turning golden, a flaming show of decay. The sofas had been pushed back to their original positions and the piles of papers and folders had been tidied into a corner. Sean was standing with a cup of tea in his hands, looking out of the bay window onto the street below. She came up behind him and wrapped her arms around his chest. They stood like that for a while, watching the gloaming sky darkening the room in slow, but inevitable degrees, listening to the final rush of birdsong before the first flickers of the streetlights. He turned to kiss her. They were gripped with a familiar urgency. She laughed as he tugged off her jacket, stepping back to fumble with the buttons of her blouse, freeing her breasts, feeling the cool air soap them.

Later, they lay on the sofa, folded together. Jazz piano was playing at low volume. The notes had a rhythm like a stream running over pebbles, moulding and smoothing as it flowed. The music seemed to bypass her conscious mind and go straight to her body, where she felt every muscle relax.

'What are we listening to?' she asked.

'Bill Evans: "My Foolish Heart". Do you like it?'

'It's lovely. I always thought I hated jazz,' she sighed.

He sat up, looking at her with an expression so full of sorrow that a lump of sadness formed in her throat, as solid as a stone.

'I'm sorry, Izzy. I'm sorry I couldn't have given you more,' he said.

'More than what?' she asked.

He gestured at the tidy room, at the two stacks of paper piled up in the corner. 'More than this. These few days.'

'That's all I expected. Maybe that's all I can handle,' she said.

He looked away and, for the briefest moment, she wondered if he felt the same.

'You're incredibly talented, Izzy. One of the best researchers I've worked with.'

She felt lightheaded with his praise. 'I'm going to apply for a job at the Policy Research Department when I graduate.'

'You'd be really good at that,' he said, kissing her on the forehead and smoothing the hair from her face. 'I've been asked to work on a story on the London Olympics. Apparently, the US wants to send hundreds of FBI agents over next summer. They're paranoid about terrorism.'

She knew what they were doing: talking about their futures and going their separate ways. She swallowed hard.

'This sounds like we're saying goodbye,' she said, determined to keep her voice breezy. He hugged her. The ferocity of his grip was thrilling but, at the same time, it unhinged her. The dam broke; she found herself sobbing.

'Hey there,' he said brushing the tears from her face with the edge of his thumb. Her face felt hot and her nose must have looked raw. She cursed her lack of control. This wasn't the way she wanted him to remember her. She fished a hanky from her sleeve and blew her nose. 'Sorry. I didn't mean that to happen.'

'It's OK. It's good to let your emotions out,' he said gently.

She smiled, remembering her own advice to him, but knew if she began crying again, she wouldn't be able to stop. 'So … what d'you fancy doing for the rest of our last evening together? Or need I ask?' She attempted a flirtatious tone, cocking her head to one side.

'It might not be our last evening,' he said, raising his eyebrows, matching her playful mood. 'Carol called. She's staying for a couple more days, till Monday.'

'Jim's leaving early in the morning for the match in Aberdeen. Won't be back until Sunday afternoon.'

'So, we've got an extra day together.'

'An extra day and night,' she corrected him.

'The weather forecast says it's going be dry but breezy tomorrow. A perfect day for …'

'… Revising for my exams?'

'Did you know that research has shown that heartbreakingly beautiful scenery boosts the latent capacity of your cerebral cortex? I'd like to take you up the majestic Ben Lui. It was the last hill I climbed with my Dad before he died. It's a very special place. The perfect place for a proper goodbye.'

He had grown serious. Their banter had stilled. She was having trouble settling the trembling in her chest. He was looking at her hand. Her wedding ring glowed on her finger like an unwelcome reminder.

'I've got some old walking boots. There's probably a waterproof jacket in the cupboard under the stairs at home,' she said.

'Come round in the morning as soon as Jim leaves for the match.'

They leaned back together on the sofa. She traced the small disturbance on his throat where his Adam's apple came close to breaking the skin. He caught her hand and kissed each fingertip until she wanted to expire.

***

Therapist: I sense you've been feeling a bit down this past week. Have you thought about doing regular exercise? It's an excellent way to lift your mood.

Jim: I look at those middle-aged jokers jogging round the streets. They look like they're about to have a heart attack.

Therapist: It doesn't have to be running. What was your favourite exercise as a child?

Jim: I liked playing football at school. Sometimes, at the weekend, the Boy's Brigade would go hill walking. I really enjoyed that.

Therapist: Hill walking is excellent exercise and we've some of the best hills in the world within an hour's drive of Glasgow. D'you think Izzy might join you?

Jim: You must be joking. She's never been up a hill in her life.

CHAPTER 28

The end, when it came, was a shock. Sean called just as she was about to leave to say he had been summoned back to London immediately. He just had time to say how sad and angry he was that they couldn't climb Ben Lui together, and then he was gone. She knew their affair was going to end, yet she felt totally unprepared. She felt a soft twist of confusion in her solar plexus and then, later, a growling, unrelenting sadness that started inside her chest and spread out to every part of her. Even her fingertips felt sad. The weekend stretched before her like a cruel test. Jim had left for the match in Aberdeen, Davy was at Cas's and Bridget was at an SNP weekend retreat in Perthshire. A voice inside her head repeated, over and over, that he was gone. Their fling was over. But, no matter how often the voice repeated itself, it was as if she was hearing it for the first time.

The celebrity magazines from her Chairman's Club research were spread out on the coffee table. She gathered them up into a pile and dropped them into the recycling bin, but when her arms were empty, she felt no lightness, only the gathering weight of loneliness. She was surrounded by the silence of her empty home. She ran a finger along the edge of the dado rail, a smudge of grime appeared on her fingertip. Dust covered every surface of this house like a thin layer of neglect.

She put on her apron, tied her hair back and did what she always did when facing a crisis – got busy. She started by wiping down the walls in the kitchen, then removing the lampshades and washing them. She pulled out all the contents from the cupboard under the sink, finding bits of wire wool, scrubbing brushes and rubber gloves that didn't match. She would have missed it if she hadn't been determined to reach right to the back: an empty bottle of Tesco Finest Scotch Whisky. The bottle's glass looked cloudy and she blew a bloom of dust from it. There was no telling if it was old, or part of a more recent transgression.

By the time she had cleaned the whole house, it was 11 p.m. and seven bottles stood on the kitchen table. Three whisky. Four red wine. One of the red wine bottles was two-thirds empty and had a cork in it. She had found it in the eaves cupboard in the spare bedroom where Jim was sleeping. She felt like a hunter displaying her kills, a sense of victory mixed with an edge of despair. She had the advantage over her prey, she had always understood a relapse was a possibility.

She wondered what else he might have lied about. His promise to give the bank back the loan of three hundred thousand pounds suddenly seemed as fragile as wet tissue paper. A brief surge of panic rose in her chest. She remembered imagining the worst case: Jim declared bankrupt; their house sold; she getting a job and buying a small flat using the money her parents had left her as a deposit. The scenario swirled around in her head, gathering the grim appearance of an actual contingency plan. She hoped the more she rehearsed it in her mind, the less scary it would become.

She sat at the kitchen table and felt something break inside her. Laying her head on her hands, she began to sob; her marriage was an empty shell, her lover was gone, her only child was forging his future with barely a backwards glance, and all that was left was the bleak disappointment of a middle-aged woman.

When there were no more tears left to cry, she got up and splashed cold water on her face. She moved like a zombie and yet, at the same time, she was clear-headed and alert. Jim was an alcoholic and would always be one. He was resolute in his belief that Rangers was trustworthy, and nothing or no-one would change his mind. She could either accept this and live with the consequences, or walk away. The empty bottles glowed in the ghostly light of the kitchen, waiting for her decision.

She emptied the dregs of each of them down the sink, put them into two large carrier bags and carried them down the side of the house. It was dry and cold in the night air. She threw the first bottle into the bin, flinching as it smashed, then threw the second one in. The sound of splintering and crashing was even louder. She hurled the others in quick succession, thrilled at the violent, catastrophic sound they made. A dog barked and then all was quiet.

She walked back into the kitchen and picked up the phone. Now she had made her decision, she was anxious to act.

'It's not too late to call?' she asked.

'Hey, Izzy. No. Not too late. It's good to hear your voice. I'm so sorry I had to rush away this morning. It's not what I'd planned,' said Sean.

'Well, you know what they say about plans, God looks at them and laughs.' She bit her lip, remembering her own attempts to plan her future.

'Talking of which … Matt's rejected the script. He's heard a rumour that HMRC are back-tracking on their commitment to prosecute. He thinks there's a chance that Rangers will ride out this rough patch and we'll be left looking like mugs.'

'You don't believe that?'

'Of course not. Oh, I don't know …'

'You said the good guys always won if they were persistent,' she said, her voice rising in protest. 'Can't we find out the source of this latest rumour? It will probably lead us all the way back to Ibrox.'

'Maybe I was wrong about the good guys winning … I don't know … Izzy, my head's in a mess.'

'Hey, Sean, this isn't like you.'

'I miss you, Izzy.'

'We both knew it had to end,' she said. She hoped saying it out loud would make her feel strong and sure of herself, but all she felt was a terrible emptiness.

'I wasn't expecting to feel this way.'

'You mean it wasn't part of your plan?'

'God's having a good laugh at me right now. Look, I've been thinking. It doesn't have to end. I can come up to Glasgow regularly,' he said.

Her legs buckled from beneath her, her heart was thumping. Every fibre of her wanted to give in, to melt. She spoke before she changed her mind. 'I'm not very experienced at this, Sean, but I think a clean break is best.'

A heavy silence crackled between them.

'Is that what you want?' he asked, finally.

'Yes,' she said.

She didn't trust herself to say anything more and hung up before her resolve abandoned her. She drew a deep, shuddering breath. There was just one more call to make. Her fingers trembled as she leafed through the phone directory. The number was easy to find. It had a one page advert all to itself. The policeman picked up straight away.

***

Therapist: This is a message for Jim: Jim, hi. I got your text saying you won't be continuing our sessions. I'd much rather we discuss this face to face. D'you think you could come in as usual next week?

CHAPTER 29

It had been over a week since Izzy had made the call to the police. She lay the newspaper out on the kitchen table, slowly turning the pages, scouring for a headline, an article, even a passing reference, but there was nothing. She turned the paper back to the front and started again. Still nothing. The sports section on the back page carried a photograph of Johnny Binooti, scoring an equaliser. His face was shining and his grin was as wide as the Clyde. Life for the club, was continuing as normal. She felt dazed with disappointment.

Davy was crashing about upstairs, getting ready for school. The spare room was ominously quiet. She had scarcely spoken to Jim since their argument about Mark. In truth, it suited them both.

She picked up the kettle and went to the sink to fill it. A bottle of whisky and an empty glass sat on the draining board. There was something brazen about the way he hadn't attempted to hide them. Her disappointment deepened into a profound resignation.

'That didn't last long,' said Davy, coming up behind her. Reaching past her, he took a banana from the fruit bowl.

'We all make our choices,' she sighed, putting the bottle back in the cupboard and rinsing the glass under the tap.

'Looks like Dad's made another crap one,' he said, picking up the paper whilst munching his banana.

'Here's hoping he'll take it a bit steadier this time,' she said.

Davy kept his eyes on the paper, saying nothing.

'I know you're angry with him, but he loves you, Davy. He loves you very much,' she said.

He looked up from the paper, his brows were knitted, his eyes fierce. 'Then why doesn't he trust me about this gap year in London? I'm working hard to get my Highers, so I'll get an offer for University. I'm not the total waster he thinks I am.'

'He's worried about you, that's all,' she said.

'It's not me he needs to worry about,' said Davy, finishing off his banana and throwing the skin into the bin.

'Mark Docherty wasn't a thug you know,' said Izzy, coming over and sitting next to him. 'He was murdered in an unprovoked attack. He was a fine boy, with his whole life ahead of him.'

'OK,' said Davy, shrugging his shoulders. 'If you say so.'

'It's good you're going to London, Davy. I'll miss you, but it's important you live the best life you can. Life's a precious, wonderful thing, and it can be taken from you in an instance, just like it did with Mark,' she said, her voice trembling.

'OK. OK. No need for the inspirational lecture. Life's short. Carpe Diem. I get all that. But maybe you should take some of your own advice and live the life *you* want to live,' he said. Picking up his rucksack, he kissed her on the cheek and hurried out the door.

It was a fine, dry day with high, wispy clouds and a blustery wind. Autumn was slipping away; the trees were bare, their branches like lace against the sky. Dead leaves rustled and cracked beneath her feet, occasionally whipping up into small flurries of wistful dancing. The air was cool with a nip of ice. She needed no reminder that winter was coming, or that life was short.

The stairs in the SOS offices were scuffed and a deep chill emanated from the stone stairway. The smell of stale noodles hung in the air from the Korean restaurant next door. The reception area was deserted. An open diary lay in the centre of the desk. In it, appointments and events were marked in a round, heavy hand, like that of a child. Today was blank. Carol was standing off to her right, her thin arms crossed, watching her carefully.

'Oh, hello, Carol. I don't know if you remember me. We met at *The Shindig*. I'm Izzy Campbell, Davy's mum,' she said. She offered her hand, but Carol's arms remained crossed. She was frowning, two vertical lines deeply drawn between her eyes.

'Come in,' she said, gesturing for Izzy to go through to her office. It was a large room with high ceilings and two cream-coloured sofas. A glass jar with wild flowers sat on the table, just like the one in her flat. The memory of being there in the kitchen, with Sean, felt like a sharp stab of loss. They sat down opposite one another. Carol's stare was accusatory and as chilly as the atmosphere between them.

'Did you make a lot of money at *The Shindig*? There was a good turnout. I thought the bands were terrific.' The longer Carol's unfriendly silence lasted, the more Izzy felt compelled to fill it.

'Look, I don't know why you're here, but I don't have much time. My husband's not well at the moment.'

'I'm sorry to hear that. I hope he gets better soon.'

Carol sighed. 'You probably know he tried to commit suicide a few months ago. Everyone in Glasgow seems to know about it. Anyhow, he was doing well. We even had a wee holiday together, but someone called Crimestoppers ten days ago to say they had information about Mark's murder, that they could corroborate that he hadn't been fighting.' Carol shook her head. 'It was enough to send Connor on a bender.'

Izzy felt her knees dissolve. Her face flushed. This was unexpected, unwelcome.

'Or maybe it wasn't that. Who knows what goes on in an alcoholic's mind?' added Carol.

Izzy felt her bewilderment deepen. 'Did the police say they would re-open the case?' she asked.

Carol shrugged. 'They're reviewing the evidence. It's funny, I don't think I care anymore. For months, I raged against those boys. I've literally pulled my hair out at the thought of them getting away with a few years in a soft prison. I've kept myself so bloody busy, trying to ignore the great big hole of despair that's my life. But, now this has happened, I realise the prospect of those boys spending another ten years in prison doesn't help me. It doesn't give me peace.'

Izzy looked down at her lap, struggling to find the right words. 'My son was at the same match. I keep thinking, it could have been him that day.'

'Ah, but that's the difference between us, Izzy Campbell. It wasn't your son that day. You've still got your lovely boy. And your lovely marriage. What the hell would you know about injustice and despair?'

Izzy's body flooded with adrenaline. 'You're not the only wife whose husband is overly fond of a drink,' she blurted.

Carol's nod was almost imperceptible. 'I don't know why I'm surprised. Connor and I put on the happy family show for years.'

'Like your husband, Jim was doing well for a while. But … well … let's just say there's been a setback.'

'Well, that explains a lot,' said Carol. 'When I saw you sneaking off with my brother-in-law backstage at *The Shindig*, I couldn't believe it. I thought, "*what a daft cow.*"'

Izzy swallowed hard, gripping the side of the chair. 'I was helping Sean with his Rangers documentary, that's all.'

'Please. Don't tell me you fell for that old chestnut? I've told him a thousand times that the Scottish establishment will never let Rangers go under, no matter what dirt he digs up on them. But he doesn't listen. Maybe it's his way of trying to makes things right for Mark.' Carol's stare hardened. 'You're not his usual type, you know. He normally goes for young media graduates fresh out of college who, when they realise he'll never commit, still have time to find someone else.'

'We had a fling. That's all. Nothing serious. It's over,' admitted Izzy. Her voice sounded strained and ragged.

'Look, I'm not judging you. I understand that, when you live with a drinker, at some point, you must decide to look after yourself, but Sean's not going to be the answer to your marital problems.'

She had told herself the same thing many times, congratulating herself on having the courage and good sense to end the affair. Yet, hearing Carol say it felt devastatingly fresh.

'I'm not looking to him or anyone else to provide a parachute out of my marriage,' said Izzy.

Carol smiled. 'I love Sean dearly. Underneath all that cynical journalist crap, he's a caring, generous person. He was a fantastic uncle to Mark. He's been a rock to me, a huge help with Connor, but in the love stakes, let me tell you, he's a gold-plated, commitment-phobe.'

She felt her face colour, a rising of frustration. 'I'm not here to talk about Sean. I've had an idea that I think might help SOS,' said Izzy.

'I'm listening,' said Carol. She was leaning forward in her chair and, for the first time since their meeting began, Izzy could sense real interest.

'You and I come from two different sides of Glasgow, but we're both mothers, both united in our disgust and anger about bigotry and sectarianism. In Northern Ireland in the 70s, it was two women who started the Women in Peace Movement. Two women who stood up and became a symbol of co-operation,' said Izzy.

'You think we could be like Betty Williams and Cairan McKeon? Bloody hell. You're even crazier than I thought,' said Carol.

Izzy let the remark bounce off her. 'There's a law due to go before the Scottish Parliament on December 11, making sectarian singing illegal at football matches,' said Izzy.

Carol nodded. 'It's likely to pass, but no one gives a damn about it and that includes the police.'

'Right. The fans on both sides think the songs are harmless banter. The police have gone on record saying it will be nigh on impossible to enforce,' agreed Izzy.

'So what's your idea?' asked Carol.

'The Bill needs a human story to raise its profile – your story,' Izzy said directly. 'Even if the police don't re-open Mark's case, couldn't we use this latest Crimestoppers' information to persuade the papers to run a story? Tell everyone that you don't want revenge on those boys? It would start a conversation, at least.'

Carol's stare was venomous and Izzy's heart flipped. She wondered if she was about to be thrown out. Carol got up from her chair and began pacing restlessly. 'We could organise appearances on TV, print, radio and social media,' she said, beginning to warm up to the idea.

'So, you think it would work?' asked Izzy. The room felt warm and she wanted to take off her coat. She looked around for somewhere to put it when she saw Carol was crying. Silent tears were falling down her cheeks. Her face was gleaming. She reached out and touched her arm. Carol smiled. 'Let's get to work, then.'

***

Therapist:	I'm glad to see you, Jim. I was worried when I picked up your message about not wanting to continue our meetings.
Jim:	Thanks for all your help and everything, but I've just come to say goodbye.
Therapist:	But why? You've made such good progress. You've abstained from alcohol for over a month. That's a real achievement. I know you were feeling down when we last met, but I'm hopeful we can work through that.
Jim:	Nah. I don't think so. I've had the odd stiffener in the past few days. Not going on benders or anything but I've slipped off the wagon. I know you'll be angry when I say this, but it's a relief. I feel like my old self again. Normal.
Therapist:	It might seem like that now, but …
Jim:	(Holds up his hand) Don't say anything more. I'm off now. You look after yourself. And thank you. I mean that. Thanks for everything.

CHAPTER 30

The snow fell like flotsam from a leaden sky. Izzy looked up, the snowflakes dizzying as they fell on her face. Clouds of vapour came from her breath as she stepped into the foyer of the East Blantyre Town Hall. Built just after the war, the building, with its cast iron radiators, was struggling to make an impression on the cold. She counted six huddled figures scattered amongst the sea of chairs and could smell the damp wool rising from their coats. She shook off the worst of the snow from her shoulders and walked briskly down the aisle, smiling cheerfully at their pinched faces.

Bridget had arrived before her. She was wearing her black and white hounds tooth coat with a huge fur collar. Her bullet head, with its sleek razor cut, looked as if it had hatched from it. Her outsized glasses were black-rimmed, her lipstick red. If anyone turned up, at least they wouldn't forget her.

'It's brass monkeys in here,' said Bridget, hugging herself. 'At least I won't be making a fool of myself in front of a big crowd.'

'If there's a small turn out, it'll be a chance for you to answer their questions in detail, to connect with people on a personal level,' encouraged Izzy.

'*If* I *get* any questions,' said Bridget, gloomily.

There was now a steady trickle of people shuffling in. 'It'll be fine,' reassured Izzy.

'How's Jim these days?'

'Don't ask,' Izzy replied.

'I'm sorry, Izzy. I've been a crap friend. Once this election's over, there'll be more time to talk.'

'I keep telling myself the same thing. Once things quieten down with Jim's work, we'll sit down and talk about the booze, our marriage, our future, but I dread the thought of it. I think he feels the same. It's easier to let things drift along and muddle through.'

'Muddling through, eh? That reminds me of your Bateson essay. Did you hear Sean Docherty on the radio last night? He was talking about the Olympics,' said Bridget. 'He thinks it'll be a huge boost to the country.'

Izzy allowed herself a small, private twist of pride on hearing his name. 'The Olympics are a shameful waste of money. I wouldn't be surprised if you get a question about that.' She chewed the inside of her cheek. She hadn't intended to sound so mean-spirited.

'It was a shame about the Rangers investigation. I guess he was up against too many powerful people.'

'Oh, I wouldn't lose hope. He always said that the good guys win ... eventually.'

'Of course they do,' said Bridget, hugging her arm and giving her a kindly look that suggested Izzy was slightly delusional. Izzy couldn't blame her. Rangers were top of the league and all the talk of financial troubles had melted quicker than the snow on her coat. Jim had bragged about Verisafe being paid on time. No problemo.

'The place is filling up, thank goodness,' said Izzy brightly. A clutch of people were shuffling uncertainly at the entrance. She gave Bridget a gentle shove. 'Go on. Greet them as they come in. Work the room, girl.'

Sean. It had been months since their affair but the memory still gave her a rush of happiness. She pulled her coat around herself, snuggled down into her seat and closed her eyes, summoning that wonderful week they had together. But her memories had begun to fade, becoming more dream-like; and like a dream, she was increasingly uncertain about what was real, or if her imagination was piecing together various fragments of memory into a fairy tale. She felt a deep sense of loss that she had no photographs, letters or any other evidence of their time together. Then a painful insight: perhaps Sean also found the memory of their relationship receding; perhaps he never gave her or their Rangers project a passing thought these days.

Bridget was speaking into the microphone. 'Get your seats, folks, we're about to get started.' Izzy could hear a slight breathiness in her voice, betraying her nerves, but she looked the picture of confidence.

Bridget's speech was short but still managed to lay out the manifesto promises of the SNP: a freeze on council tax for five years (a cheer went up); increased funding for the NHS (a shout from the back: 'not enough'); more money for apprentices and a commitment to break the money-fixing cartels of the big energy providers. She made a brief mention of the passing of the anti-sectarian legislation and gave Izzy a wink. But the biggest cheer was for the up-coming referendum on Scottish Independence. Bridget finished with her rallying cry: 'It's time for change.'

Izzy got out her notebook, ready to note down any questions, pleased to be doing something practical. A man at the back stood up: 'My granny can no longer cope at home on her own. What assurances can the SNP give she won't have to use up her savings, or sell her home, to pay for care?'

Bridget's eyes danced. 'Your granny will be in safe hands with us. We'll guarantee free care for all our elderly citizens, irrespective of their financial situation. It's a sign of a civilised society when we look after our elderly with total respect and the highest quality of care.'

The man sat down, looking satisfied. That provoked a flurry of other questions relating mainly to people's personal lives, their jobs, the tax system. One or two asked about debt problems and Izzy took a special interest in their faces; it's possible she'd see them later at the Bureau.

'We've time for one last question,' announced Bridget.

Izzy was on the point of putting her notebook in her bag when she heard a familiar voice: 'I work as a volunteer at the Citizens Advice Bureau.'

Alan was on his feet. He was wearing a puffer jacket that was so bulky he probably took up two chairs. She was surprised she hadn't spotted him earlier. 'There are parts of Blantyre East where we've some of the highest levels of debt, drug and alcohol abuse in the western world. What do the SNP plan to do to stop this spiralling descent into poverty?'

There was a murmur of approval, an appreciation of the gravity of the question. 'Well,' said Bridget slowly, 'the question I ask myself is, what have Labour done in all the years they've been in power to change that? The answer is, "clearly not enough." So, let me paint you a different future. Imagine if Scotland was in control of its destiny, if the revenue from North Sea oil flowed into our coffers and not Westminster's … if we could raise more income tax, particularly from higher rate taxpayers … We would have the resources, the will and the expertise to reverse those shameful statistics. We would be a proud nation again.'

The audience were on their feet. Stamping. Clapping. Cheering. Someone started singing *Flower of Scotland*. Bridget joined in, singing into the microphone and encouraging the rest of the audience to sing with her. Izzy shoved her notebook in her briefcase and stood up and sang along with the rest of them.

O flower of Scotland
When will we see yer like again
That fought and died for
Yer wee bit hill and glen
And stood against him
Proud Edward's army
And sent him hameward
Tae think again

One or two voices kept singing the next verse but a burst of applause drowned them out. Izzy wasn't sure if the applause was for Bridget or for the idea that Scotland could reverse years of supposed oppression. It struck her that *Flower of Scotland*, with its anti-English sentiment, was as much sectarian in spirit as the football songs that had just been outlawed. She kept these thoughts to herself. It was unlikely that anyone in their right mind would call for the unofficial Scottish National Anthem to be banned, even if it was on the bigoted side.

The audience seemed unwilling to disperse. A large crowd was clustering around Bridget, vying for her attention. Izzy picked up her briefcase and was walking towards them when she was struck by a thought; the election was in a week's time and Bridget was going to win – she was going to be the next SNP Scottish Member of Parliament for Blantyre East. Was that another of her fairy tales? She shook her head. No. She was certain.

***

Jim:

I love my wife, you know. She's beautiful and clever. I mean, she's as clever as fuck. She's studying for a degree in Social Sciences. What about that?

Barman:

You're a lucky man.

Jim:

(Stares into mid space) I don't deserve her.

Barman:

You should go home to her. Looks like there'll be more snow. The boss is talking about closing early.

Jim:

She's had to put up with an awfy lot from me, you know.

Barman:

Give her a call. Maybe she'll come and collect you.

Jim:

I'm going to make it all up to her. I'm going to take her to Australia on holiday. Just the two of us.

Barman:

Sounds like a better plan than staying here, pal.

CHAPTER 31

Izzy didn't see him at first. He was standing in the shadows by the door. He wasn't wearing a coat and his arms were wrapped round his body, shivering and swaying from side to side. She was consumed by a terrible, familiar disappointment and reminded herself that she was not responsible for Jim's behaviour, yet despair had already begun seeping into every pore. The town hall was still full of people and, thankfully, Bridget was still surrounded by her new-found fan club.

'Where's your coat?' she asked. He looked at her with a glazed expression. He's probably left it in a pub, she thought. She took him by the arm and guided him to a seat by a radiator. His fingers felt cold and blubbery and she began to rub them to get the circulation going.

'It's summer in Australia, you know,' he said.

She looked up and frowned.

'What about it, Izzy? A wee holiday Down Under. Just you and me. Wouldn't that be lovely?'

She stopped rubbing his hands and looked him straight in the face. 'What's the matter, Jim?'

'Maybe Australia's a bit too far away. What about Italy, Izzy? You've always wanted to go to Venice. It could be our second honeymoon.'

She smiled indulgently. 'We never had a first honeymoon. Two nights in your Uncle Andy's caravan at Ardrossan when it rained non-stop with a leak above our bed, doesn't count.'

Jim looked down at his feet. 'I don't know why I'm talking about holidays. I'm in trouble, lass.'

'What kind of trouble?' Her mind was racing, full of terrible scenarios, all of them dreadful; all of them possible.

'The club's hit a spot of bother. They've asked me to hold off invoicing them for last month's work. A temporary cash flow problem. I haven't got enough cash to cover the wages.' He was blinking, trying to focus on her face. He looked on the verge of tears.

'Have you spoken to the bank?'

'That bunch of bawbags?'

She sighed and summoned her patience. 'What about a loan? They said they'd lend you three hundred thousand months ago, and that was before you were getting regular income from the club.'

'Nae chance. I've already spent it,' he said. His voice was becoming hoarser, more desperate.

'What d'you mean, spent it?'

'The three hundred thousand; it's gone, spent, vamoosed,' he slurred, shrugging hopelessly.

Her dwindling patience evaporated. 'But you promised me you would give it back. You promised, Jim,' she said, in a voice loud enough to make a few people turn in their direction.

'I need the money now,' he cried. He grabbed her arm, his fingers pressing painfully into her flesh. She pulled away from him. Bridget was looking towards them; her sharp stare was fixed on them both.

'Please, Jim. People are watching,' she whispered, rubbing her forearms. She pulled down the sleeves of her coat to hide the red marks where his fingers had been.

'As soon as you give me that passbook, I'm out of here,' he said, hissing under his breath. Small pearls of foam had gathered at the corners of his mouth.

'What are you talking about? What passbook?' she whispered. Fingers of fear were gripping her heart.

'Don't play dumb with me, Izzy.'

She felt the strength drain from her legs. 'You mean the £10,000 Mum and Dad left me?'

'It would only be for a few weeks. The club's promised me they'll pay double next month, plus interest.'

'Promises from Rangers? I'd be more inclined to believe the exact opposite,' she said bitterly, remembering Sean conclusion from when they'd met at the Necropolis. She could hear her dead parents' voices and her own voice of common sense clamouring in her head, telling her not to give the money to Jim; that it was their only lifeline. Jim looked wretched, as if the voices inside his head were telling him the same thing.

'If you want me to beg, Izzy, I'll beg. I'll get down on my hands and knees right this minute if that's what it takes,' he said. Desperation was clouding his eyes.

'There's no need to do that,' she said quietly.

Jim grabbed her hands, his eyes swimming with tears. 'I promise you, Izzy. I'll pay you back. And once we're through this bad patch, I'm taking you on that holiday to Australia. No arguments.'

'Just go, Jim,' she said. She barely had the strength to speak.

'No. Honestly, Izzy, I promise,' he assured her.

'If you want to promise me anything, promise you'll go back to your counsellor. Get some help with the drinking. And when this election is over, you and I need to sit down and talk, Jim. I mean, really talk.'

'I love you so much, Izzy,' he said crushing her in an embrace.

***

Therapist: Jim? I wasn't expecting you. I'm sorry but I've got another appointment.

Jim: Nae problem. I told her I would come and see you and now I have. Box ticked.

Therapist: Jim, I can see you've been drinking.

Jim: That's fucking perceptive of you.

Therapist: Please come back when you're sober. We can talk then.

Jim: I don't understand why everyone thinks we can solve anything by talking.

CHAPTER 32

Excitement drifted up from the counting floor like rising heat. From Izzy's position on the visitors' balcony, she had a birds-eye view of the crowds of people swarming below. A stage had been rigged at the front, a single microphone marking the spot where the result would be announced and where the winning Member of Parliament would make their speech. It was after midnight, and Izzy felt as excited as a child who had been allowed to stay up past their bedtime.

She had put Jim and all their problems in a far corner of her mind, determined to keep them there until tomorrow. But, for now, she wanted to savour the atmosphere, to soak in the way the air fizzed with tension. The last time she had felt this level of anticipation was … well … it felt like a lifetime ago.

'I thought you could use a coffee,' said Carol, handing her a paper cup. She had been in the media centre next door, taking part in a programme about the future of Scottish politics. One of a series of fill-in slots whilst they waited for the result to be announced.

'How was the interview?' asked Izzy.

'They only wanted to talk about Scottish Independence. No one's interested in anti-sectarian legislation. I gave Lothian Police video evidence at the last Rangers versus Hibs match, of supporters singing those disgusting songs. What do you think they said?'

'Video phone evidence isn't admissible in court,' replied Izzy. She'd heard the story many times before.

'Bastards,' said Carol.

Izzy smiled. 'So let's not waste another second talking about them. The atmosphere down there's electric.'

She leaned over the balustrade, captivated by the sense of anticipation, the knowledge that she might be witnessing history.

'Sean's coming back to Glasgow tonight,' said Carol casually.

Izzy's body numbed, as if it had been over-charged and then short-circuited. She sipped her coffee, the heat flowing down her throat, but her mind remained frozen.

'He's covering the election results,' added Carol.

Izzy looked wildly around the visitors' gallery. Was he already here?

'He'll be at the Election Party after the results are announced. He says he needs to speak to you,' said Carol.

'I wonder why?' she asked. Her heart was doing somersaults in her chest. She pushed her hair behind her ears and smoothed down the sleeves of her jacket, letting out a long breath to stem the onslaught of nerves that was about to overwhelm her.

'If you don't want to speak to him, I'll tell him to bugger off,' said Carol

'It's fine, I don't mind,' she said, trying to sound casual, though her heart was beating painfully.

Officials were gathering by the stage, wearing their high-viz jackets. In another context, they could have been mistaken for council road workers. TV cameras were being wheeled in, presenters talked urgently into microphones. Bridget looked up towards the gallery and Izzy waved and smiled back. Bridget's face was rigid with a crazy, joyful terror.

***

Izzy stood beside the canapés, where she had a good view of the party. The room was rammed and there was a constant flow of people coming and going. She would need to keep her wits about her if she was to spot him. Someone had given her a glass of champagne and she stood stroking the stem, her pulse pounding. She hadn't expected to like it, but the way the sweet flavour burst inside her mouth and how the bubbles tickled her nose, was a pleasant revelation. She took another sip, surprised to see her glass filled to the brim. She couldn't remember it being topped up.

'Hey, Izzy.'

Her heart stopped, yet she was still breathing. How was that possible? He looked just as she remembered him. Wildly attractive. 'Hey, you,' she croaked, clearing her throat to recover her composure.

'It's good to see you. You look well.' She felt a ruffle of irritation. Did he think she would just crumble, just lay down and die? The lyrics of the song continued in her head ... *No. No. Not I, I will survive.*

'Can we go somewhere quieter to talk?' he asked.

'Sure,' she said lightly, 'plenty of quiet places to talk here.' She laughed. How witty she could be. He was taking her by the arm through the throng of people to a corner by the door. God, he smelled like a dream.

'Bridget smashed it didn't she,' she said, lifting her glass of champagne to the sky and taking another swallow, wrinkling her nose, a happy giggle escaping from her.

'Overturning a Labour majority by twelve thousand votes? Yes, I would say she definitely smashed it,' he agreed.

She squeezed his arm. Having him so close had cocooned her in a joy that felt impregnable. 'She looked beautiful when she gave her speech.'

'She's not a conventionally beautiful woman,' he said, choosing his words carefully, 'but I know what you mean.'

'She's like a caterpillar that's turned into a butterfly. Or more like a larva turning into a dragonfly because it's taken her a few years to metamorphose herself.' Her mouth struggled with the word "metamorphose". It came out like a long mumble of m's. She made a mental note to herself: *Do not use clever words.*

'Butterflies and dragonflies have short lives. Scotland needs to think long term if it wants to be an independent nation,' he said. His expression had become serious.

A laugh burst out from her. 'No long faces allowed tonight. This is a party. We won, remember.'

'Izzy, listen to me,' he stressed, his expression business-like, determined. 'Rangers is going bust. It'll be announced in the papers any day now.'

'Oh Sean, not that old chestnut,' she said, laughing. 'Now, promise me, no more talk of the Billy Boys, OK?'

'Izzy, maybe you should have some fresh air,' he suggested, gently turning her round and opening the back door. Cold blasted her in her face. 'Woah,' she said reeling backwards.

Her mouth flooded with saliva, champagne was rising from her stomach. The first wave of nausea hit the back of her throat. She pushed him away and staggered out to the pavement. She tried breathing deeply, hoping it would steady her. Instead, it made the world swing wildly around her.

'Oh God,' she cried, bending over, feeling the first uncontrollable retch, smelling the vomit as it hit the ground.

She was vaguely aware of someone holding her hair back from her face. A quiet voice reassuring her: 'It's OK.'

She walked a few metres away and leaned against a wall. The smell of sickness was in her hair and her clothes. She was clutching a hanky in her hand but had no idea how it got there. She felt dazed and strangely indifferent. Who cares what people thought of her?

'I couldn't find your coat and bag. Carol said she would bring them back to the flat,' said a voice close by. She felt a coat being draped around her shoulders. It was way too big for her and enveloped her in the smell of ozone with a touch of citrus; she could even hear the sound of waves crashing to the shore. Sean was looking at her with concern. She lifted her face to be kissed but moving her head brought on another wave of dizziness.

'C'mon,' he said taking her hand.

'Where are you taking me?' she asked, though she didn't care. She was enjoying this game. He could take her anywhere he wanted.

She was woken by an incessant buzzing. A fly was close to her ear. Opening her eyes, she blinked in the daylight. She was lying in a bed and the room looked familiar, though she couldn't place it. Gingerly, she turned her head. Someone was lying in the bed beside her. Her heart and head were drumming as she took a longer look. Sean was curled up in a foetal position, fast asleep. She looked under the bedclothes. She was in her underwear, though she had no memory of taking off her dress. Sean was naked except for his boxer shorts. She lay back on the pillow, slowly remembering the events of the night before. Getting drunk, being sick. Her mouth felt so dry it was as if it belonged to someone else. The drumming in her head was getting louder. She closed her eyes, expecting shame to consume her. Instead, she felt a surge of happiness so huge she wanted to bounce on the bed like a child on a trampoline.

She turned to look at his back, astonished at how the bones of his vertebrae paled the skin at points. She didn't want to wake him, she only wanted to smell his skin and feel the heat of his body. He rolled over and smiled, his eyes were the colour of jade. He lifted himself up on one elbow. His hair was dishevelled and he was smiling sheepishly. They had never woken up together in the morning before and she felt recklessly happy.

His phone began to ring.

'Do you have to answer that?' she asked teasingly, stroking his shoulder.

He squinted at his phone. 'It's Bridget. It'll be for you,' he said. 'I'll make us some coffee.' He slipped out of his bed. His body was lean and beautiful. It was hard to concentrate on what Bridget was saying.

'Izzy? Thank God.'

'Hey, congratulations on being MSP for Blantyre East,' said Izzy, 'but why are you calling me on Sean's phone?'

'Because yours is going to voicemail,' Bridget said.

'What?' asked Izzy looking around for her handbag. Her coat. Her phone. They were nowhere to be seen.

'Jim's in a total panic. When he couldn't get through to you, he called me. You were meant to be staying with me, remember?'

'I'm beginning to remember …'

'I said you'd popped out to buy us a coffee, so you need to call him back right away. He sounded desperate.'

Izzy leapt out of bed and pulled on her dress. Sean was in the kitchen. He had put on the TV and was watching the news, a satellite sports channel with a ticker tape display scrolling along the bottom of the screen in a continuous loop.

Rangers Football Club go into administration. Future of the club uncertain.

The presenter was beside himself with excitement. 'This is a colossal story for a colossal club. The current Champions of the Scottish Premier League have gone under. Rangers is a massive club and this news will have massive ramifications.'

Stunned, she turned to Sean. 'I have to call Jim.'

He held out her handbag and coat. 'Call me if I can help.'

***

Celtic supporter 1:	Thanks, Jimmy, for the pint. You may be a Hun, but you're an exceptionally good Hun. Now Rangers are finished, come on over to us.
Jim:	Over to the dark side?
Celtic supporter 1:	The green side.
Celtic Supporter 2:	Hey, Jimmy the Hun, d'you know what size bra your wife wears?
Jim:	That's none of your business, pal.
Celtic supporter 2:	Two handfuls. Or maybe that's the size of her arse.
Jim:	That's fucking outrageous.

Celtic Supporter 2: Who's calling who fucking outrageous?

Celtic Supporter 1: C'mon lads. Settle down. Let's get another round in.

CHAPTER 33

Izzy's taxi was stuck in a queue of traffic deep in the Clyde Tunnel. She leaned forward to see if anything was moving, but the cars were at a standstill, a long string of brake lights twinkling prettily ahead. She thought about the enormous weight of water pressing down on the tunnel walls. It would take the smallest of cracks for the pressure to force a fissure wide enough for the river to come rushing through. Trapped in the back seat of this taxi, she wouldn't stand a chance. Her head throbbed, her eyes felt sore and crusty. A fluttering of panic was beginning in her chest. Jim hadn't answered his phone and no-one knew where he was. The idea that he might do something stupid had wormed its way into her brain and had stayed there. She had to find him.

The club had put out a message on social media for fans to go to Ibrox, where it was rumoured that the Chairman would be speaking. She had spoken to Davy and they'd agreed to meet there to look for Jim. She could hear concern in Davy's voice, too, despite his attempt at indifference.

'Are you a Rangers fan?' Izzy asked the taxi driver, thinking a bit of small talk might help quell her rising anxiety.

'A two-horse race between Celtic and Rangers? Totally tedious.'

'It looks like it might be a one-horse race from now on,' said Izzy, sadly.

'Then Celtic will have to take up show-jumping,' said the taxi driver, laughing. He was still chuckling when she got out of the taxi half an hour later.

There was a steady trickle of fans making their way to the main entrance, their faces blank with shock, bewilderment; stunned to the point of listlessness. Barriers had been put up, like it was a match day, and small knots of policemen in high-viz jackets stood about as if waiting for instructions. There was a film crew collaring anyone who looked as though they would speak to them. She spotted Davy standing by one of the burger vans.

'I don't think Dad's here,' he said.

The smell of fried food turned her fragile stomach. 'When did you last see him?' she asked.

'We watched the election results together at home last night. After Bridget's speech, I went to bed. I got up about 11 this morning, but he was gone. I didn't think much about it until you called. Then I switched on the TV and realised all this had happened.' He finished off his burger, wiping his greasy fingers on the side of his jeans.

'Let's try Verisafe. He might be in the office,' suggested Izzy.

'OK. But I think we'd be better off looking in the pubs,' said Davy.

Bill was sitting at Jim's desk; the other offices were deserted. It looked like a bank holiday or a scene from a post-apocalyptic film. 'I've sent everyone home,' explained Bill. 'No one's seen Jim all day,' he added sadly. Then, smiling, 'Try not to worry, Izzy. He's probably drowning his sorrows in a pub somewhere. I've asked a couple of the fitters to look for him. Best for us to go home in case he turns up there.'

They rode in Bill's car in silence. Davy was looking out of the window, his earphones in, caught in the trance of his music. Bill was driving steadily, his eyes fixed on the road. Izzy's head still ached and a mild nausea persisted in her stomach. Thoughts rushed round her head. It was strange to have so much energy in her brain when her body felt sluggish, as if she was moving underwater. One clear thought stood out. The good guys might have won when it came to Rangers, but that victory meant that Jim had lost. It terrified her to think what that might do to him.

She knew as soon as she opened the door that the house was empty. She put on the TV and the three of them stood listening to the satellite sports channel; the ticker tape was still going round and round, repeating that the club had gone into administration, as if it couldn't quite believe it itself.

'I'll make something to eat,' she said.

Davy took out his earphones. 'He'll turn up eventually, Mum. He always does.'

The three of them sat in the kitchen eating a shepherd's pie that she had taken out of the freezer and heated up in the oven. She pushed around a pile of mash and grey looking meat with her fork, making a mental note never to cook this type of food again. Davy and Bill had finished and were eyeing up her plate. She divided it between them.

She checked her phone for the hundredth time. Still nothing from Jim. She scrolled down Sean's messages; he was asking if she was OK, if she needed anything from him. In his last text, he offered to go looking in the pubs for Jim, but she knew he couldn't help. Whatever Jim was up to, it had nothing to do with Sean.

'Everyone was so shocked,' said Davy as he licked the last remains of potato from his fork. 'Some of the fans were actually crying, big men with shaved heads, tattoos and beer bellies, crying like children. It's like a death to them, I suppose. A sudden death. They knew nothing about the club's troubles.'

'Selective hearing,' replied Bill. 'There was plenty of warning. It's just that no one wanted to hear it. Your mum saw all this coming, but no one listened to her.'

Izzy opened the freezer. There was a supermarket cheesecake at the back, covered in a thin coating of ice. The thought of its cloying sweetness brought bile to the back of in her throat. She popped it in the microwave to defrost it and cut two large slices. Bill and Davy tucked in as if they hadn't seen food all day.

'Delicious, Izzy. Did you make this yourself?' asked Bill.

'So, how come you know so much about Rangers, Mum?' asked Davy.

'I did a bit of research when we went to The Chairman's Club,' she said.

'She did a lot more than that,' said Bill. 'She knew all about the management buyout and the club's finances. Your mum's got a journalist friend who was working on a documentary about the Rangers at the time. Isn't that right, Izzy? They wanted Jack Marshall, the venture capitalist, to give an interview reassuring people there was money to pay their debts.'

'Who's this journalist friend?' asked Davy.

Izzy gazed out of the window. 'No one you know,' she said wearily.

Davy and Bill were hacking at the remains of the cheesecake, shifting the last crumbly wedges onto their plates. 'So, Bill, how does this affect Verisafe?' asked Davy.

It was a reasonable question. She was curious about Bill's response herself.

Bill looked down at his feet. 'We don't know the full extent of the club's troubles. Their petition for administration takes five days to go through the Court of Session.'

He was hedging, fluffing.

'What's the worst case scenario?' asked Davy.

'Let's not go there until we have to,' Bill cautioned, taking his time to carefully put his spoon and fork together on his plate. 'I thought my Annie made a good cheesecake, but this beats hers hands down, Izzy.'

Davy and Izzy exchanged a glance. Things looked bad.

'I need to go, Mum,' said Davy. 'Band practice starts at nine. You'll be all right on your own?'

'I'll stay with your mum until your dad gets back,' Bill offered.

Bill and Izzy sat in silence after Davy left. She poured him a cup of tea. He looked disappointed. He probably would have preferred a whisky.

'I didn't like to say too much in front of the lad,' started Bill, 'but we're in trouble.'

'You'll never make a poker player,' she answered.

'This will finish us. Thirty-seven employees. Mostly youngsters with families. I don't know how we're going to tell them.'

Izzy got up and looked out the window. 'Where the hell are you, Jim?' she asked the night air.

'He'll turn up soon and wonder why we worried,' soothed Bill.

The doorbell chimed. It sounded like a death knell.

'I told you,' said Bill.

'I'll go,' she said, her feet moving without seeming to touch the ground. She hardly knew what she feared most – a policeman telling her Jim was dead, or Jim himself, dead drunk. She opened the door. The person she least expected was standing in front of her.

***

Jim:	Say that again, you fucking Fenian shite.
Celtic supporter 2:	You followed the Billy Boys right down the fucking drain.
Jim:	Go to fucking hell.
Celtic Supporter 2:	That's the only fucking place that's going to welcome you, Hun Scum.
Jim:	We're not fucking finished. We don't do walking way.

Celtic Supporter 1:	Now now, lads. Can we have a bit of calm round here?
Jim:	No fucking surrender! Hear me? No fucking surrender!
Celtic Supporter 2:	Yer a sad wee fucking cunt.

CHAPTER 34

Sean was breathing heavily, as if he'd been running. He stood back and Izzy saw the slumped figure lying on the doorstep.

'Bill,' she shouted, 'come and help.'

The two men lifted Jim's arms over their shoulders and dragged him into the hallway. He was wearing his office suit with his shirt hanging out at the back, his feet trailing. She wasn't sure if he was conscious. They laid him in an armchair in the lounge and Izzy closed the curtains. Curiously, she was relieved. A drunk Jim she could cope with.

'Bill, this is Sean Docherty. The journalist friend I told you about,' said Izzy.

Bill looked at Sean suspiciously. 'Thanks for your help, Sean,' he said.

'Where was he?' asked Izzy. Jim was out cold, a bruise forming over his left eye.

'The Gallus Bar in Parkhead,' said Sean, 'surrounded by celebrating Celtic fans. They'd been plying him with drinks all afternoon. It wasn't looking so friendly by the time I got there.'

'What made you look for him there?' asked Bill, warily.

'A mate of mine runs the pub. Called me to tell say they had stray Hun who was drowning his sorrows. Thought it would make a good story, I suppose.'

'A stray Hun, eh?' said Bill, his hostility now obvious. He turned to Izzy in bewilderment, wondering, no doubt, what she was doing with friends like him.

Jim stirred in his seat, 'I'm awfy sorry. I'm awfy, awfy sorry. That's all I can say,' he slurred, flailing his arms. Izzy went up close to him, his breath was pure alcohol. He was struggling to keep his eyes open, his pupils were dilated and his mouth loose. His head fell onto his chest as if his neck had snapped. He was frowning, as if he was trying to work out what had slayed him.

'I'll make some black coffee,' she offered.

'Don't go, Izzy darling, don't leave me. You promised me you'd never leave me,' he wailed. His eyes were now wide open, concentrated on her, gripping her arm. She turned and caught Sean's eye; his expression was inscrutable.

'Just getting some coffee,' she said, extricating herself from Jim. He stroked the back of his neck then rubbed his face vigorously, as if washing himself awake. 'Who the fuck are you?' he demanded as he tried to sit upright, pointing at Sean.

'This is Sean Docherty. He brought you home from the Gallus bar,' said Bill, pulling Jim up to a seated position on the chair.

'Never heard of him,' said Jim, slumping back into the chair, as if the effort to speak had exhausted him. 'Sean Docherty? What sort of name is that? A Fenian bastard? In my house?' An animal-like energy filled him and he hurled himself at Sean before Izzy or Bill had time to react. 'No fucking surrender!' he shouted. His bear-like figure was smothering Sean's as he tried to punch and kick him, but the blows were mis-timed and ineffectual. Sean pushed him away as easily as if he had accidentally bumped into him. Jim fell, landing heavily on his back, spread-eagled on the carpet.

'C'mon, big man, get yersel' up,' said Bill, heaving him to his feet and back onto the chair.

Jim's eyes burned with anguish. 'What's going on, Izzy? Why's that wee shite still here?'

'No need for talk like that, Jim,' said Bill. 'Izzy, get him a coffee.'

'I don't want a fucking cup of coffee. I want him out of my house,' he said. He seemed suddenly sober.

'I'll go,' said Sean.

She felt assailed by helplessness, her loyalties utterly divided. Bill and Jim were staring at her, as if she had become unrecognisable. Sean was walking out of the room. A voice in her head was shouting: *choose happiness*. She felt reckless with selfishness.

'Wait, Sean,' she said, biting her lip. 'I'm coming with you.'

She turned to get her coat just as Jim launched himself at her, punching her in the face. She felt her head jerk sideways and then she was falling … falling. He grabbed a handful of hair at the nape of her neck and pulled it so hard, it felt like her scalp was separating from her head. She tried to cover her face with her arms but she could feel more punches landing on her throat, her neck … the small indentation between her collarbone. Bill and Sean must have hauled him off, because, suddenly, it was over.

She got to her feet, breathing heavily, too shocked to cry or feel pain. She touched the back of her head and felt a small bald spot where her hair had been ripped out. She was leaning into Sean, grateful for the support. Bill was staring at her, his face ashen, his lips parted in horror.

***

Jim: My life's a fucking mess. I assaulted my wife, I've alienated my son, I bankrupted my business, even my bloody football team went under. One big fucking mess.

Neil: It must seem like that to you now, but

324

we're glad you decided to sign up for the programme.

Jim: I'm beyond help, pal.

Neil: We've all felt like that at some point on our journey.

Jim: What journey have you been on?

Neil: We're all recovering alcoholics here at the Whitehill Centre. I went through the same programme you're now embarking on, five years ago.

Jim: I'm not even sure what I've signed up for. It was my counsellor who said I should give it a try.

Neil: This is a twelve-week residential rehab programme based on the principles of AA.

Jim: AA. Alcoholics Anonymous? Isn't that some sort of religious sect?

Neil: No, but we do believe there is a higher power than ourselves.

Jim: Christ. I'm sorry, pal, but I'm not religious. I mean, I support Rangers, so I'm definitely Protestant, but I don't believe in God or any of that mumbo jumbo.

CHAPTER 35

Tucked away in the quiet border town of Galashiels, thirty miles south of Edinburgh, the handsome villa that housed the Whitehill Centre looked like it might once have belonged to a prosperous mill owner. It was only when Izzy got up close that she saw the modern extension at the back, with the unmistakeable look of a hospital wing.

Davy dawdled beside her, kicking the gravel on the driveway. She took his arm and steered him inside. The waiting room was in the old part of the house, wood-panelled and dark. An oak desk was covered with pamphlets offering information about reflexology, yoga and meditation. There was a scattering of wide-winged armchairs on a dark tartan carpet, the fibres of which were permeated with the smell of mince and potatoes. Izzy and Davy stood uncertainly, waiting for someone to appear. She felt as nervous as she had been on her first day at school, waiting to meet the headmaster.

'Izzy? Davy? I'm Neil, how are you?' Neil was in his late thirties, plump-cheeked and almost completely bald. He was shorter than both Izzy and Davy, and dumpy looking in his black, collarless jacket and matching trousers. He held out his hand. His fingers were short and fleshy, reddened at the knuckles, as if they had been in hot water too long. He had an aura of calmness, verging on the serene. 'Let's take a seat over here, shall we, and have a chat,' he said.

Izzy sat down, feeling some of Neil's calmness spread itself to her. She glanced out through the rain-smeared windows to a sweep of lawn and a copse beyond it. The grounds were immaculate, a lovely setting for troubled minds.

'Would you like some mint tea, fresh from the garden?' asked Neil. Izzy shook her head. 'What about you, Davy?' Davy shook his head, too.

'Right, well, I'll get to the heart of things. As you know, Jim admitted himself voluntarily last week, on the advice of his counsellor in Glasgow.'

'Good for him,' muttered Davy.

Neil ignored Davy's sarcastic tone and pressed his short fingers together in a steeple gesture. 'At Whitehill, we believe the only path to recovery is one of total abstinence. Jim has agreed to embark on a twelve-week programme. During this time, we discourage visits from family and friends. Our intention is to give Jim all the support he'll need to succeed. We will, of course, keep you regularly informed of progress.'

'Twelve weeks?' said Izzy. 'That's a long time.'

'Some of our clients need even longer than that,' added Neil.

'Can we see him today?' asked Izzy.

'He's expecting you,' said Neil gently.

'You go,' said Davy, 'I'll wait here.' He picked up a *Scottish Field* magazine and pretended to be fascinated by a photograph of a stag posing majestically in a glen.

'C'mon, Davy. This may be the last time you see your dad in three months,' she said.

Davy shrugged and returned his attention to the magazine. She wished it was as simple as Davy thought: a wronged wife, physically abused by her alcoholic husband. Izzy hadn't told him she had been unfaithful. She wondered if telling him now would be a good idea, but Neil's optimistic face broke her train of thought. 'He's in the garden.'

She felt nervous. She hadn't seen Jim since the night of the fight. Would he be angry or full of contrition? She felt a muddle of emotions herself; furious about his drinking, repelled by his violence towards her and, at the same time, ashamed at having provoked it. She inhaled the sweet smell of newly cut grass and hoped the beauty of the place would calm her jittery heart.

Jim was sitting on a bench at the top of the lawn. His back was straight, his hair glistened with gel, his jaw was freshly shaved and his black moustache neatly trimmed. Only, something about his eyes was different. It took her a moment to realise what it was. There was no inner light, he looked defeated. Pity welled inside her.

'I didn't think you'd come,' he said.

'Of course I'd come,' she said, picking up his hand, stroking those familiar blunt fingers. 'How are you?' she asked, before gently putting his hand back in his lap where it stayed, still and lifeless.

'Has Bill told you?'

'Yes,' she said.

'The house will have to go as well.' He was barely able to finish the sentence.

'I've spoken with the building society. We don't have to move out for three months.'

'You loved that house so much ...'

'Davy will be going to London soon. I hope to get a job in Edinburgh after I graduate. We'll both be fine,' she said. Her speech had the poise that came from frequent rehearsal.

'I'm so sorry, Izzy,' he said, looking up at her. The whites of his eyes were yellowed with jaundice. She dreaded seeing a flicker of hope in them, dreaded him thinking there was a possibility of reconciliation. The silence between them grew.

'I know our marriage is over. I knew that the moment I took my hand to you. I'll never forgive myself for that.' His voice was hoarse with emotion. 'I don't deserve you, Izzy. I've lost you and I've only got myself to blame.'

She sat quietly for a moment. 'Don't talk about blame, Jim. It doesn't help. We've both done things that were wrong. We've still got Davy to think about.'

He laughed a dry, hopeless laugh. 'Davy will never want to see me again.'

She patted his hand, noticing for the first time that the skin around his nails was bitten raw.

'I suppose you're still with that journalist fellow ... he must be having a field day with all this Rangers scandal ... I suppose he's going to write a book about it ... has he asked you to write it with him? Sorry, Izzy ... you don't have to answer that. I've no right to ask about your life. There's just one thing I must say to you, though ...'

She closed her eyes, expecting some thinly-veiled warning about the reliability of catholic journalists.

'... Tell Davy I love him. Tell him I'm sorry I wasn't a better dad to him.'

His head dropped onto his chest, his shoulders trembling as he sobbed. Her throat ached with a huge, howling sadness at seeing him so reduced, so despairing. 'Get yourself better, Jim. Davy loves you. He'll come around in time. I'm sure of it.' She chewed her lip. It was a lie. She wasn't sure that Davy would forgive his father, but, in that moment, she wanted to believe it more than anything else in the world.

He turned away and dried his face on his handkerchief. She reached out to touch his arm, but he waved her away, as if he was impatient for her to leave. Black clouds raced across the sky, the air darkened and the first spots of rain began to fall.

***

Jim: I'm not sleeping. I'm having terrible dreams.

Neil: Tell me about them.

Jim: I'd rather have some sleeping pills.

Neil: Carl Jung, the psychologist, thought dreams are like hidden doors into the most secret recesses of the soul.

Jim: He sounds like a bampot.

Neil: Maybe these dreams are serving a purpose?

Jim: Now *you're* sounding like a bampot. In my
                       dream, I see that dead boy's face. That white
                       face and those dark brown eyes pleading
                       with me. Then, sometimes it blurs into
                       Davy's face. I wake up in a panic thinking
                       they're both dead, and I've stood by and
                       done nothing to prevent it from happening.

Neil: How does that make you feel? Guilty?
                       Powerless? Sad?

Jim: All of that.

Neil: You think you could have done more to
                       save the Celtic boy's life? That you could
                       have been a better father to your son?

Jim: (Crying) Yes. Yes.

Neil: That's a terrible burden to carry.

Jim: It's like a physical pain. I'm so alone. (Blows
                       nose, looks out to space)

Neil: Yet, you're not alone. You're here,
                       surrounded by people who care for you
                       and, of course, there's a force bigger than
                       all of us …

Jim: Oh yeah. A God who sends me dreams so
          I can feel shite about myself.

Neil: Or maybe a God asking you to face up to
          the fact that you're normal; a flawed human
          being? Maybe a God that's ready to forgive
          you if you can forgive yourself?

CHAPTER 36

The Scottish Parliament looked like a jumble of blocks a child had knocked over. Bridget pushed the door open and Izzy found herself in a wide space of polished marble, granite and oak-panelled walls. Light flooded in from above and below through unexpected nooks and crannies. It was if they had landed in a fantasy film set. They looked at each other in wonder.

'The old part of the building is Queensberry House. It was a lunatic asylum in the 19th century, and the offices were converted from a brothel. You couldn't make it up,' said Bridget, happily.

The debating chamber was ultra-modern and looked like a cross between a theatre and an art installation. Hull-shaped forms hung from the ceiling and the windows were framed by tubular pipes that looked like a giant game of pick-up sticks. They climbed the stairs to the back row, just like they did when they attended lectures at Glasgow Tech.

'Jim must be nearly finished with his programme at the Whitehill Centre. How are things between you two?' asked Bridget.

'Jim's doing well but he's staying on at the Whitehill for another three months. We exchange the odd text and email; there's no hard feelings between us, but our marriage is over.'

'So, the way is cleared for the mice to play?'

'Sean's busy writing his book about Rangers. He's called it "The Downfall Dossier", after that file I used to carry around with me.'

'How bloody touching,' replied Bridget. 'I hope he does more than that. Make sure you get proper credit, Izzy.'

'He's having to go back to London for the summer. He's got a job covering the London Olympics.'

'And you're OK with that?'

'Absolutely not. The London Olympics are a scandalous waste of tax payer's money.'

Bridget fixed her with one of her penetrating stares. Izzy did her best to match it. 'Of course I wish he wasn't leaving, but I've always known his work is massively important to him.'

'Didn't you fancy going with him?' asked Bridget.

'Honestly, Bridget, Jim and I have only just separated,' she said, attempting a light laugh. 'Best to take things slowly.'

'I thought you two were all loved up?'

'We are. He'll be coming up to Glasgow regularly. We'll make it work. He's an amazing person, Bridget. Intelligent, supportive, open-minded. A bit of a clever arse at times, but the sex more than makes up for that. Sorry … that was too much information.'

'There can never be too much information as far as I'm concerned, when it comes to sex,' replied Bridget.

'We talk, Bridget. We talk about everything and anything. He's interested in what I have to say. It feels amazing to be taken seriously, for your opinions to matter.'

'Did you tell Sean it was you who called Crimestoppers about Mark?' asked Bridget.

'No. The only person I've told is you. I wanted to tell him, but he doesn't like talking about Mark or Selina, his fiancée who died. It's like he's hiding a part of himself away. Not just to me, but to himself.'

'D'you think part of him still loves Selina?'

Bridget's questioning was beginning to feel uncomfortable, like a relentless tickling.

'He'll talk about her when he's ready to talk. I'm not going to push him.'

'It's a tough gig, competing with a ghost,' murmured Bridget.

'There's no point telling him about Crimestoppers because my call has served its purpose. The truth about Mark is out there. SOS got the publicity they needed to kick-start the anti-sectarian campaign. Now, will you stop interrogating me? Sean and I are fine. Everything's good,' she said, taking Bridget's arm and walking briskly down the steps of the debating chamber and into the courtyard. A muddle of people swilled around them, chatting happily.

'When will you hear about the job at The Policy Research Department?' asked Bridget.

'Soon, but I'm not feeling confident. There were three of us on the shortlist and the other two were both men, younger and better qualified. One of them had a PhD in Social Anthropology.'

'A PhD in Bollocks is no substitute for common sense and experience,' said Bridget. 'They'd be mad to turn you down.'

'I'm so proud of you, Bridget. You always said you wanted to play big, and now, here you are.'

'I'm proud of you, too, Izzy.'

'I'm small change compared to you.'

'We're all small change, but never doubt that small change can add up to something massive.'

'D'you remember our first day at Glasgow Tech?' asked Izzy. 'How scared we were?'

'I'm still terrified,' said Bridget, 'but I'm getting better at hiding it. I don't look up to the top of the mountain and think, that's too bloody high, no way I'll ever get to the top. I just focus on each step at a time.'

'When you put it like that, it doesn't seem so scary,' said Izzy.

'Promise me, Izzy, when they offer you that job, you'll accept it. You and I can achieve anything we bloody well want, if we just ...'

'... Take it one step at a time.'

***

| Jim: | Admitting that I'm a flawed human being has been a relief. Still not too sure about the God stuff but, as I haven't been able to stop drinking on my own, maybe I should take all the help that's out there. |
| Neil: | God won't do the work for you. You need to be fully committed to doing that yourself. |

Jim: I've never shied away from hard work.

Neil: Could you face up to everything you've
                ever done wrong? Write it down? The
                people, the places, the times?

Jim: I've done so many things I'm ashamed of. I
                took a loan from the bank of three hundred
                thousand pounds against the value of my
                home without telling my wife. Now she's
                been evicted and has had to get a job to
                support herself. What sort of husband does
                that?

Neil: It's not just the big things I want you to
                think about, but all the little things, too,
                like any bad thoughts you've had, any
                grudges, rudeness you've shown to others.

Jim: That'll be hundreds – thousands – of things
                in my case.

Neil: Termites are small creatures, but they do
                more damage than all the natural disasters
                of the world put together. Being conscious
                of all the small ways you've behaved badly
                will help you fully face up to yourself.

Jim: Just the thought of writing all that down
                makes me want to run a mile.

Neil: It seems intimidating, I know, but it starts with you writing down the first name. That's all. A single name.

CHAPTER 37

The red sandstone of the Merchant City glowed pink in the evening sky. The sun, like a flaming ball as it dipped. Izzy watched the sun set, wishing she could slow it down, though she knew it was inevitable and there was beauty in that, too. She buzzed the entry phone at the Bureau. No reply. She buzzed again, frowning. She was sure Shona and Alan had told her to arrive at 8 p.m. for the handover meeting.

'Hullo,' came Alan's gruff voice. The one he reserved for clients. 'We're closed. Come back on Monday at nine.'

She had to smile; he must know it was her. 'It's me, Izzy,' she said.

The door buzzed open and she began to climb up the satanic stairs, swallowing a lump of dismay at the thought this might be for the last time. She pressed the reception bell. There was a long delay. Sometimes, Alan could take a joke too far.

'SURPRISE!' The voices hit her like a gust of wind. Faces, individually familiar but collectively overwhelming, swam in front of her. Shona was powering her way towards her. 'You didn't think you'd get away that easily, did you?' she laughed, taking Izzy over to the table where they kept the information pamphlets. A space had been cleared for bottles and paper cups.

'Blame Alan. He's been planning it ever since you handed in your notice,' she said, holding out a cup of fruit juice. 'He's kept it small. Just a few folks from the Bureau and some of the SOS lot.'

She felt like a bride as colleagues and friends milled around her, wishing her good luck for the future. Some even commented on how nice she looked in her navy trouser suit.

'Speech … Speech,' someone yelled.

Izzy looked blank.

'OK, seeing as you insist,' said Shona, coming to her side. She held a piece of paper in her hand and waved it about in the air like a flag.

'As we all know, Izzy has taken up a new job in the Policy Research Department in Edinburgh. I'd like to get hold of the person who offered her the job and tell them they have just made the best decision of their life.'

This was greeted with hoots of laughter and leg stamping.

'When I first met Izzy, she told me she was an ordinary housewife and mum. Studying for a degree was a big step for her. She's worked incredibly hard and I'm sure I speak for all of us when I say how proud we are of her achievements and how much everyone here in the Glasgow Office will miss her.'

'Hear, hear,' shouted someone, followed by a final warm round of applause.

Izzy sipped her drink and looked down at her feet, concentrating on a small square of carpet, trying not to cry. That was the sort of speech people gave when you were leaving a place and never coming back.

Carol appeared by her side, clapping softly. 'Nice speech,' she said.

'A bit over the top,' said Izzy.

'She's right, we'll all miss you. I'll miss you.'

'I'm forty miles away, not four thousand. This new job will give me exposure to some influential people in social policy making. I can do even more for SOS than before,' said Izzy. Carol looked sad. Unconvinced.

'Sean seemed a bit down last week when I spoke to him on the phone. He's missing you.'

'And I'm missing him. He's hoping to come up for a holiday after the games are over.'

'You're both so busy.'

'It keeps the spark alive,' answered Izzy.

'Seriously? You don't mind being on your own for so much of the time?'

'At first, yes, but I've got used to it. I've got the space and time to develop my career. Sean's been incredibly supportive.'

Carol paused and looked thoughtful, then slapped Izzy on the back. 'Who would have guessed it? He's met his match.'

Izzy's office was just as she had left it that morning: cleared out and tidy. The terminal screen was blank, the filing cupboard locked. She sat on her chair and stroked the wood of her desk, tracing the grain with her fingers as a blind person might, committing it to memory.

'End of an era,' she said out loud.

Perhaps it was a small movement in the air that made her look up. He was standing in the doorway. She felt caught in time warp; a heart-stopping moment of recognition.

'Mr Docherty?' she asked.

'I'm not too late, am I?' he asked.

Then they were laughing, kissing, and he was whispering in her ear: 'I want you right here, right now.' She would have been happy to lie back on the desk for him, hitching up her skirt, and felt a pinch of disappointment when he pulled away and sat on her desk.

'What a lovely surprise,' said Izzy, sitting next to him.

'Couldn't keep away from you,' he said, kissing her neck. The creases at the sides of his eyes had deepened; the blue vein on his temple darkened. He looked pale, as if he had been ill.

'D'you ever wish we could spend more time together?' he asked her, pushing a lock of hair behind her ears and stroking her cheek.

'Of course, but it's not possible so there's no point wishing it,' she said, catching his hand and kissing his palm.

'If you want something badly enough, anything's possible,' he said, taking her hand and kissing her palm in return. His eyes were ablaze.

'Has something happened?'

'I've been offered my dream job, Izzy. A two-year secondment to the New York Times.'

She gasped. 'New York? That's amazing,' she heard herself saying as her insides began to collapse.

'But, there's a problem,' he added.

She nodded. Could their relationship survive? Could any relationship survive over such a long distance? New York was a long way from Edinburgh. Her mind was already whizzing forwards. Video calls, mobile phones ... they would be earning enough money to afford a flight or two. He was right, if you wanted something badly enough, anything was possible.

'I don't want to go on my own,' he said quietly.

She felt her heart clench.

'I don't want any more flying visits. No more fitting in between schedules. I love you, Izzy. Please, say you'll come with me.'

He looked as hopeful as a child and hugged her tightly. She breathed in his smell, her body responding as it always did, but there was a clear voice in her head that was unaffected by his closeness, by the seduction of the idea. It was saying: *No, no, no.* The sounds of the party tinkled in the air. Such happy sounds. She wished she was back in the room with them all.

'But, Sean, I've accepted the job in Edinburgh. I've signed a contract.'

A frown floated across his features. 'But you haven't started. Call them and tell them that you've had a better offer.'

'I can't do that, Sean. I'm sorry.'

'Why not?' he asked.

She felt her resolve flame into a reckless heat of selfishness. It burned with a clear conviction. 'Because I've been offered the job of my dreams, too.'

***

Jim: I've made my moral inventory of all the people I've wronged. It's an awfy long list.

Neil: You would be kidding yourself if it wasn't.

Jim: Strange how good it's made me feel. It's a kind of magic to have admitted and written down all my sad, dirty past.

Neil: Are you ready for the next step?

Jim: To contact everyone on the list and ask for their forgiveness?

Neil: Yes.

Jim: And what if people tell me to fuck off.

Neil: That's a possibility.

Jim: I suppose I'll just keep trying. Ticking off the list, one name at a time.

CHAPTER 38

Izzy took the stairs two at a time. Breathless, she fumbled with the key in the lock. Inside, she threw down her coat, kicked off her shoes and lunged forward to switch on the computer. The machine hummed but the screen stayed blank. Seconds ticked by. She pressed the space bar but it did no good. The machine was going to warm up in its own good time, and there was nothing she could do to hurry it. At last, the desktop picture flowered into view: a photograph of her and Sean on Brooklyn Bridge on a freezing day last December. They were wearing matching fair isle knitted hats, their noses scarlet with cold. She smiled; how cute they looked together.

The Skype icon was bouncing as if waving to attract her attention. She settled in her chair, pinched her cheeks and fluffed up her hair. She longed for a coffee, regretting that she hadn't made herself one before starting the call. After all, what difference would a couple more minutes make? But she had resisted the impulse; she was already late.

Sean's face appeared on the screen. He had a two-day beard and his hair looked like it needed washing. His eyes were downcast, as if he was reading something.

'Ah, so you've finally decided to show up,' he said, not looking up.

She felt a brief rise of irritation. 'Better late than never,' she said, trying to sound bright.

'I suppose so,' he agreed. He didn't sound convinced.

Her heart sank. Please don't let it be one of those calls.

'Hey, don't be mean. I didn't go to the pub after work even though the rest of team wanted me to. We've had our research paper on social housing accepted for the conference in Rome,' she said, her bright tone sounding more brittle.

'I didn't realise I was such an interruption to your busy life.'

She took a deep breath, suppressing her disappointment that he hadn't congratulated her on the paper's success. 'Let's start again, shall we?' she suggested. 'So, how are you?'

'Knackered. The editor is being a right sod about the latest draft of the Rangers book. I've been working on it every evening after work and he still thinks I need to do more,' he replied.

Exasperation seized her. She waited a couple of seconds to calm herself. 'Poor you,' she said, trying, but failing to keep an edge of sarcasm out of her tone.

'There's only a small window of opportunity for these things, Izzy. The club's still in the news but it won't last forever,' he said.

'You do look tired. Maybe we should try Skype sex?' She leaned in and planted a big kiss on the screen, laughing.

He looked irritated, then immediately calm. 'Izzy, I've been thinking,' he said. She waited. Her breath held. 'I can't go on like this.'

Irritation boiled up inside her. It travelled up through her body and out of her mouth. 'What do you expect me to do about it, Sean? Drop my entire life and come running into your arms?' She felt a jab of remorse. She might have done that in the past, but not now.

'Would that be so hard for you to do?' he asked.

She leaned back in her seat. Stunned. She couldn't speak.

'I love you, but we both know this long-distance thing isn't working. It's time to make a decision,' he said.

'You mean, it's time for me to make a decision. Giving up my job would be a massive thing for me. I'm surprised you don't see that,' she said.

'There's an intern job at the United Nations in the International Relations department. It doesn't pay anything, but it would be brilliant experience,' he said.

'I see,' she said. She felt numb, yet curiously awake.

'Izzy, I think about you all the time, wishing you were here. New York is an amazing city. You'd love it,' he added.

She nodded dumbly.

'I never thought I'd want to share my life with someone again, but you've changed all that.'

Unease and dread was growing in her chest. Thoughts swam crazily in her head. She would be handling this so much better if she'd had a cup of coffee.

'You mean after Selina died?' she said. Inexplicably, she felt a fury break out from her. 'Why can't you say her name? You've shut her away in a special place in your mind, in your heart. You can't bear to talk about her, can you? Not even with me.'

He looked bewildered, and then thoughtful, as if trying to work out if it was worth the effort to understand her or if it was better to say nothing and let the storm pass.

'It's true, isn't it? Admit it,' she yelled.

'Are you jealous of Selina?' he asked. 'Because, let me tell you, you've no cause to be jealous.'

She was trembling with agitation. 'You've never trusted me with your deepest feelings, Sean. About Selina. About Mark. Even your mother. It's no coincidence that I've never met her, is it?'

'My mother? Christ, Izzy. What's she got to do this?' He had taken off his glasses and was rubbing the bridge of his nose. 'I don't understand what you want from me,' he admitted sadly, raking his fingers through his hair.

Hot tears were spilling down her cheeks. She was amazed at the depth of her outpourings, but was powerless to prevent them. 'I want us to know each other in the deepest, most intimate way two people can. But that can only work if you lower your defences and allow me in.'

'I don't understand anything about this conversation, Izzy. I've said I love you and I want us to live together,' he said. 'I think you're being … irrational.'

She felt her love for him contract, like an open flower closing into a tight bud. 'Maybe I am. Maybe the rational thing to do is to call it a day.' She felt sick, her vision blurring.

'Maybe we should,' he agreed. There was a heartbeat of hesitation. She felt sure he would back down, suggest they talk later when they were less tired, but the video link vanished and she was left with the desktop picture of their happy faces raised to a weak winter sun on Brooklyn Bridge.

***

Neil: You'll be leaving us shortly. Have you thought about where you might go? What you might do?

Jim:	I'm separated from my wife, as you know. She lives in Edinburgh now. My son's in London. There's no place that calls me except ... well ... it's a daft idea.
Neil:	Sometimes daft ideas are the best ones.
Jim:	I've always had a soft spot for the Isle of Arran.
Neil:	I don't blame you. It's beautiful.
Jim:	Don't laugh, but I've been helping with the market garden here.
Neil:	Why would I laugh?
Jim:	I've always hated eating vegetables, but now I'm thinking I might spend the rest of my life growing them.

CHAPTER 39

Eighteen months later; August 2014.

Izzy hung her head over the side of the ferry, letting the breeze whip her hair, feeling the ozone power through her body like special fuel. The Isle of Arran lay dead ahead, the craggy outline of Goat Fell dominating the skyline, its heather-sided slopes wrapped around the peak like a warm blanket. It had taken her less than two hours to arrive at this perfect gem of Scottish beauty, as wild and remote as any of the islands in the far north.

She spotted Jim right away. He was standing a little way back from the crowd on the pier, with his characteristic pose: stocky, straight-backed and legs planted. Even from this distance, she could see he had let his hair grow long and he had a full beard and moustache. He was wearing dun-coloured overalls with the sleeves rolled up, as if he had taken a break from ploughing a field. He waved as she walked down the gangway. It was an enthusiastic gesture, as if he was either greeting an old friend or a stranger. She supposed she was an odd mix of the two.

They sat in silence as the Land Rover rattled along the road north of the main ferry port of Brodick. She felt self-conscious. Her jeans, sweater and white trainers looked too smart, too new, compared to his work overalls. The taste of salt and seaweed floated in the breeze through the open windows. It was a smell so inviting, she wanted to ask if they could take a walk on the beach, but Jim's face was set in concentration, discouraging her from suggesting a change to his plan.

'Here we are,' he announced. 'Welcome to my salvation.'

The cottage had been freshly whitewashed, the walls layered with decades of paint that had become so smooth, she wanted to reach out and stroke the surface. The small window frames were painted black and the slate roof was in good condition. It was a mild day, but a curl of smoke rose from the chimney.

'I can see why you call this a place of salvation,' she said. 'It's beautiful.'

'I wasn't referring to the house,' he said. 'Come round the back.'

The market garden stretched out along a valley that tapered off at the end. Her immediate impression was of order and tidiness. Rows of vegetation, marked off in squares, was interspersed with cages wrapped in netting to protect the plants from birds. Jim picked up a plastic crate. 'The local hotel needs some tatties tonight. We can pick a few extra for ourselves whilst we're at it.'

She followed him down a furrow. He pulled up a leafy plant, gently loosening the soil with his thick fingers. 'Treat them like eggs,' he explained. His voice was slow and kind, but with an authority like that of a kind teacher. 'They're lovely with a bit of fresh mint and a balsamic dressing,' he added, carefully placing the potatoes in the crate, where they lay like shiny pebbles.

It was hard to believe that this was the same man who had once complained bitterly when she'd put a touch of cinnamon in his apple pie. He was looking at her closely. 'Your freckles are coming out. They always did that the minute you went out in the sun.'

She felt herself blushing. The mention of her freckles felt as intimate as if he'd remembered some detail of their love-making.

'You've done wonders with this place, Jim.'

'And this place has done wonders for me,' he said quietly. He seemed caught in a private dream and then, just as quickly woke up from it. 'Davy and Cas came to see me when they were up visiting her mum. I suppose they told you.'

'They said they really enjoyed their visit,' she said.

'They're both vegans now, you know. They loved the garden. I told them they won't taste better veg anywhere else in the world.'

'It wasn't just the garden they loved,' she added quietly.

'I'm so proud of the way they're sticking with the band even though they didn't get that record deal.' Tears had begun to fall down his face. She suppressed a cry of alarm, but he was smiling broadly, wiping his face dry with the sleeve of his shirt, as carelessly as if he was mopping up some perspiration.

'They've got their own YouTube channel, you know,' she added.

'I love them both to bits,' he concluded happily.

They stood, side by side, looking towards Goat Fell. The mountain was outlined against a bright sky, the bracken foothills a deep purple. 'It's so beautiful here,' she said. 'Tranquil. Safe'. It was the perfect description. Jim was safe here and she was glad.

'The turning point for me was when I finally understood that I couldn't give up drinking on my own, that I needed to believe in a higher power. Not God in the religious sense, but a bigger spiritual force. It's been a big help to me.' Perhaps it was the warmth of the sun, or his obvious contentment, but she had no trouble believing that a higher spiritual energy would help you kick an addiction.

'The programme at Whitehill teaches us to face up to your past – honestly admit all the terrible things you've done. And I did some terrible things, Izzy. I was like a tornado destroying everything in my path.'

'It was the drink, Jim. You were always a good man underneath.'

He shook his head. 'No, underneath I'm the same daft bugger, but I'm trying to live a better life and part of that is to ask for your forgiveness for all the terrible things I've said and done.'

'Oh, Jim,' she breathed, swallowing hard. She could feel tears of her own beginning to form. She had forgiven him the day he'd signed himself into the Whitehill clinic. 'Of course I forgive you, Jim. Completely. Without hesitation.' Her words had the solemnity and beauty of a vow.

He looked relieved. 'Davy's forgiven me, too. I'm very blessed. Being at peace with the past is a wonderful thing. To leave nothing in the unsaid,' said Jim.

'To leave nothing in the unsaid? Is that what we're doing now?'

'I need to ask you, Izzy, was it you who called Crimestoppers about Mark Docherty? I read the article in the paper about Carol not wanting revenge and you were the only person I could think of who would have made that call.'

She felt surprised, a little guarded. 'I'm sorry, Jim. I know I promised you I wouldn't tell the police ...'

He nodded. 'You told me it was the right thing to do, and you were right. I called Carol Docherty myself the other week. I told her that I had witnessed what happened that terrible day, that I would go to the police and make a statement if that's what she wanted. She was very gracious. She said there was nothing more I could've done to save Mark's life, but she was glad that I'd had the guts to call,' he finished.

'You've spoken to Carol? I've lost touch with her in recent months.'

'She tells me she and Connor are still married but it only works if they live apart. I don't pretend to understand it. In my way of thinking, if you're married, you live together, under the same roof, in the same bed,' he said authoritatively.

They worked in silence until the crate was nearly full. He stood up and stretched. 'There's no chance for us, is there, Izzy?'

He said it not as a question, but more as a statement of fact. There was no hope of a reconciliation. It lay between them as solid and as real as the crate of potatoes.

'No, there isn't, Jim,' she agreed softly.

'Will you be wanting a divorce, then?' he asked. It was a mild request, as if he was asking if she wanted sugar in her coffee.

'No. There's nobody …' she said quickly.

'It didn't work out with Sean, the journalist fellow, then?'

She felt a sour, sharp taste in her mouth remembering the aftermath of that Skype call; the sniping and recriminations.

The way their love had petered out and died. 'Sean and I broke up eighteen months ago. But what about you?'

He grinned, hitching the crate of potatoes under his arm, and began walking back to the house. 'There's a lovely lass at the hotel. A recovering alcoholic like myself. I was thinking of asking her out …'

'Go on yersel' son,' she said lobbing a small potato at him.

He ducked, laughing. 'Carol told me Sean has moved back to the UK, he's staying with her in Glasgow.'

She stood, blushing furiously.

'Now, how about I show you the herb garden and we can pick some mint for these tatties?' he suggested.

CHAPTER 40

Clyde, the giant green mascot for the Commonwealth Games, was greeting shoppers. He was wearing a green and red tartan kilt, had purple hair and a grin that took up most of his face. People were flocking to him for selfies, as if he had super powers. A group of beautiful girls in mini kilts and high-heels surrounded him. 'Welcome to Glasgow,' cried one of them.

'Where are you from?' asked Izzy.

Her blonde hair was streaked with purple dye, the same shade as Clyde's. 'Poland,' she answered, cheerfully.

The city seemed cleaner and brighter than when Izzy last visited. The sun bathed everything in a continental warmth. She could have easily been in an Italian piazza, not George Square in August. A man was handing out leaflets, urging people to vote in the upcoming referendum for Scottish Independence. He had badges in every available space on his waistcoat that read: YES. She took a leaflet from him but, inside, she felt an edge of despair. Was Scotland hardwired for division? Scots and English; Catholic and Protestant; Rangers and Celtic; YES and NO. Well, today wasn't about creating division, it was about healing one.

They had arranged to meet at the Waterstones bookshop café in Buchanan Street. A poster of Mel Gibson advertising a special showing of Braveheart at the Film Society was stuck on the window. The film was almost twenty years old, a Hollywood version of Scottish nationalism that bore little relation to historical fact. It was all mildly depressing.

She was early and had no trouble finding a table. From her position on the mezzanine level, she had a clear view of the front door and would see him the moment he arrived. The thought, was momentarily paralysing. She wanted to rehearse her opening lines but her brain wasn't co-operating.

She saw him standing outside the front door and her heart began to race; her tongue felt as if it was too big for her mouth. He was weaving his way between the piles of books on the lower sales floor. His hair was shorter and lighter in colour, as if it had been bleached by the sun. He looked a little thinner, but other than that, he was just as she remembered him; attractive, arousing.

'Hey, Izzy,' he said, sitting opposite her. They didn't touch. Not even a London kiss. He smiled, a cool, guarded, wait-and-see type of smile.

Her face was burning; it was probably the colour of a roasted pepper. She cleared her throat. 'I've thought about this moment for a long time,' she started. 'How I'd feel. What I'd say. But now you're here, my mind's gone completely blank.'

'I have that effect on a lot of women,' he said with a straight face. She smiled and he smiled back, a little warmer this time.

'I thought I might see your book, *The Downfall Dossier*, downstairs,' she said. 'But maybe it's not out yet? I imagine there'll be a lot of controversy when it is. No one's been prosecuted for the mismanagement of the club, have they? It's a disgrace, really.'

'Izzy,' he said gently. 'Could you stop chattering for a moment? It's good to see you.'

A comforting voice inside her head was telling her to relax; this wasn't going to be a disaster.

'It's good to see you, too,' she said.

'The book's due out next month. It's taken way longer than it should have, but the publishing industry moves at glacial pace.'

'The Rangers story is still big here. There's a lot of anger about the denials of any wrongdoing. Hopefully, the book will stir things up again,' she said.

'Talking of stirring things up, I'm wondering how much longer I'll have to wait before you tell me why you wanted to see me,' he said, frowning.

She felt herself become animated, edgy. 'I wanted us to say goodbye in a good way. To leave nothing in the unsaid between us.'

His frown deepened. 'Leave nothing in the unsaid? I don't know what that means. You want me to say I'm sorry things ended the way they did?' he asked.

She felt her resolve flounder, suddenly unsure of what she expected of him. 'How things ended between us was terrible. I never got a chance to say thank you. You helped me believe in myself. I wouldn't be doing what I'm doing today, if it hadn't been for you.'

He leaned back in his seat. His forehead had cleared and he was smiling. 'The irony is, I never understood the implications of that. I thought you'd give up your life in Edinburgh, your new career, and join me in New York with an unpaid, crappy intern job. What an idiot I was.'

'If you'd asked me earlier, before getting the job in Edinburgh … but, afterwards …'

'Afterwards it was too late. I understand that now, but, at the time, all I felt was bitterness and rejection. And all that stuff you said about me being emotionally guarded? Not being able to talk about Selina or Mark?'

'Or not taking me to visit your mother,' added Izzy, interrupting. 'That was ridiculous I know, I'm sorry.'

'No, you were right. I had never been called out on it before, that's all. I had a spell in therapy after we broke up, to try and understand what went wrong. I absolutely accept that I find feelings – intimacy – difficult, but I'm working on it. What was the term you used, when you worked in the Bureau, about facing up to reality of your situation?'

'A breakthrough moment,' said Izzy, laughing.

'So, thank you, Izzy. Thank you for giving me that breakthrough moment,' he said, laughing with her.

'Jim told me you've moved back to the UK,' she said.

'I've sold my flat in London. I'm staying with Carol until I've sorted out where I want to live.'

She gulped. 'That's a big change.'

'I'm going to write full time. I've got a new book deal. An investigation into Russian state-sponsored doping of Olympic athletes. I'm going after Putin,' he said. His eyes were lit by a familiar energy.

'Quite a step up from Jack Marshall,' she said, feeling a mixture of awe and tenderness towards him.

'What about you, Izzy?'

'I'm still in Edinburgh, still loving my job. Maybe too much sometimes. I've lost touch with Carol and my other Glasgow friends.'

'You know you'd be welcome to visit, anytime.'

Was this an invitation? She gripped the edge of the table to steady herself.

'Carol would love to see you,' he added.

'Tell her I'll call soon,' she said, sipping her coffee and swallowing down a small disappointment.

'I'm glad we had this conversation, Izzy. It feels good. We can both move on with our lives with no hard feelings, right?' he said brightly.

'We've made peace with our past,' she agreed. Her face felt numb, her smile rigid.

'Except … we can't say we've made peace with the past until we've done one final thing together.'

Thoughts fluttered like moths in her head. Sex? Dinner? A visit to Ibrox for old time's sake?

'The Rugged Peak shop is next door. We can buy climbing boots and some gear there. It doesn't shut for half an hour.'

A slow realisation. 'You want to climb that hill? The one you climbed with your dad? The one we weren't able to because you had to go back to London early?'

He nodded. He looked pleased with himself. She had forgotten the power of that smirk: to irritate; to enthral.

'The majestic Ben Lui. That way we'll have left nothing in the unsaid and, more importantly, we'll have nothing left in the unclimbed either.'

***

Sean parked the car in a lay-by off the A80. It was early in the morning but it was already full of walkers and climbers. She got out of the car and stretched. She looked up at a clear blue sky that was so wide, it was in danger of swallowing her up.

'High pressure is sitting over the country. It should be a fine day. Most of this lot will be walking the West Highland Way,' he said. 'The shortest way up Ben Lui is from the other side via Glen Lochy. I reckon we're the only two taking this route.'

The mountain, with its elegant Alpine profile, dominated the valley. Even from five miles away, it looked intimidatingly high. She took a deep breath and smiled weakly.

The winding path towards the base of the mountain was flat and easy. Bracken and grasses waved in a mild wind, which carried a peaty smell from the boggy wetlands. The water in the burn changed from cobalt blue to a raging white as it rushed over stones. Sheep stopped grazing as they passed and fixed them with looks of deep boredom. She felt the tension inside her unwind, thinking calmly: *I can do this.*

He was talking in a quiet voice, explaining their route. They would take the easiest way up, round the left-hand side of the corrie and up the ridge to the summit. She was comforted by the reassurance in his voice, the closeness of his presence, the gentleness of the weather; it was unlikely to become wild and threatening on such a glorious day.

They started climbing upwards. Breathing became harder but, to her surprise, she managed to keep up with him. As they climbed, her lungs gradually lost their capacity to take in air and became so small and tight, they felt like two withered balloons inside her chest. She stopped, bending over, gasping for breath. She lifted her face to the wind and a gust of air turned the perspiration on her skin to a film of frost. Her new boots had begun to hurt. Sean looked as fresh as if he had just started.

'Have some water,' he suggested, offering her a bottle.

It took an effort to get going again. Her legs had stiffened and her confidence was crumbling, but as she got moving, she found a rhythm of sorts returning. She was slower now, but still moving steadily. Sean had stopped up ahead and was waiting for her to catch up. As soon as she reached him, he started off again without her. She didn't know what hurt most, her legs, her lungs or the fact he hadn't waited for her to fully recover.

As they climbed, clouds began to materialise from the west and the blue sky gradually disappeared. Suddenly, she found herself trapped in thick cloud, barely able to see the path in front of her. The mist was catching in her throat, making her cough and she had to stop. There was a terrible quality to the silence in that milky light, as if all sound had abandoned her.

Blindly, she stumbled upwards. The cold stung her ears and fingers. Her nose had begun to drip. She longed to get the warm jacket out of her rucksack but worried that, if she stopped walking, she wouldn't be able to start again. There was no sign of Sean. She thought about calling out to him, but suspected he was too far ahead to hear her. Her frozen fingers fumbled for her phone. She would call him and say she was turning back. She switched on the phone but there was no signal. Feeling foolish, useless, she put it back in her pocket.

Her first instinct was to collapse in a heap and weep. Boo hoo, but then what? She slapped the sides of her legs to try to bring some warmth into her limbs. Dry-eyed and determined, she summoned Bridget's brave face telling her not to look up to the top of the mountain and panic; but to concentrate only on taking the next step. She looked down at her legs and willed them to move.

'Izzy?' It was Sean's voice but she couldn't tell where he was calling from.

'Sean,' she yelled back, but in the lifeless murkiness, there was nothing except the sound of her own ragged breathing. She began climbing again: agonisingly; slowly. Above, she could see a subtle change of light and, a few minutes later, she found herself surrounded by the blue clearness of a magnificent sky. She looked down; banks of cloud rippled around her feet, as solid and as regular as cobblestones. A great happiness roared within her.

There was a rushing and a spraying of stones as Sean slid down the path to her side. 'Are you all right?' he asked gently.

'The white-out was so sudden, it frightened me,' she said. He was hugging her roughly, rubbing her arms to get some warmth into them. She was aware of the heat from him and the heat generating between them. Time rolled back.

'Put on your jacket. It'll get even colder the higher up we go,' he warned her.

He helped her with the coat and rubbed her hands until some life came back into them. She wanted to kiss him, partly in gratitude for helping her and partly because, when he was this close, she always wanted to kiss him.

'Isn't it incredible?' he said. They stood side by side looking down on the sea of clouds. He was taking photographs and his camera lens projected a mini rainbow onto the surface of the clouds. She knew the physics behind this prism phenomenon but, in this high place, with its winds and weather system, it felt almost mystical.

'D'you think you can make it to the top?' he asked, pointing upwards.

The ridge to the summit lay to her right. In the crystal air the path zig-zagged upwards. She felt so strong and happy, she thought she could run up it.

Two walkers were sitting on the summit cairn, huddled against the cold wind, eating sandwiches with a proprietorial air. Sean and Izzy headed past them to a small gully on the leeward side where the wind had died and the sun had recovered some of its warmth. The world was at their feet. Trails of rivers snaked through the valleys below, like silver ribbons, and mountain ridges stretched in waves towards the sea.

'Hungry?' he asked.

'Starving,' she admitted.

'We'll have to make do with rice crackers, hard boiled eggs and hummus.' He pulled off his beanie hat; his hair was standing up with static.

'You look like "Oor Wullie,"' she said, flattening his hair down, realising, too late, that this was the sort of gesture a girlfriend would make. She shifted her gaze and looked out to the horizon. 'You know Jim believes in a higher spiritual force these days? Looking around, it's easy to believe that something bigger than all of us created this beauty.'

Disconcertingly, Sean was not looking at the view. He was looking at her. 'I know today is about saying goodbye, moving on with our lives ...' he began.

Saying goodbye. The crumbs of the cracker tasted like dust in her mouth.

'... But I want you to know that I don't regret a single moment of our time together.'

'Even the crap stuff at the end?' she asked teasingly, recovering her composure.

'What we had, Izzy, was as amazing as this view,' he stated, putting his arm round her shoulders.

'Who'd have known you'd end up being the romantic one,' she replied, leaning in tight to his side. Minutes passed. The silent space around them was huge, taking them back to their past, where nothing was forgotten. 'When I was in that mist, I was frightened. All I could think of was turning back. I had no idea this bright blue sky was above me. Just a few yards away,' she said.

'Even on the greyest of days, there's always a blue sky above the clouds,' he told her.

'Did we turn back too early, Sean? D'you think that, if we'd kept going, we'd have found our way through to the blue sky?'

'I don't know, but we found it today, didn't we?' he replied, picking up her hand and threading his fingers through hers.

'We did,' she agreed, marvelling at the way their hands fitted together.

'I'm going down to Brighton next weekend to see Mum. She's been nagging me to visit ever since I got back from the States,' he said. 'I don't suppose ...'

'... Don't suppose what?'

'I don't suppose you'd like to come with me?'

She watched her icy breath mix with his; the air was as clear as a sacred promise. The sky had such a glittering beauty, it seemed she was staring into a limitless world, shimmering with possibility.

'I'd like that,' she said. 'I'd like that very much.'

POSTSCRIPT

After Glasgow Rangers Football Club was liquidated in May 2012, a new club was formed, called The Rangers Football Club. They were forced to play in the lowest division, eventually returning to the Scottish Premiership in August 2016, where their bitter rivalry with Celtic was rekindled. Although six former directors were charged with 16 charges of criminal fraud surrounding the mismanagement of the club, to date there have been no prosecutions and no one has been held to account for their part in bankrupting the club.

Alcohol consumption in Glasgow has continued to rise. In 2016, it was calculated, by NHS Scotland, that every adult in Glasgow over the age of sixteen drinks the equivalent of 41 bottles of vodka a year.

The Citizens Advice Bureau (now called Citizens Advice) continues to offer an advice lifeline to over 2.5 million people in the UK annually. The charity relies on government grants and charity donations for its survival. Due to austerity cuts in local and national government budgets, its funding remains precarious.

ACKNOWLEDGEMENTS

Thanks to Pauline for her invaluable insight into the work of volunteers at Citizens Advice; to Paul for accompanying me into the inner sanctum of Ibrox without arousing any suspicion; to Andy for sharing the reality (and pain) of a fan's perspective; to Fiona for her brilliance in coming up with a title and to all my friends and family who have supported me with their encouragement and love. But above all, my appreciation goes to the wonderful city of Glasgow – its people, its culture and the unsurpassable scenery that surrounds it. Always an inspiration.

Printed in Great Britain
by Amazon